## "You gave a stunning presentation, Captain. Yours is a harrowing tale."

A flicker of a shadow came over his eyes at her use of the word. It was instantly replaced by the cavalier expression. "Ah, but so heroic and inspiring."

"It makes it unfair that your leg pains you so much."

She expected him to give some dashing dismissal of the judgment, but he paused. He looked at her as if she were the first person ever to say such a thing, which couldn't possibly be true. "Why?" It was said in the oddest tone.

"I…" She fumbled, not knowing the answer herself. "I should think it a terrible shame. It seems a very brave thing you've done."

"Wars need heroes," he said, "and those of us in the wrong place at the wrong time find ourselves drafted into that need. I don't ponder whether I limp from justice or bravery, Nurse Sample. I just try to walk."

His smile had a dark edge to it as he walked away. With an odd little catch under her chest, Leanne noted that while he hid it extremely well, he still limped.

**Books by Allie Pleiter**

Love Inspired Historical

*Masked by Moonlight*
*Mission of Hope*
*Yukon Wedding*
*Homefront Hero*

Love Inspired

*My So-Called Love Life*
*The Perfect Blend*
*\*Bluegrass Hero*
*\*Bluegrass Courtship*
*\*Bluegrass Blessings*
*\*Bluegrass Christmas*
*Easter Promises*
   \*"Bluegrass Easter"
*Falling for the Fireman*

\*Kentucky Corners

Love Inspired Single Title

*Bad Heiress Day*
*Queen Esther & the Second Graders of Doom*

## *ALLIE PLEITER*

Enthusiastic but slightly untidy mother of two and RITA® Award finalist Allie Pleiter writes both fiction and nonfiction. An avid knitter and unreformed chocoholic, she spends her days writing books, drinking coffee and finding new ways to avoid housework. Allie grew up in Connecticut, holds a B.S. in speech from Northwestern University and spent fifteen years in the field of professional fundraising. She lives with her husband, children and a Havanese dog named Bella in the suburbs of Chicago, Illinois.

# Homefront Hero

## ALLIE PLEITER

Love Inspired

Recycling programs
for this product may
not exist in your area.

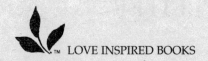

LOVE INSPIRED BOOKS

ISBN-13: 978-0-373-82916-3

HOMEFRONT HERO

Copyright © 2012 by Alyse Stanko Pleiter

www.LoveInspiredBooks.com

Printed in U.S.A.

Have I not commanded you?
Be strong and courageous. Do not be afraid;
do not be discouraged, for the Lord your God
will be with you wherever you go."
— *Joshua* 1:9

To Suzanne,
a brave hero and a warrior in her own right

## Acknowledgments

A wise writer brings lots of good counsel
with her into a historical manuscript.
In addition to John M. Barry's invaluable book
*The Great Influenza,* I owe thanks to many other
good people who served as sources: Paula Benson,
Dr. John Boyd of the 81st Regional Support
Command, Susan Craft, Kristina Dunn Johnson
at The South Carolina Confederate Relic Room
and Military Museum, Mary Jo Fairchild at
the South Carolina Historical Society,
Mary J. Manning (and the entire outstanding
museum) at the Cantigny First Division
Foundation, Nichole Riley at Moncrief Army
Community Hospital, Stephanie Sapp at
Jackson Army Base U.S. Army Basic
Combat Training Museum, Christina Shedlock
at the Charleston County Public Library and
Elizabeth Cassidy West and the other dedicated
librarians at the South Caroliniana Library at the
University of South Carolina at Columbia. Any
factual errors should be laid at my feet, not at the
excellent information these people provided me.

## Chapter One

*Camp Jackson Army Base*
*Columbia, South Carolina*
*September 1918*

"I still can't believe it." Leanne Sample gazed around at the busy activity of Camp Jackson. Even with all she'd heard and seen while studying nursing at nearby University of South Carolina, the encampment stunned her. This immense property had only recently been mere sand, pine and brush. Now nearly a thousand buildings created a self-contained city. She was part of that city. Part of the monumental military machine poised to train and treat the boys going to and coming from "over there." She was a staff nurse at the base army hospital. "We're really here."

"Unless I'm seein' things, we most definitely are here." Ida Landway, Leanne's fellow nurse and room-mate at the Red Cross House where they and other newer nurses were housed, elbowed her. "I've seen it with my own eyes, but I still can barely believe this place wasn't even here two years ago." Together they stared at the layout of the orderly, efficient streets and structures, rows upon rows of new buildings standing in formation like their soldier occupants. "It's a grand, impressive thing, Camp Jackson. Makes me proud."

Leanne had known Ida briefly during their study program at the university, but now that they were officially installed at the camp, Leanne already knew her prayers for a good friend in the nursing corps had been answered. Different as night and day, Leanne still had found Ida a fast and delightful companion. Ida's sense of humor was often the perfect antidote to the stresses of military base life. As such, their settling in at the Red Cross House and on the hospital staff had whooshed by her in a matter of days, and been much easier than she'd expected.

Still, "on-staff" nursing life was tiring. "There was so much to do," Leanne said to Ida as she tilted her face to the early fall sunshine as they chatted with other nurses on the hillside out in front of the Red Cross House. "Too many things are far more complicated in real service then I ever found them in class."

"A free afternoon. I was wondering if we'd ever get one. Gracious, I remember thinking our class schedules were hard." Ida rolled her shoulders. "Hard has a whole new meaning to me now." This afternoon had been their first stretch of free time, and they'd decided to spend an hour doing absolutely nothing before taking the trolley into Columbia to attend a war rally on the USC campus that evening.

"However are you going to have time to do this?" Ida pointed to a notice of base hospital events pinned to a post outside the Red Cross House. "I feel like I've barely time to breathe, and you're already lined up to teach knitting classes."

"I've managed to find the time to teach you," Leanne reminded her newest student.

"Don't I know it. I tell you, my mama's jaw would drop if she saw I've already learned to knit. I guess you've found right where you fit in the scheme of things around here."

Ida was right; Leanne had found her place on base almost instantly. As if God had known just where to slot her in, placing an opening for a teacher in the Red Cross sock knitting campaign. If there was anything Leanne knew for certain she could do, it was to knit socks for soldiers. She'd run classes for her schoolmates at the university; it seemed easy as pie to do the same thing here. And it would help her make friends so quickly—hadn't she already? In only a matter of days the vastness of the base seemed just a wide-open ocean of possibilities.

Of course, there were others who were less thrilled at the opportunities ahead of Leanne—namely, her parents. Mama and Papa had come to see her settled in, and they hadn't left yet. They'd already stayed on in Columbia two days longer than planned. Papa attributed it to "necessary business contacts" here in the state capital, but Leanne knew better. Mama wasn't at all calm about the prospect of her daughter being an army nurse. Leanne had agreed to meet her parents for a last luncheon before they caught their train, a final goodbye off base before tonight's rally. In truth Leanne worried that despite already-packed bags, Mama would invent some other reason to delay their return to Charleston.

Ida must have read her expression. "Oh, stop fretting about your mama and papa, will you? Don't give them reason to stay one more minute. You're in for a ten-hankie bout of tears no matter what, so best just to get it over with. Don't you give them one inch of reason to stay off that train."

Leanne couldn't argue. She'd declared to herself that even Mama's fits of worry would not be permitted to dampen the eager wonder she felt to finally be in service. Leanne squared her shoulders and straightened her spine. "I am a United States Army nurse. I am an educated woman—" she shot a sideways glance at Ida as she adjusted the colored cape that designated her as a leader of the newly graduated nursing class "—and I am a force to be reckoned with."

"I'll say an amen to that!" Ida flashed her generous smile that widened further as she pointed to a large new bill posted in a spot all its own. "Speaking of forces to be reckoned with, I reckon our evening will be highly entertaining." She peered closer at an announcement for the "rousing patriotic speech" to be given by "a true wartime hero." "'Hear the daring exploits of Army Captain John Gallows,'" Ida read aloud. "'Thrill to the tale of how he saved lives at the risk of his own.' Well, where I come from a gallows is something to be feared."

Leanne could only laugh. Some days Ida sounded as if West Virginia were the wild, wild West. "Oh, that might still be true here. The Gallowses are a very formidable Charleston family."

"Have you met them?"

"I've not had the pleasure, but I believe our fathers

know each other back in Charleston. A fine family going back for generations."

Ida leaned back and crossed her arms while eyeing the dashing photograph of Captain Gallows that illustrated the announcement. "Fine indeed. He's certainly handsome enough." She adjusted her stiff white apron as if primping for the photograph's admiration. Ida did like to be admired, especially by gallant army officers. "I can't think of a better way to spend our first free evening off base. Perhaps he'll let me sketch him."

"Why is it you want to sketch every handsome man you meet?" Leanne teased. Already she could see it might prove hard to keep her artistically inclined roommate focused on her duties. Ida was a free spirit if ever there was one, and while she took her nursing very seriously, her adventurous nature already pulled her too often away from her tasks.

"I'd be delighted to sit for you," came a deep voice behind them. "Especially if you are so partial to handsome war heroes."

Ida and Leanne spun on their heels to find the very man depicted in the photograph. Complete with the dashing smile. Even out of his dress uniform—for he wore a coat, but not one as fancy or full of medals as the one in the photograph—he was every bit the U.S. Army poster-boy hero. His dark hair just barely contained itself in its slick comb-back underneath his cap. He carried himself with unmistakably military command—Leanne suspected she'd have known he was an officer even in civilian clothes. He certainly was very sure of himself—a long moment passed before Leanne even noticed he leaned jauntily on a cane.

Ida planted one hand on her hip. "Well—" her voice grew silky "—no one can fault you for an excess of modesty. Still, my daddy always said a healthy ego was a heroic trait, so I suppose I can let it slide, Captain Gallows." She drew out the pronunciation of his name with a relish that made Leanne flush.

Captain Gallows was evidently all-too-accustomed to such attentions, for he merely widened his dashing smile and gave a short bow to each of them. "How do you do?" He pointed to the sign. "Say you'll attend tonight's event, and my fears of facing an audience full of dull-faced students and soldiers will be put to rest."

"Are you one of the Four Minute Men, then?" Leanne asked. Her father had been asked to serve on the nationally launched volunteer speakers board, called "Four Minute Men" for the prescribed length of their speeches, but Papa had declined. Still, from the superlatives on his bill, Captain Gallows could go on for four hours and still hold his audience captive.

"The best. They give me as long as I want. They tell me I'm enthralling."

"I have no doubt they do. I'm Ida Lee Landway, and this is my friend Leanne Sample. We've just joined the nursing staff at the base hospital."

The captain tipped his hat. "How fortunate for our boys in the wards. Miss Landway, Miss Sample, I'm delighted to meet you. Tell me what I can say to convince you to come to the rally."

"Oh, it won't take *much,*" Ida cooed.

"We were just on our way over to town early and already planning to attend," Leanne corrected. "No persuasion will be required." He certainly seemed a cocky sort, this Captain Gallows.

"I'm not so sure," he replied with a disarming grin. "I was on campus this morning and one of the students told me she would come, but she would bring her knitting. Not the kind of response I'm used to, I must say. I'm trying to see it as a patriotic act, not an expectation of my inability to fascinate."

Definitely a cocky sort. "Don't take that as an affront at all, Captain Gallows. I'm meeting my parents for luncheon and I have my knitting with me right now."

"Well, I can't say I haven't longed for a sharp pointy stick in several conversations with my own father."

Leanne didn't find that especially funny. "The Red Cross encourages us to knit everywhere we can, Captain Gallows." She tried not to glare as she pointed to the bag currently slung over her shoulder. "I assure you, I knit even in church, so the presence of anyone's yarn and needles need be no dent to your confidence. Our boys need socks as much as the army needs our boys."

Gallows tucked a hand in his pocket. "Duly noted, ma'am." He turned to Ida. "Does the Red Cross know what a fine champion they have in nurse Leanne Sample?"

"They ought to," Ida boasted. "She's been here a week and already she's teaching two knitting classes at the hospital."

"Impressive," Gallows replied. "I'm sure the fellows here at the hospital have told you there are days when a pair of warm, dry socks are the highlight of the week. I suppose if I just remember that while you all are staring down at your needles instead of up at me, I'll be just fine."

The man enjoyed being the center of attention—that much was clear. "You needn't worry. Most of us can stitch without even looking. I've knit so many pairs of socks I think I could probably knit in my sleep by now."

"Not me," Ida said. "Leanne's a good teacher, but I fear for the feet that'll have to put up with my socks. I'll have to stare down a fair amount—" she paused and batted her long auburn eyelashes "—but not the *whole* time."

"Well, then." Gallows rocked back on his boot heels. "I have my orders. I'm to be enthralling but not distracting. Have I got it right?"

"I have no doubt you do such a job very well," Leanne replied, not wanting to give Ida another chance at that one. "Good day, Captain. We've a trolley to catch, but we'll also catch your enthralling-but-not-distracting presentation this evening."

Gallows tipped his hat. "You do your bit, I'll do mine."

# Chapter Two

Captain John Gallows planted his feet—or rather one good foot, one bad foot and the tip of his cane—on the porch of the Camp Jackson officers' hall. He'd envisioned his homecoming so very differently.

Still, he was in South Carolina, if not yet in Charleston. And home, in the form of his formidable and sharp-pointy-stick-worthy father, had come running to him.

"John." His father pulled open the door before John even set hand to the knob. He gave John a stiff clap on the back. The force made John put more weight on his bad leg than he would have liked. "Our boy, our hero, home for a bit from the grand tour of rousting up recruits, hmm?"

His father undoubtedly considered talking up war a poor substitute for winning one, but John shook off those thoughts as he shook his father's hand. "You know me," he said, applying his most charming smile, "ready to open my big mouth for a good cause."

"Welcome home, dear," John's mother cooed as she emerged from the hall behind his father. "Oh, look at that medal." She smoothed out the front of his uniform and the medal for bravery that continually hung there now. "My son. Decorated for valor." The pride in her voice was warm and sugary.

John had saved six lives, but only really in his efforts to keep his own. That didn't feel like bravery. He wasn't even supposed to be on that navy dirigible except for a favor he was granting to his commander's buddy. Still, John could spin a rousing tale and history had thrown him into a dramatic scenario. As such, John had been healed up quickly and delivered to several American cities to give speeches. He was eager to return to fighting, but hoped this recruitment tour would better his chances at being admitted to pilot training. Pilots, now those were the real heroes. If doing his best to stir up the patriotic spirit wherever and whenever asked got him closer to that kind of glory, he'd gladly comply.

"How handsome you look," Mama went on. "How much older than twenty-two. You walk differently, even."

John winked. "That would be the cane, ma'am," he joked, swinging it the way Charlie Chaplin did in the movies. He tipped the corner of his hat for effect.

Father made some sort of a gruff sound, but she laughed. "No, that would be the *man,* son. I'm not talking about your gait, but the way you carry yourself. With wisdom. Authority."

"Flattery. Don't you think you're just a little bit biased?" he teased her.

"Of course I am," she said, reaching up to lay a hand on each of his shoulders. "Oh, I am just so glad to have you home!" She hugged him tight. "And for so long a leave! Why, I wouldn't be surprised if they had this nasty business sewn up before y'all even had a chance to get back over there."

"Now, Deborah," John's father replied in his "let's be sensible" voice, which had the desirable effect of removing Mama's hands from John's shoulders, "I hardly think they'd want Johnny back here making all those speeches if the end is near." His father's gaze flicked down momentarily to the black cane. "Besides, you're here to get the best of care while that leg heals."

"How is it?" Mama asked, following Father's gaze.

It hurt. All the time. But John had figured out early on that truth wasn't always the desired answer. "I'll be fine," he said, employing his now-stock reply to all such questions. Most days, it was the truth. Yet every moment since the train had pulled into Columbia, he'd felt odd…as if his body suddenly found his home state a foreign land.

Mama tucked her hand in John's free arm. "To think of my boy, dangling up there over the water, saving lives at the risk of his very own." Her voice trailed off and she leaned her head against his shoulder.

*Saving lives at the risk of his very own.* The words came directly from the press wire he'd seen. From the paper they'd read when they'd pinned the medal on him. From the leaflet that papered the cities where he spoke. Funny, all that bravery sounded like it belonged to someone else, even though John had vivid memories to prove otherwise. No man forgets hanging upside down from the stay wires of a dirigible a mile up and a mile out to sea. An army captain, in the *air* and out to *sea*. A fluke of circumstance that turned into a near-death disaster. He'd take the memory of nothing but air between himself and his death to his grave, even if he never spoke of it again. He *wished* he could never speak of it again, never again hear himself be lauded for an act that had no selfless heroism to it at all. It wasn't admirable to go to drastic lengths to save an airship when the alternative was crashing into the ocean with it.

"A heroic tale, surely," Papa boasted. "I imagine the ladies think even more highly of you now."

Father was right in that respect. The only thing ladies liked more than a man in uniform was a decorated hero in uniform. And John—like every member of the well-bred Gallows family—was a social success even before he slipped into uniform. He'd not lacked for company for one minute of his hospital stay, the voyage home, or his multi-city speaking circuit. "Well, now," he quipped, "hard to say. The nurses are supposed to be attentive. It's their job."

"I have the feeling 'above and beyond the call of duty' has a new meaning." Oscar Gallows laughed. He'd been a dashing soldier in his own day, Mama always said. "Seems to me y'all won't hurt for company one bit."

"Do you have to stay at the camp?" Mama asked... again. "Why can't you come home to Charleston? You'd be so much more comfortable at home with us."

"The hospital reconstruction therapists are here, Mother. And I am still on active duty. I've got to go where they send me."

Mama pouted. "Tell them to send you home to your mama's good care."

"That's no way for a Gallows to serve, Deborah.

John has duties to perform even while he heals. You wouldn't want him to finish up the war as a mere spokesman, would you?"

Oscar Gallows began strutting toward the general's house where they had a luncheon engagement before John's big speech tonight. His father walked quickly, giving no quarter to John's injured leg.

John wasn't surprised. A Gallows gave no quarter to anyone, least of all himself.

"It's so *dry* here." Leanne watched her mama mop her brow and frown over her glass of tea. "And dreadfully hot without any kind of breeze. I don't know how you don't just shrivel up."

In truth, Columbia was a lovely town. It held the University of South Carolina and the state capitol—both as fine cultural centers for the region as any of which Charleston could boast. While it lacked the sea breeze, it also lacked the rain-soaked humidity that sent Charlestonians running out of their city to their beach houses. "I'm half a day to the coast, Mama. And no, I won't shrivel up. For goodness' sakes, I'm a nurse… I imagine I've learned how to care for myself in the process."

"That place is just massive," Mama moaned, casting her glance across town in the direction of Camp Jackson. Mama had made it clear, over and over and despite Leanne's many statements to the contrary, that she had fully expected Leanne to return to Charleston after completing her courses at the university, not join the service as she had done. "And so drab." Mama put a dramatic hand to her chest. "What if they decide to send you overseas?"

"They won't send me overseas, Mama. I'm needed here. Can't you see what an opportunity this is?"

Papa, who had been rather quiet the entire trip, put a hand on Mama's shoulder. "She needs to do her part, and far better here than over there. She'll learn a great deal." Leanne had the distinct impression he was half lecturing himself. "Honestly, Maureen, Columbia is not that far from Charleston."

"Not far at all, Papa," Leanne assured him. "And I'll be able to feel so much more useful here." She'd learned a great many things already, and was about to learn a great deal more. The world was changing so fast for women these days—there was talk of voting and owning property and pursuing careers in literature and painting, serving overseas, all kinds of things. Awful as it was, the war gave women the chance to do things they'd never done before. The lines of tradition were bending in new and exciting ways, and if they would only bend for this time, she couldn't bear to miss exploring all she could in a town that was right at the heart of it all.

Leanne yearned to know she'd made a difference—in lives and in the healing of souls and bodies. She felt as if she would make too small a contribution in Charleston now that the university had shown her how far a life's reach could be. Leanne wanted God to cast her life's reach far and wide.

As they finished their luncheon and walked reluctantly to the train station, Mama smoothed out Leanne's collar one last time.

"I'll be fine, Mama, really. I'm excited. Don't be sad."

Mama's hand touched Leanne's cheek. "I'll pray for you every day, darlin'. Every single day."

Leanne took her mother's hand in hers. Mama's promise to cover her in prayer ignited the tiny spark of fear—the anxiety of God's great big reach stretching her too far—that she'd swallowed all day. Her assignment in the reconstruction ward of the camp hospital, helping soldiers recover from their wounds, was so important, but a bit frightening at the same time. She swallowed her nerves for the thousandth time, willing them not to show one little bit. "I'd like that," she said with all the confidence she could muster. "But I'll be home for Thanksgiving before you know it. And I'll write. I'm sure the Charleston Red Cross will keep you so busy you'll barely have time to miss me."

"I miss you already." Mama's voice broke, and Leanne gave a pleading look to her father. The Great Goodbye—as she'd called it in her mind all this week— had already taken an hour longer than she'd expected.

"We've lingered long enough, Maureen." Papa took Mama's hands from Leanne's and tugged her mother's resistant body toward the station platform. Leanne thought that if he waited even five more minutes, Mama might affix herself to a Columbia streetlamp and refuse to let go. "It's high time we let our little girl do what she came to do." He leaned in and kissed Leanne soundly on the cheek. "Be good, work hard." It was the same goodbye he'd said every single morning of her school years. It helped to calm the tiny fearful spark, as if this was just another phase of her education instead of a life-altering adventure.

"I will." Leanne blew a kiss to her mother, afraid that if she gave in to the impulse to run and hug Mama, Papa would have to peel them tearfully off each other.

"Write!" Mama called, the sniffles already starting as Papa guided her down the platform toward the waiting train. Leanne nodded, her own throat choking up at the sound of Mama's impending tears. Papa had joked that he'd brought eleven handkerchiefs for the trip home and warned the county of the ensuing flood.

Leanne clutched the hanky he'd given her as she stood smiling and waving. As sad as she was to see them go, she couldn't help but feel that this was a rite of passage, a necessary step in becoming her own woman. Childhood was over—she was a nurse now. Part of the Great War. Part of the great cause of the Red Cross and a new generation of women doing things women had never done before.

*It is,* she told herself as she turned toward the university auditorium where she'd promised to meet Ida, *a very good sort of terrifying.*

## Chapter Three

It could have been any of the dozens of halls, churches, auditoriums and ballrooms John had been in over the past month. He paced the tiny cluttered backstage and tried to walk off the nerves and pain. He tried, as well, to walk off the boyish hope that his father had stayed for the presentation. Foolishness, for not one of these maladies—physical or mental—would ease with steps. He knew that, but it was better than sitting as he waited impatiently for his speech to start.

If only he could run. It would feel wonderful to run, the way he used to run for exercise and sheer pleasure. More foolishness to think of that, for it would be torture to run now. John's uncooperative leg ignored his persistent craving to go fast. The fact that he went nowhere fast these days proved a continual frustration to his life-long love of speed. He'd been aiming to drive those new race cars when the war broke out, and he'd heard some of the race-car drivers were trying to form a battalion of pilots. Airplanes, now there was the future—not just of warfare but of everything. Nothing went faster than those. When the army had hinted he'd have a chance at the Air Corps, he'd signed up as fast as he could.

And he did end up in the air.

On the slowest airship ever created.

John's only chance at air travel came in the form of a diplomatic mission on a huge, sluggish navy dirigible—the furthest thing from what he'd had in mind. Still, as he was now about to tell in the most enthralling way possible, even that fluke of history had managed to catapult him into notoriety.

Pulling the thick red velvet curtain to the side, John couldn't stop himself from scanning the sea of uniforms for the one he would not see: Colonel Oscar Gallows. Mother had surely pleaded, but even as a retired colonel Father wasn't the kind of man who had time to watch his son "stump" for Uncle Sam. How often had the colonel scowled at John's oratory skills, calling his son "a man of too many words"? *And not enough action—* Father had never actually said it, but the message came through loud and clear.

John consoled himself by scanning the audience for the scattered pockets of female students and army base nurses. Nearly all, as Nurse Sample had predicted, were knitting. He tried to seek her out, looking for that stunning gold hair and amber eyes that nearly scowled at his swagger. It was clear her friend Ida was taken with him—women often were, so that was no novelty. Leanne Sample, however, fascinated him by being indifferent, perhaps even unimpressed. He scanned the audience again, hoping to locate her seat so he could direct a part of his speech especially to her. Her kind were everywhere, a sea of women with clicking needles working the same drab trio of official colors—black, beige and that particularly tiresome shade of U.S. Army olive-green.

There she was. My, but she was pretty. Her thick fringe of blond lashes shielded her eyes as she bent over her work. She seemed delicate with all that light hair and pale skin, but the way she held her shoulders spoke of a wisp of defiance. He made it a personal goal to enthrall her to distraction. To draw those hazel eyes up off those drab colors and onto him.

In full dress, John knew he'd draw eyes, and easily stand out in this crowd. And if there was anything he did well, it was to stand out. Gallows men were supposed to stand out, after all. To distinguish themselves by courageous ambition. Ha! Even the colonel seemed to realize that John's path to notoriety had only really been achieved by climbing up and falling down on a ship he should never have been on in the first place. This from a man who'd spent his life trying to stand out and go fast. His life had been turned on its ear in any number of ways since this whole messy business began.

The university president tapped John on the shoulder. "Are you ready, Captain Gallows?" John could hear the school band begin a rousing tune on the other side of the curtain.

He did what he always did: he dismissed the pain, shook off his nerves and applied the smile that had charmed hearts and reeled in recruits in ten American cities. "By all means, sir." He left his cane leaning up against the backstage wall, tilted his hat just so and walked out into the myth of glory.

\* \* \*

Proud.

Did Captain John Gallows earn such arrogance?

Yes, he was heroic, but the man's self-importance seemed to know no bounds. As he told the harrowing tale of his brush with death, dangling from airship stay wires to effect a life-saving repair while the crew lay wounded and helpless, Leanne could feel the entire room swell with admiration. Women wanted to be near him, men wanted to be him. His eyes were such an astounding dark blue—rendered even more astounding against the crisp collar of his uniform—that one hardly even noticed his limp. He didn't use his cane on stage, but Leanne reasoned that they'd arranged the stage in such a way as to afford him the shortest walk possible to the podium. The way he told the story, however, it was a wonder the audience didn't break into applause at his very ability to walk upright. While his entanglement in the dirigible's stay wires had saved his life, it had also shredded his right leg to near uselessness. He never said that outright, but Leanne could read between the lines of his crafted narrative. She guessed, just by how he phrased his descriptions and avoided certain words, that his leg still pained him significantly—both physically and emotionally. He did not seem a man to brook limitations of any kind.

"Now is the time to finish the job we've started," he said, casting his keen eyes out across the audience. "Our enemy is close to defeated. Our cause is the most important one you will ever know." Captain Gallows pointed out into the audience, and Leanne had no doubt every soul in the building felt as if he were pointing straight at them—she knew she did. "When you look your sons and daughters in the eye decades from now, as they enjoy a world of peace and prosperity, will you be able to say you did your part? Can you say you answered duty's sacred call?"

Cheers began to swell up from the audience. The young students off to her left began to stand and clap. Next to her, Ida brandished her newly employed knitting needles as if she were Joan of Arc charging her troops into battle. Despite her resistance to Gallows, Leanne felt the echo of a "yes!" surge up in her own heart. Her work as a nurse, her aid to the troops and even her leisure hours spent knitting dozens of socks for soldiers answered her call. Homefront nurses were as essential to the cause as those serving overseas. She understood the need for combat, but wanted no part of it. Leanne longed to be part of the healing. And beyond her nursing, she was using her knitting, as well. She'd taught hospital staff how to knit the government-issued sock pattern, and she'd teach her first class of patients later this week. When those classes were off and stitching, she would teach more. For there was so very much to be done.

When someone behind her started up a chorus of last year's popular war song "Over There," Leanne stopped knitting and joined in. It felt important, gravely important, to be part of something so large and daunting. To be here, on her own, both serving and learning. The whole world was changing, and God had planted her on the crest of the incoming wave. While her grandmother had moaned that the war was "the worst time to be alive," Leanne couldn't help but feel that Nana was wrong. Despite all the hardship, this was indeed the best time to be young and alive.

If Captain Gallows wished to stir the crowd to the heights of patriotic frenzy, he had certainly succeeded. More than half the students in the room were now on their feet, cheering. Even Leanne had to admit Gallows was a compelling, charismatic spokesman for the cause. Perhaps she could be more gracious toward his very healthy ego than she had been earlier that day.

Captain Gallows made his way off the stage as the university chorus came onstage to lead in another song. She could see him "offstage" because of her vantage point far to the left, but he must have thought he was out of view for his limp became pronounced and he sank into a nearby chair. As the singing continued, she watched him, transfixed by the change in his stature. He picked his cane up from where it lay against the backstage wall. Instead of rising, as she expected him to do, he sat there, eventually leaning over the cane with his head resting on top of his hands. He looked as if he were in great pain. From the looks of it, his leg must have been agonizing him the entire speech. And surely no one would have thought one lick less of him had he used the cane.

Leanne watched him for a moment, surprised at the surge of sympathy she felt for this man she hardly knew and hadn't much liked at first, until the dean of students approached Captain Gallows. Instantly his demeanor returned to the dashing hero, shooting upright as if he hadn't a pain or care in the world. That was more in line with the behavior she expected of him. So which was the real John Gallows—the arrogant, larger-than-life hero—or the proud, wounded, struggling man she'd caught a glimpse of the moment before? There was no way for her to tell now. The captain and the dean walked off together, and Leanne remembered there was a reception of sorts for him afterward. As one of the Red Cross knitting teachers, she'd been invited. She hadn't planned on going at first, for she hadn't a taste for such things and it would be awkward since Ida hadn't been asked. She'd go, now, if just to help make up her mind as to what kind of man he truly was.

"You know, I think I will go to that reception after all," she said as casually as she could to Ida as they packed up their things to exit the hall.

"Well, now, who wouldn't?" Ida didn't seem the least bit slighted by her lack of an invitation. Some days Leanne wished for Ida's confidence and, as Papa put it, "thick skin." Instead of sulking, Ida only offered her an oversize wink. "Tell the good captain he can recruit me any day," she whispered, visibly pleased at Leanne's startled reaction.

"It's a good thing I won't and he can't," she replied, hoping no one else heard the scandalous remark.

"Says you." Ida laughed, and sauntered away.

Yes, he was a hero. Yes, he was vital to the cause. Still, Leanne couldn't see how even the most rousing of Gallows's speeches could overcome her distaste for the man's monumental air of self-importance.

## Chapter Four

Leanne was just barely ten minutes into the reception, not yet even to the punch bowl, when Gallows swooped up behind her and took her by the elbow.

"Save me," he whispered as he nodded to the library shelf to their left. "Pull a book off the shelf this very minute and save me from Professor Mosling, I implore you." She couldn't help but comply, for Leanne knew that calling Professor Mosling long-winded was an understatement. Mosling thought very highly of himself and his opinions, and shared them freely with unsuspecting victims. At great length and with considerable detail. Last month she'd been cornered for three quarters of an hour by the man as he shared his views on the use of domestic wool for socks. Mosling raised an arm with an all-too-hearty "There you are, Gallows!" Leanne snatched the largest book within reach and angled her shoulders away from the man.

"Really, Captain Gallows, there is much to be said for—" she realized in her haste she'd neglected to even scan the massive volume's title "—*Atlantic Shipping*

*Records of the Cooper River.* I find it a most fascinating subject," she improvised, finding herself stumped.

"As do I," replied Captain Gallows, his eyes filled with surprise and a healthy dose of amusement even though his voice was earnest. "Please, do go on."

Go on? How on earth could she "go on"? "As I'm sure you know, the Cooper River runs right through Charleston, providing a major seaport thoroughfare…" It felt absurd; she was stringing together important-sounding words with almost no sense of their content. Still, Gallows's eyes encouraged her, looking as if she was imparting the most vital knowledge imaginable.

"Do forgive me," Gallows said to the professor, "but I simply cannot tear myself away from Miss Sample's *fascinating* explanation."

The ruse worked, for Mosling huffed a little, straightened his jacket and then seemed to find another suitable target within seconds. "Oh, yes, well, another time then."

"Indeed," said Captain Gallows, actually managing to sound sorry for the loss despite the relief she could see in his eyes. "Very soon."

As soon as Mosling had left, Gallows took the huge text from her and began to laugh. *"Atlantic Shipping Records?* A most unfortunate choice. I could probably better explain these to you than the other way around."

Leanne raised an eyebrow, not particularly pleased to be roped into such a scheme. "I was rather in a hurry and quite unprepared."

"Perhaps I should have asked you to teach me knitting." He looked as if he'd rather read *Atlantic Shipping Records* from cover to cover than take up the craft—

as if he found it a frilly pastime better suited to grand-mothers in rocking chairs.

"Many men have, you know. There was a time, cen-turies ago, when knitting was purely a man's craft. And you can't argue that every hand is needed. Perhaps we can arrange a lesson for you yet." She couldn't for the life of her say where such boldness had come from. Perhaps Ida was rubbing off on her.

"If anyone could…" The fact that he didn't finish the sentence made it all the more daunting.

Leanne chose to shift the subject. "You gave a stun-ning presentation, Captain. The boys were on their feet cheering by the end of things."

He leaned against the bookcase, and while she had the urge to ask him if he'd like to sit down, she had the notion that he wouldn't take to such a consideration of his injury. "You stopped knitting there for a moment. I saw you."

He made it sound as if her pause revealed secrets. "I was inspired. It is a harrowing tale."

A flicker of a shadow came over his eye at her use of the word. Only for a sliver of a second, however, and it was so instantly replaced by a cavalier expression that it made her wonder if it had been there at all. "Ah, but so heroic and inspiring."

"It makes it unfair that your leg pains you so much." She hadn't planned on making such a remark, but some-how it jumped out of her.

She expected him to give some dashing dismissal of the judgment, but he paused. He looked at her as if she were the first person ever to say such a thing, which couldn't possibly be true. "Why?" He had the oddest tone of expression.

"I…" she fumbled, not knowing the answer herself. "I should think it a terrible shame. It seems a very brave thing you've done, and I would like to think God rewards bravery, not punishes it."

"God? Rewarding me for being caught on a failing airship?" He laughed, but far too sharply. "The very thought." He took the book from her, snapping it shut before replacing it on the shelf between them. "You have a very odd way of thinking, Nurse Sample."

What did the captain think of his "fate"? Or his Creator? Did he even acknowledge Him? Unsure what to make of Gallows, Leanne pressed her point. "Odd? By thinking God is just or by thinking you brave?"

That got a hearty laugh from him. He spun his cane in his hand, almost like a showman, and stared at her a long, puzzling moment before he said, "Both."

She wasn't going to let him go at a clever dodge like that. "How so?"

Gallows's face told her the conversation had ventured into difficult territory. "Are you always so pointed in your conversations?"

"Would you prefer we return to *Atlantic Shipping Records?* Or I could get the good professor to rejoin us…"

"No," he cut in. He pulled a hand over his chin, groping for his answer while she patiently waited. Leanne found herself genuinely curious—and surprisingly so— as to what this man truly thought of himself when no one else was watching. "Wars need heroes," he said eventually, "and those of us in the wrong place at the wrong time find ourselves drafted into that need. I've been too busy staying alive and playing hero to worry about who did the drafting or why. I don't ponder whether I limp from justice or bravery, Nurse Sample. I just try to walk."

His smile had a dark edge to it as he turned and walked away. With an odd little catch under her chest, Leanne noted that while he hid it extremely well, he still limped.

Ashton Barnes was a big, barrel-chested man who barked orders with the intensity of cannon-fire. He'd been one of Colonel Gallows's protégés, rising fast and far to head up a logistical marvel like Camp Jackson even though he was barely pushing fifty. The general's balding head stubbornly held on to what was left of his white-blond hair, the rounded pate in stark contrast to the rectangular metal glasses he wore. Fond of cigars, hunting and blueberry pie, Barnes was the kind of larger-than-life commander a bursting enterprise like Camp Jackson required.

Every soldier knew Barnes as firm but fair, and even though one might consider Barnes "a friend of the family," John knew better than to think his last name bought him any leverage with the general. His talents earned him the man's eye, not his pedigree, and John had seen Barnes at the rally, sizing up his performance from the back corner. He'd known the job they'd given him to do yesterday, and he'd done it well, so John wasn't surprised to receive a summons to the general's office this morning.

While he also prided himself on good soldiering,

drama and attention were John's strongest weapons to wield. He'd known within the first ten minutes how to draw this particular audience into the cause. Really, what young man doesn't want a chance at heroism? Doesn't yearn to know he's stepped into the destiny life handed him? The kindling was dry—it was only his job to strike the match and set it aflame. In his more whimsical moments, John sometimes wondered if his father was at all amused that John's "gift for instigation," as Mama always put it, had been put to such a virtuous use.

No sense pondering that. Father was undoubtedly back in Charleston and it was General Barnes's approval that mattered at the moment. When John walked into the general's office and stood at attention, Barnes gave him a broad smile. "Outstanding speech. I could have piled all the 'Four Minute Men' into one uniform and not done as well. We had two dozen new recruits before lunchtime today, and while I haven't talked to the navy I suspect they did just as well." He gestured toward the chair that fronted his desk. "At ease, son, get off that leg of yours."

John settled into the chair. "I'm glad to see you pleased, sir." He'd always liked Ashton Barnes, but he was smart enough to be a little afraid of the man and the power he wielded.

"I am. I am indeed. I knew you were the man for the job." Usually a straight shooter, John didn't like the way the general watched the way he laid his cane against the chair. Why did people always stare at the cane? Why never the leg? Or just at him? The general at least did him the courtesy of acknowledging the injury.

That reaction was always easier to bear than those who did a poor job of pretending to ignore it, like his father. Barnes nodded toward John's outstretched right leg. "How *is* the leg getting on?"

John stared down at the stiff limb. It never bent easily anymore so he'd stopped trying in cases where there was enough room. "Fine, sir. I'm better than most."

"I suspect you are." Barnes took off his glasses and pinched the bridge of his nose. "I don't like to see our boys coming home in pieces like this. Victory can't come soon enough, in my book."

The general had handed him the perfect opening, and John was going to take it. "I mean to go back, sir. As soon as I can."

"So your father tells me."

So Father *had* spoken with Barnes. John had suspected it—expected it, actually, given the colonel's clear-but-unspoken distaste for his current assignment. It struck John as ironic that Oscar Gallows's long, deep shadow lent John half the "marquee value" his current speeches produced. The Gallows family name got him this job as much as his silver tongue. After all, Gallowses were pillars of Charleston society long before John had been lauded as a hero.

While it goaded John that his father had lobbied the general behind his back, anything that sped up his return to combat was a welcome development. "I don't think it'll take more than three or four weeks here for me to finish healing up. Maybe two if that brute of a therapist has me doing any more exercises. I'm grateful for the chance to toot the army's horn, but with all due respect, I'd rather be back in France."

The general steepled his hands. "Much as I'd like to appease your father, or you, your doctors haven't cleared you for duty."

He didn't say "yet." John didn't like the omission one bit. Father probably caught that one as well, which may have been why he'd skipped the rally. Wounded out of the service wouldn't play well with Oscar Gallows.

It didn't play well with him, either. He'd throw the cane away tomorrow and grit his teeth until they fell out before he'd listen to any doctor tell him he couldn't go back up and finish what he'd started. He had no intention of being left behind among the wounded, even if others thought him a hero. His heroism was unfinished business, as far as John was concerned. He needed to be back in the fight, not sitting over here spouting rousing tales while his battalion earned a victory. "They will soon enough. Sooner on your recommendation, sir."

"I won't say you haven't been valuable overseas, but you're of no value at all if that leg fails you when you need it most. I admire your eager spirit, John—" Barnes knew what he was doing when he intentionally used his given name like a friend of the family would— "but don't let your impatience get you killed. You'll go back when you're ready, and I'm of no mind to send you off a minute before."

It was the closest thing to a promise he'd had yet; John wasn't going to let this "friend of the family" go at a mere hint. "But you'll send me? When I'm ready?" He was ready *now*.

"I imagine I will, yes." He spoke like a true commander—leaving himself the tiniest of escapes just in case.

He may never get another chance like this. The colonel had obviously asked for it. *He'd* asked for it. He'd just given the army several weeks of record-breaking recruitment speeches. John stood, without his cane. He extended his hand. "I'd like your word on it, sir. I'll give speeches until I'm blue in the face, I'll rouse up recruits out of the sand, but I want to know you'll send me back when I'm ready."

Barnes hesitated for a moment, John's message of "I will hold you to this" coming through loud and clear. "Very well," he said after an insufferable pause. They shook on it. John had his guarantee. He wouldn't end the war as a campaign poster. He'd go back where he belonged and make a name for himself on the battlefield, where it really mattered. "Thank you, sir."

"I'd say you're welcome, Captain, but I'm not so sure."

John allowed himself the luxury of picking his cane back up, even though it shot pain like a bolt of lightning through his hip to bend over so far. "I'm sure enough for the both of us," he said when he was upright again, making sure none of the strain showed in his voice.

"You should know it would help, Gallows, if I could have your cooperation on a—shall we say an unconventional little campaign of ours."

Now it came out. Give and get, push and pull. Why was he surprised the general had a trick up his striped sleeve? "Anything you need, sir."

"Don't be so agreeable, son, until you've heard what it is the Red Cross has in mind."

John sat back down again, the ache in his leg now matched by a lump in his throat.

## Chapter Five

A few days after the rally, Leanne sat in the hospital meeting room helping an older nurse struggle through her first cumbersome knitting stitches. "Yes—" she smiled at the confused grimaces given by many of the women around her "—it does feel funny at first. Give it a few days, and you'll be amazed how quickly you take to it."

Another nurse held up the yarn Leanne had distributed at the beginning of class. "It's drab stuff, don't you think? I'd rather go to war in red socks. Or blue."

"As long as they're warm and dry, we don't much care what color they are," came a voice from behind Leanne's shoulder. She turned to find Captain Gallows poking his head into the room.

"Captain Gallows, have you decided to take up knitting?"

"Well, since my job is to encourage, I thought I shouldn't stop at soldiers." He stepped into the room and leaned against the doorway. Leanne suspected he was well aware of the fine figure he cut standing in such a cavalier manner. Around her, stitching ground to a halt. The young woman Leanne was currently sitting next to actually sighed and dropped her knitting to her lap. "Knit as if our lives depended upon it, ladies," Gallows said with a gallant flair, "for I dare say they do. An army fights on its feet, you know."

"Y'all sound like the Red Cross poster," a hospital cook to Leanne's left remarked, holding up the very beginning of a sock.

"Good for me." He grinned. "That means I've gotten it right. It seems I *am* your poster boy. Or will be, next week."

"How very fortunate." Ida, who had stopped into the class to have Leanne correct a mistake on her current pair of socks, nearly purred her approval. "How so?"

Gallows sat down, and for the first time Leanne noticed how a shred of annoyance clipped his words. "I'm your new student." There was the tiniest edge to the way he bit off the *t* in the last word.

"You?"

"Under orders, it seems." He looked at the yarn as though it would infect him on contact.

Leanne dropped a stitch—something she never did. "Am I to understand that you've been *ordered* to learn how to knit?" She tried not to laugh, but the very thought of gallant Captain Gallows struggling with the turn of a sock heel was just too amusing an image, especially after the way he'd acted earlier. He may have long, elegant fingers, but they'd tangle mercilessly under so fine a task. Not only had he been dismissive, but Leanne was sure the captain hadn't nearly the patience for it. He'd make a ghastly student.

Her assessment must have shown on her face, for his

look darkened. Even though this was very obviously not his idea, he didn't take to being doubted or dismissed. Oh, others might be fooled by his very good show, but Leanne could tell he wasn't the least bit happy at the prospect of…whatever it was he'd been ordered to do. Which, actually, she wasn't quite sure of yet. "You're to knit Red Cross socks?"

"More precisely, I'm to be photographed learning how to knit Red Cross socks. I suppose as long as the rascals get the shot they want, whether or not I actually master the thing is beside the point."

"Not to me," Leanne countered. No set of cameras was going to turn her beloved craft and service into a three-ring circus. No, sir, not with this soldier.

"Leanne's never failed yet—every student she's had has managed at least one pair of socks," said the woman to Leanne's right with an enormous grin.

"If not dozens," Ida added, her grin even wider. "I doubt she'll let you be her first failure. Especially not on—did you say camera? Photographs?"

It was starting to make sense. Although many people had taken up the cause, the Red Cross was still woefully short of knitters. They'd been trying to convince more males to take up the needles in support of soldiers, and hadn't had much luck. Capturing photos of someone with Captain Gallows's reputation learning to knit would go a long way toward convincing other men to do likewise. They'd never find a more convincing spokesman. But goodness knows what they'd done to secure his cooperation, for she was sure he wasn't pleased at the prospect by any means.

"I'm evidently the man to convince America's men to knit. Or at least America's boys."

"Our dashing hero put to the needles." Ida giggled. "Why, it's a fine idea when you think of it. I know I can't wait to see your first sock, Captain. I expect you could auction it off to the highest bidder and raise loads of funds for the Red Cross."

"I declare, Ida, you're brilliant." Leanne jumped on the idea. If nothing else, it'd force the captain to see the project through, not just sit long enough to knit on film, but to actually learn the thing. And that was a most entertaining prospect. "I think you've hit on the perfect plan."

"You're joking." Gallows balked. "It'll be a hideous thing unfit for service to any soldier's foot."

"All the more reason that it should serve in some other way, then." Leanne couldn't suppress a wide smile. "We could set up a booth to auction it off at the Charleston Red Cross Christmas Banquet in November. My mama's on the committee. I think a deadline would be a grand motivation for your progress, don't you?"

Gallows stared at her, half amused, half daunted. "I don't think the general knows who he's dealing with. That's downright mischievous, Miss Sample."

"Oh, no," said another of the women. "I think it's the best idea ever. I wouldn't be surprised if Leanne's class size doubled the moment folks found out."

"And you do your best work with an audience, Captain Gallows. You told me yourself."

"Did I?" He had the look of a man who knew he was cornered. Leanne couldn't hide the delightful spark of amusement and conquest she felt at turning the captain's monstrous ego to a useful purpose. The woman was right—her classes would swell with new students once word got out that the dashing Captain Gallows was a fellow knitter. And with an audience to watch his triumphs and failures, he'd simply have to succeed. Perhaps even excel. And wouldn't that be something to see?

"I am undone," he said, throwing up his hands. "Overthrown. When you keep your appointment with the general this afternoon, I hope you won't throw me to the wolves. Or is it the sheep in this case?"

"The general?"

"You're to see General Barnes at two o'clock. He wants to explain his idea to you, but I have the most peculiar feeling it is you who'll be doing all the explaining. The man ought to be warned."

Leanne blushed. "You overstate my influence, Captain Gallows."

"No," he countered, giving her the most unsettling look, "I don't think I do." He got up—with a grimace of pain Leanne doubted anyone else noticed—and saluted the group. "Press on, ladies. Next week I join the forces. Until then."

He made his way out the door, but Leanne was not done with this conversation. She told the group to continue knitting and caught up with the captain a ways down the hall.

"You're serious?" she said as he turned, suddenly wondering if the whole thing had been one of Ida's pranks.

"I assure you," he replied, "I'd hardly make something like this up. I'm not at all sure my dignity will survive the day."

So he had been cornered into it. By what? She motioned for them to continue walking. "If you don't mind my asking, what on earth could make you agree to something like this?"

He gave out a slight sigh. "Let's just say the general has something I want, and like most good commanders, he's wielding it to his advantage." He chuckled and leaned back against the wall. He made it look cavalier, but Leanne suspected by the way he cocked his right hip that he was very good at finding obscure ways to take the weight off his leg. "Blackmailed into needlework. I'll never live it down."

"What, exactly, is the general proposing?"

"I'm sure he'll tell you at two o'clock."

"I'm sure you'll understand that I'd rather know *now*."

Gallows took off his hat and sighed. "It seems a hoard of photographers from *Era* magazine will be invited to take pictures of you teaching me to knit. They'll write an article saying how easy it is, and how much everyone's help is needed, probably even publish a copy of the Red Cross pattern or whatever it is you call the directions. I'll go on and on in dashing terms about how important it is, and how every boy should step up to the plate and do his bit. You'll be famous for a spell and I'll hold up my end of the bargain—which evidently now will involve producing an actual sock, thanks to your quick-witted friend back there. I should think it all is rather obvious."

Leanne crossed her arms over her chest, not caring

for his tone. "I should think it all rather obvious that I ought to have been *asked*. I don't much care for being made a spectacle of, Captain, even if it is your favorite pastime."

"No one asked me, either. I'm following orders."

"And you strike me so much like a man who always does what he's told." Leanne turned to head back to her classroom.

"I'm not!" he shot back. "Not unless it gets me what I want."

Leanne merely huffed. No one seemed to give one whit about her opinion in all of this. She marched off to her classroom without a single look back.

# Chapter Six

Captain Gallows sat entirely too close. Leanne shifted her chair farther away from him as they sat in the Red Cross House parlor. Then she set her knitting bag on a small table and pulled it between them for good measure. Their first photo session was in three days, but he'd pestered her nonstop until she'd agreed to give him an off-camera lesson first.

"I still don't know about this," she said. They were two minutes into the lesson and she was already regretting giving in to his persistent demands. "You're supposed to be photographed learning how to knit."

"And I will." While Gallows's smile was worthy of a matinee idol, it was a genuine one—or at least, it seemed to be. He had another manufactured smile—she'd seen him employ it during the reception after his first appearance. That smile was just as cinema-dashing, but it never reached his eyes with the same intensity. It stopped somehow at the edges of his mouth.

She could see the distinction between his "public" and his "private" smiles as clear as day, but others didn't seem to. It bothered her—and she suspected it bothered him—that she could tell the difference. It felt like too much information to know, like walking into a room that ought to have been locked. Why did she, of all people, see through his facade? Worse yet, he knew she recognized her effect on him. And it bothered her that he knew she knew. The whole business felt like an emotional house of mirrors—awareness reflecting back onto confusion upon discomfort. Knitting was supposed to be calming.

Leanne picked up the set of needles she'd selected for him. They were slightly larger than the usual sock needles, but Captain Gallows needed something substantial that wouldn't get lost in those large hands. "Some would say learning ahead of the photographs that are supposed to *show* you learning would be cheating." Where was the nerve to talk to him like that coming from? One simply didn't tease a war hero as if he were a little brother. Certainly not this war hero. Still, the spark he would get in his eyes when she did was an irresistible lure.

He raised an eyebrow, the gleam emanating full force. "I'm not cheating. I'm *rehearsing*."

"Really?" She gave him an expression she hoped showed her dislike for the way he wrangled semantics to his advantage.

"Remember, it's my job to make this look easy."

It bothered her that he actually had a point. The Red Cross cause would only be served by his mastery. "This, of course, places no small amount of pressure on my teaching skills."

His eyes sparkled. "Let's not dwell on how much is at stake."

Leanne handed him the yarn and needles, and despite the fact that they had looked so enormous in her own grasp, they looked nearly small in his. He turned the objects over in his hands, peering at them as if with the right look they'd give up secrets. He shifted his eyes from the dull green yarn to look at her. They were an exquisite indigo, his eyes. A deep-sea blue, like mussel shells or the last hour of a summer's evening. "Wait a minute, there are four needles here. My mother knits with only two. You're not pulling one over on me or anything, are you? It *is* easy?"

So his mother knitted. She tried to imagine little Johnny Gallows sitting at his mother's feet while she knitted him a Christmas sweater and couldn't bring up the image. The man in front of her looked like he'd never been small—or innocent—a day in his life.

He certainly looked far from childlike now. It was as if his personality only intensified the closer one stood. And he was so fond of standing close. She moved her chair back an inch. "Oh, some take to it naturally." She made her voice sound more casual than she felt. If he'd noticed her retreat, he didn't show it. "Minnie Havers," she went on, "why, she had her first sock done almost within the week. Took to it like a fish to water. Others, well, I'd say it's more of a struggle. And no, Captain, I quite assure you all socks are knitted with four needles like these. Surely a man of your aptitude should master it in no time."

John held up the needles. "No time, hmm?"

"Most do. Well, most *women,* that is. I haven't taught my first class of soldiers yet. Those start next week."

"I am your first male student?" He enjoyed that far too much.

Leanne cleared her throat rather than answer. "I find it's a matter of dexterity. Do you have a great deal of dexterity, Captain Gallows?"

She regretted the question the moment she asked it. "I've been told I have the hands of a surgeon." He said it in a way that made Leanne sure she didn't want him to elaborate.

"Let's get started." Leanne had never actually taught a man to knit before. Normally it involved a lot of her holding the yarn and needles together with the student, repositioning fingers, adjusting the tension of the yarn. Touching. She'd never given it a moment's thought before, but now it meant touching a *man's* hands. *This* man's hands. The air between them was charged enough as it was. It seemed foolish, but Leanne was afraid to touch him. It would cross some kind of line she hadn't even realized was there.

She attempted, in response, to teach him without touching his hands. This resulted in nothing short of disaster. His frustration built on her tension, tangling their composure tighter than the yarn in their fingers.

"It feels like wrestling a porcupine," Captain Gallows grunted when a needle slipped through the stitches and fell to the carpet at his feet. "The annoying little sticks won't stay put." She knew it would pain him to reach over and fetch the needle, so she bent and picked it up as quickly as she could. The look on his face—reflecting the limitation she knew he would never speak of—almost made her shudder. Captain Gallows was obviously used to mastery of anything he attempted, and the effort required to do what he clearly deemed a simple task simmered dark behind his eyes.

"It's much more difficult for larger fingers." While she'd meant the remark to soothe his feelings, it did just the opposite. He looked as if he'd snarl at the yarn within minutes. A shameful corner of her heart enjoyed watching the arrogant captain meet his match, but the part of her that could see through his bravado winced at causing him further pain. No one likes to have their weaknesses displayed. "You know," she confessed in the hopes of easing his nerves, "you were right to keep this first lesson between us." Under any other circumstances the phrase "between us" would have been harmless. When "between us" meant between her and Captain John Gallows, however, the words darted between them like an electrical charge.

He grunted again. "Ease up, Captain. Hold that yarn any tighter and you'll lose circulation in your fingers."

He dropped the knitting to his lap and closed his eyes. "If I'm going to make a complete fool of myself in front of you, we might as well drop the formalities. Let's just watch *John* Gallows fail at knitting for the moment, rather than the spectacle of *Captain Gallows* botching needlecraft, shall we?"

Leanne wasn't sure what drove her to lead his hands back down to the needles, and gently position them in the correct way. It wasn't a wise choice. They were tanned, strong hands; large and well-groomed. It was the warmth of them that struck her most of all. She wasn't sure why that surprised her. Perhaps because it served as a reminder that he was human, flesh and blood with fears and feelings like any other man. She'd forgotten that he'd been dragged into this bargain as much as she. He shifted his weight in a way that told her his leg was starting to ache, but anyone could see he wasn't giving in until he'd done a respectable stretch of successful stitches. He was making a genuine effort.

She tried again to reposition his fingers. Some odd little shudder went through his hands when she touched him. Or was it her hands that shuddered? Or had she merely felt a tremble but not seen it? She forced a casualness to her touch as she showed him again how to wrap the yarn around his right index finger—the one with the long scar down the side. "You don't need to strangle it, Captain, just let this finger do the work."

"John," he corrected as he fumbled his way through a stitch—labored but correctly done. "At least off camera."

"Well, John." The familiarity felt more daring than she liked, even though she worked to hide it from her voice. "It feels odd to *everyone* at first, not just war heroes." John rolled his shoulders and scowled as he produced a second stitch—also correct but less forced. "See? There's no need to mount a battle here." She leaned over to adjust his far hand again, catching a whiff of his aftershave. He smelled exotic and sophisticated.

"This must get easier." She couldn't tell if it was a question or a demand.

"Yes." She felt the first smile of the afternoon sneak across her lips. "It does."

He looked up at her for the first time. Were she knitting at the moment, she would have surely dropped a stitch. He would have enjoyed that. "It must. I've seen young boys do this."

"That is the idea, isn't it?" And it was. It wasn't just some general's folly to decide to convince America's boys to knit. The clicking needles of American women and girls simply weren't enough. The Red Cross was so desperate for woolen socks that this "farfetched scheme" to recruit boys was, in fact, important to brave men risking their lives across the ocean.

"And you'll teach injured soldiers to do this?" he asked. "To pass the time in the hospital as well as meet the need for socks?" What he hadn't realized was that five tidy stitches had worked their way onto his needle while he spoke. While many might accuse John Gallows of great arrogance, his only knitting sin was the universal fault of trying too hard.

"Yes, that's the idea. It's been done successfully in some other hospitals, so I am eager to try it here."

"Done successfully, you say? Well, then, I simply can't allow this to elude me, can I? My own grandmother," he went on, "who can barely see well enough to know which Gallows is who, can do this." Three more stitches.

"Your grandmother knits?" *Keep him talking*, Leanne urged herself, realizing that talking was the key to keeping him from overthinking the simple stitches.

"Constantly. I have several holiday sweaters in the most atrocious patterns you can imagine. And a few scarves that could scare away the enemy." He looked down, a little stunned to realize he'd made it all the way to the end of the double-pointed needle. "Now what?"

She didn't have to force herself to take his hands

and show him how to switch to the next needle. And while she didn't dare look up at him while she touched those hands, she could feel his smile behind her. "See, just like that. All lined up like soldiers, they are. Well done."

He said nothing until the silence forced her to look up at him. When she did, Leanne felt it burrow its way under her ribs and steal her breath. "Well taught, Nurse Sample."

"Leanne," she heard herself say, but it was as if Ida's daring nature had inhabited her voice. "Off camera."

## Chapter Seven

"**O**ne more inch…just one inch farther…*ugh!*" John growled in exasperation at the joints that would not bend to his will. It was as if the plaster cast on his leg had never come off—the stubborn limb refused to regain the needed flexibility. He gripped the bench harder and set his teeth against the pain, leaning into another push. It was probably no accident that the "reconstruction clinic," the gymnasium on base that housed the staff and equipment designed to rehabilitate wounded soldiers, was olive-green rather than hospital white. To John, the gymnasium was no less a battle-field than the front line. It reminded him that he was a soldier—and that a soldier belonged on the front lines, where he intended to return as soon as possible, even if he had to thrash his leg into submission every step of the way.

"Whoa there, stallion. You're not going to get what you want out of that leg by beating it up." Dr. Charles Madison pushed John's leg back down. John hated how easily the small doctor could do it, too. The weakness in his leg made him crazy, and Madison had a gift for showcasing just how much strength John had lost.

"It doesn't bend a single inch farther this week." Complaining felt childish, but John's frustration stole his composure as easily as the dirigible stay lines had shredded his leg. Patience was not a virtue Gallows men either possessed or cherished. John pulled himself upright with something just short of a snarl.

"This isn't the kind of thing that goes in a straight line." Dr. Madison, his Bostonian accent sounding entirely too fatherly, sat down on the bench next to John. He set his clipboard down with a weariness that spoke *do we have to go over this again?* without words. "It's going to be back-and-forth. And if you push it too far too fast, I promise you it will be more back than forth. Flex your foot."

John shot him a look but obeyed. The doctor could make "flex your foot" sound like "go sit in the corner."

"You've got more rotation than you did last week. You tore nearly every tendon from your hip down. It's a wonder you've still got use of the leg at all, Gallows. Those tether lines could have ripped the whole thing off."

"Yes, yes, I'm so *fabulously fortunate*." John launched himself up off the bench and hobbled to the bars on the wall nearby. Did Madison think he didn't know that? And if those lines—those horrid steel lines that felt like they were slicing his leg off from the inside out while he dangled—had severed his leg, where would he have been? Falling thousands of feet out of the sky to drown in the ocean. If he lived through the fall. The mere thought of that terrifying, helpless hanging sensation, those minutes of absolute dread that felt like hours of twisting over what he was certain would be the site of his death, sent that icy sensation through his chest again. He hated this sniper-fire fear of that memory which could attack him without warning. A wrong comment or even the slightest hint of falling— and he slipped all the time these days—would catapult him back to those moments in the sky. Somehow he knew that if he ever had to hang upside down again for any reason—some exercise or calisthenic someone dreamed up to rehabilitate him—he'd stop breathing altogether. Die of remembered fright on the spot. Just the kind of way every war hero ought to behave.

"For a talented spokesman, I wonder sometimes if I ought to punch you for the thoughtless things you say." Madison cornered him against the wall and pinned him with severe eyes. "Look around you, son. Wake up and see just how fortunate you are. That imperfect leg you so despise is at least *still there*. You've your wits about you and the admiration of many. Take a walk with me over to another hall of the hospital—the one with no visitors—and see some of the ghosts we can barely call men. Complain to them as they sit in chairs mumbling because not only their arm but their mind is gone."

John was in no mood to be smothered by the silver lining of his own survival. Madison didn't get like this often, and it bothered John to no end when the doctor lectured him on his advantages. He needed no reminding. "I know I ought to be glad I'm alive," he mumbled with reluctance. That was, in fact, part of the problem. Part of the thing niggling at the back of his mind, taunting him on the edges of sleep. He was alive. He was fortunate. More than that, he was lauded and admired. He just never felt like he earned it. And that wasn't the sort of thing one mentioned to anyone. Humility was one thing—and another one of those virtues not especially prized by Gallows men. Feeling like a fraud? That was another. "I let my frustration get the better of my mouth."

John had been down that particular hospital hallway. He knew soldiers who, once maimed, wanted nothing more than to get back out on the front lines so they could be shot down and end their misery. They wouldn't put their families through the shame of suicide, yet they couldn't face the prospect of a lifetime without a limb or an eye or whatever. Those men clamored back to the battlefield with a dangerous "death wish."

He wasn't one of those. John wanted back in the battle so he could prove to himself he was the hero everyone seemed to think he was. Whatever he did— and honestly, he didn't even clearly remember most of it—up there to those dirigible lines was sheer, terrorized survival, not heroism. Grab this or fall. Secure that or risk it ripping off and taking him with it. He climbed out onto that airship not because he wanted to be brave, but because it was try something or die. He was working only to save himself, and that other lives would benefit from his actions was the last thing on his mind. That wasn't the kind of thing one ought to get a medal for. The fellows who had risked their lives to pull in wounded mates, who went back out into gunfire to drag their captain to safety? Those were the men who should be making speeches and wearing medals. He wasn't here stirring up patriotism because he was brave. He was here because his name was Gallows, he had a silver tongue, took a good photograph and had somehow managed not to die.

Ida tossed her nurse's hat down on her bureau. "You know, I thought I was an admirer of the male physiology."

Leanne looked up from the outline of reconstructive exercises she'd been studying. "You're not?"

"I think how God put us together is one of the most amazing things ever. Y'all would think there's no way to make it tedious." Ida leaned back in her chair and looked up at the ceiling, her long auburn mane tumbling down behind her. She had a gift for striking dramatic poses.

They sat in their shared bedroom at the Red Cross House. It was comfortably furnished by army standards, with a pair of beds, bureaus and desks much like the dormitory rooms she'd had at the university. It had color and comfort, two things the bland army housing clearly lacked. She found she couldn't fully approve of the way the U.S. Army piled soldiers into barracks that looked more like hospital wards than homes. The standardized, militarized buildings utterly lacked the pleasant feel of the Red Cross House. Not that the Red Cross House was perfect, but Leanne had come to appreciate privacy for the dear commodity it was in military life. It made her grateful she enjoyed Ida's company so much. "I take it you're not fond of your current rotation?"

"I have babysat my five-year-old cousins and heard less complaining. And I declare, I could be tending a ship of pirates and hear more civilized conversation. To think I thought being surrounded by soldiers would be a good thing!" She flung out one hand as if addressing the universe. "I had to smack one private's hand three times for attempting to get…too private."

Leanne laughed at Ida's pun. "Your sense of humor serves you well." Ida's vibrancy made her a grand friend to have in trying times. "I imagine you're just the kind of care some of those boys need. Have you drawn any of them yet?" Ida was an immensely talented artist. She'd tacked a few of her better sketches up on the wall of their room and Leanne thought they rivaled some of the things she'd seen framed on the best walls in Charleston.

Ida opened one eye from her dramatic recline and shot Leanne a look. "I have not. They don't merit my talents. Truly, I'm not askin' for chivalry. Just a little civility would be fine with me. Goodness knows, with the work I put into seeing them healed and healthy, it's the least they could do. A man's broad shoulder is one of the finest things God has ever made, but I had to muck out the gouges in one today that rivaled a Tennessee swamp. By rights, he should owe me nothing less than a fine dinner for my troubles."

"Have you been to Tennessee, Ida?"

Ida groaned. "I feel like I have now. At least that one had the decency to pass out eventually. At the start, he was fighting me like I was the enemy." She pulled herself upright. "And speaking of pain and chivalry, how was your knitting lesson with Captain Gallows?"

Leanne winced. She'd hoped to avoid this conversation with Ida, who was quick to insert a romantic intention into just about any male-female interaction. Leanne hadn't really decided what to make of John Gallows, and she didn't want Ida jumping to all kinds of conclusions. "Well—" she planted her eyes on the outline "—I did change my mind about it being unnecessary. As it turns out, Captain Gallows did most certainly need a dress rehearsal."

Ida raised an eyebrow.

"Really, I'm not sure he had any more trouble than any other first-time student, but it did seem to fluster him more than he liked." She remembered the look on his face, amazed how it still surprised her for reasons she couldn't quite work out.

"Fluster?" She leaned on her desk, planting her elbows in a "tell me all about it" pose.

Leanne looked down to see she'd written "John?" above an illustration of leg exercises. She quickly crossed it out and turned the page. The last thing she needed to do was to refer to Captain Gallows by his given name in front of someone with Ida's imagination. "I believe the captain is used to mastering things quickly, that's all. He'd thought it would be easier—I did, too, actually—but even with larger needles his big hands make it difficult. It took longer than either of us thought it would."

"But you succeeded in teaching our brave hero?"

Leanne wasn't sure she succeeded at anything except bringing herself into a further state of confusion. Still, she was relatively certain Gallows would look more in command of his stitches at the first photo shoot tomorrow. He'd actually been right. Had they just taken photos, it would have been clear to her or any other knitter that he wasn't really knitting. It was painfully obvious to her when people pretended to knit in paintings or photos—their needles were always pointed upward, waggling about in a way that couldn't possibly produce stitches. John had wanted to make sure he was knitting so that it looked real in the photographs. While she'd first chalked that up to vanity, she'd realized it was a sort of integrity. An honor she hadn't really attributed to the man with the gleaming cinemastar smile. "Yes," she said feeling a regrettable hint of color come over her cheeks. "We made it work and I think tomorrow will be a success."

"You'll be famous. Have you thought of that?"

Leanne sincerely doubted anyone even noticed her in the same room with someone like Captain Gallows. "Not really."

"I heard the quartermaster talking about the supplies he needed to get for all those *Era* magazine people. They're talking about putting Captain Gallows on the cover." She nodded at Leanne. "If he's on, *you're* on. We're gonna have to get your hair done up right and everything. Have you even given a moment's thought to that?"

Leanne had actually thought about what she wanted to wear. Not because of the cameras, but because of something John had said. Something about sky-blue being his favorite color. She had a blouse the color of the sky. Mama had said the color suited her especially well. The sleeves had a delicate ruffle at her wrists, which she supposed would be the only part of her to make it into a photo of any kind.

Yesterday, her planned obscurity didn't bother her at all. As a matter of fact, General Barnes had said something to the effect that she'd "hardly be noticed" and she'd been almost relieved at the assurance. Today, after the supreme teaching effort required to get Gallows to any kind of competency, she found herself miffed. No one had ever asked what she thought of this campaign. Of course she agreed with the need to get more people knitting for the soldiers. And it was dreadfully difficult to convince boys to pick up the yarn and needles with images of their doting grandmothers clouding their vision. But it all seemed so…so…contrived. As if both she and John had been tricked into something far beyond their original intentions by people who didn't really care about the true purpose.

John seemed to actually care. He covered it up well, but she could see it in the way he chose his words, the way he would try over and over to get the stitches right. But she had the niggling sense that his ego wouldn't allow anyone to know he cared. Would he let go of all that bravado if they knew each other better? Did she want to know John Gallows better?

Would he even take the time if given the chance? Leanne found she couldn't be sure he took this as seriously as she. She took this very seriously, and it bothered her that no one else seemed to. Certainly not the general nor any of the *Era* staff. They'd made no effort to get in touch with her directly, and learn more about the knitting program. Clearly the publicity angle involving the captain was all that interested them. It was probably just another way to sell magazines. And could she really be sure of John's motives? John Gallows was known in Charleston as a charmer who collected—and then dismissed—female admirers. What if he'd been behind it from the beginning, picked her out for what he hoped was a compliant spirit? Yet another damsel who would merely swoon under his spell? She felt her annoyance rise just picturing those magazine people angling lights and asking for wider smiles. Sky-blue? Suddenly Leanne wanted to wear bright red. To stand out. To stand up.

"Leanne!" Ida was off her chair, facing Leanne, waving her hands as if flagging down a battleship. "Where'd you go, honey? Y'all are frowning like we're at a funeral. It's just hair."

Leanne slapped her notebook shut. "Yes, I want you to do my hair up nice. And would you lend me that bright yellow dress you have? The one with the buttons on the cuffs?"

Ida swung back on one hip, eyes wide. "Not fading into the background tomorrow, are we?"

"Absolutely not. The method might be a bit…unorthodox, but the cause is important. No one's going to push me and all the other dedicated knitters out of the picture tomorrow. Not while I'm around. There's more to what we're doing than Captain John Gallows, and the American people need to know that."

Ida stood up, saluted and winked. "Yes, ma'am!"

## Chapter Eight

John's leg was screaming at him from inside perfectly pressed trousers. His shirt collar tightened around his neck like a starchy, menacing hand. At least in war, no one gave a fig what a man looked like or how he stood, as long as he got where he needed to be. Here, he was waging a battle with the barbed wire under his skin while smirking and making small talk with a dozen people who had no idea what torture it was to bend his right leg at a natural angle. And hold it for the endless seconds it took to get the right image. They'd been at it for hours, and already he was coming to hate the funny accordion-faced camera as much as he loathed the pointed metal knitting needles. People said the camera loved him, but he did not return the affection.

"You were right," Leanne remarked after the first handful of photos. "It would have been dreadfully hard to learn under these conditions." A man in a plaid vest had repositioned her hands dozens of times, and even John could hear the frustration in Leanne's words. Obviously the wonder born of buzzing activity and bright lights had died down quickly for her, made worse by the tactless positioning of photographers who made it very clear they weren't too worried about getting her in the shot.

Which was a waste, for she looked beautiful today. John could tell she'd taken extra care with her hair and dress. "You should wear that color more often," he ventured when one assistant all but pushed her out of the way. The bright yellow made the peach of her skin fairly glow. He yanked his hat back from some apple-cheeked boy charged with brushing nonexistent lint from it. "Clark, I want Miss Sample in the next shot."

Clark Summers looked up from his camera with a dubiously raised eyebrow. "Do you now?" His tone implied that what Captain Gallows wanted didn't much matter at the moment.

Someone fired off one of those flash contraptions, making Leanne jump. The photographer rolled his eyes as if he considered working with such innocents penance for some earlier photographic sin.

"I do," John replied. He poured so much Gallows command into those two words that the hat boy sat down in deference. "Surely you don't plan to slap me on some magazine cover without a pretty girl by my side. I'm supposed to recruit young lads to the cause, aren't I? You don't expect me to do that without a lovely lady on hand to admire my efforts?"

John regretted those last words the minute he'd said them, but his leg was making it hard to think well. Miss Sample's spine shot straight and the needles dropped to her lap. Worse yet, her foot began tapping. Nothing good ever came out of a lady tapping her foot, ever. The fire he had suspected was lurking under all that peaches-and-cream was sneaking out under all this scrutiny. He liked that, although John was convinced that amusement could well be the death of him. If his leg didn't kill him first.

He made up his mind, then and there, to ensure he saw Leanne Sample someplace much closer to his own territory. Someplace where he held most of the cards. He smiled as it came to him just where that was.

The captain had nerve, she'd give him that much.

It wasn't that she minded being pulled out of the standard nurse's rotation—those shifts could be dreary, indeed—it was that she hadn't been given a choice at all. The smug grin on John Gallows's face as she signed the clipboard admitting her to the reconstruction gymnasium pressed down on her, glossy and manipulative. Clearly he thought he'd done her some kind of favor. While other nurses might fawn over the chance to work so closely with such "a hero," Gallows's manipulative nature canceled out any gratitude Leanne could muster.

She walked straight toward him, hoping her annoyance showed as she held his gaze. "You press your advantage with entirely too much ease, Captain Gallows."

He sat lengthwise on a bench, slowly hoisting a small weighted bag on his ankle. He was pretending it took no effort. "Not at all. We're allowed to request specific attendants. I requested you."

Leanne stood over him crossing her arms over her chest. "I fear I'm not sufficiently qualified to supervise your exercises." She stopped short of saying "given the extent of your injuries" because she knew that would bother him. Then again, perhaps he deserved to be

bothered after the way he'd behaved at their photographic session yesterday.

John leaned back on the bench, the white of his exercise shirt stretching across his chest. "Nonsense. You'd
only be taking temperatures and walking lads out on
the lawn anyway. I know you like a challenge." It really
was a crime what white did for the man's eyes.

"You do not know me at all, Captain. If you did,
you would know I'm not one to play favorites. Or be
played as one." She wouldn't give him one inch of the
satisfaction of thinking that she'd been even the smallest bit flattered by his special request of her—she was
rather ashamed of it herself. She wasn't blind to the
way women looked at John Gallows, how they flocked
around him like gulls to a fish boat, circling and diving
for scraps of regard. There was something regretfully
pleasing in being singled out, even by him. But her mission here was so much more important than any small
boon to her vanity, and she was aggravated with herself
for forgetting that—and aggravated with him as well,
for making her forget.

She watched his eyes narrow the slightest bit as the
orderly pulled his leg farther up, noticed the teeth grit
inside his constant smile. "Would it help you to know
I had a practical reason for requesting you?"

She raised an inquiring eyebrow.

The leg started its descent and she could see his grip
on the bench loosen. "They're going to stuff my leg
into horrid packs of ice this afternoon, and I'll have to
sit there like a landed fish at market." He nodded at the
large orderly currently removing the weighted bag from
his ankle. "No offense to Nelson here, but I'm going to

need more distraction that he can provide. And it might prove a good time to practice my—" he hesitated a fraction of a second "—new skill."

"Your *knitting?*" She emphasized the word. The public spectacle of his knitting had been his doing, after all. She was going to see that he owned up to it. Nelson looked down, hiding his smile in the business of taking weights out of the bag.

"You enjoyed shouting that." There was too much tease in his voice for it to be an accusation.

"I did not shout. And you're enjoying the way you've shanghaied me."

"Nurse Sample, there you are. I see you've met your new assignment." Dr. Madison came up behind her. "Well, of course you've already met, that's the thing of it, isn't it?" He looked over the top of his round glasses at Leanne. "You've your work cut out for you, but I suspect you already know that."

This was how Papa's horses must feel at market. "Tell me, Doctor, will I ever have the pleasure of being *consulted* before pressed into service regarding our esteemed captain?"

Dr. Madison blinked. Evidently it had never occurred to him that giving personal attention to a celebrity rather than clocking time in the hospital wards might not thrill her. Surely it would never occur to Gallows. Madison looked at her for a second, flicked his gaze to the captain, who shrugged. "Yes, well, there it is." He made some kind of notation on his chart and went on as if he'd never heard her. "You're to take three laps around the track, Gallows, followed by the ice for thirty minutes, then a rubdown."

Leanne's eyes went wide. "Not by *you* of course," Captain Gallows assured her. "Whatever else I may be accused of, I am always a gentleman. Nelson over here, however, is a brute. It's more of a pound-down, I promise you."

Dr. Madison handed her the clipboard. "Three laps, one slow, followed by one quick, then the final slow. Long strides, no cane."

Captain Gallows grinned as he pulled his khaki shirt back on. "I'll have to lean on *something,* Doc."

Dr. Madison smiled and turned toward the next bench. "Oh, I'm sure you'll improvise."

Nelson gathered up his things, scurrying out of the way of the captain's grand plan. Leanne felt neatly cornered. Part of her was irritated at his manipulation. A large part. Then again, she remembered Ida's groans about the unpleasant lot she'd been assigned in the wards. Perhaps it was best to look at this with gratitude. Thirty minutes in an ice bath sounded rather painful; could she really blame Captain Gallows for seeking the most distraction possible? And if he actually was planning on knitting, well then she could take satisfaction that her classes for soldiers recognized knitting's ability to distract a man from tedium or pain. And Gallows was in pain, even if he worked hard to hide it from the world. She could see his pain. Maybe she *alone* could see it, and he knew that. Perhaps he felt he could drop the bravado, let his guard down a bit with her. She was here to learn to help soldiers heal, after all—why not this particular soldier?

Why not? The shameless grin on his face as he held his elbow out to her was why not. "Shall we promenade,

Nurse Sample?" One would think from his tone that *he* was escorting *her* around the walking track, not the other way around. Honestly, the man's showmanship knew no bounds.

She slipped one arm into his elbow, holding the clipboard with the other. "What shall we talk of while you *exercise,* Captain?" She felt the hitch in his step, the flinch in his arm when he put unaided weight on his leg. He made sure it wasn't visible to an observer, but it was impossible to hide with her arm in his. She suspected he hadn't counted on that. She suspected he also didn't intend for her to hear the soft curse he muttered under his breath—but hear it she did.

"Anything you choose," he said aloud.

Finally, something in *her* control. "Let's start our discussion, then, on why it is inappropriate to take the Lord's name in vain as you just did."

He made a small groan. "I asked for distraction and you offer a lesson on manners?"

"Courtesy is a most engaging subject, Captain. Take, for example, the fact that most people of faith do not take kindly to a casual use of God's name. I'll ask you to refrain from such language in my presence," she couldn't help adding, "as any true gentleman would."

"Well, I am nothing if not a gentleman." They turned the first corner. He clearly hated being forced to go so slow; impatience and frustration radiated out of his body. "I'll admit, however, to a…" He paused, selecting careful words. "…a respectful indifference to spiritual matters."

"Truly? I was told there were no atheists in foxholes."

"I've done precious little time in foxholes, thank… thank *goodness,*" he corrected himself with a nod toward her. "And I'm not an atheist. I believe God exists, but I don't bother Him with my petty schemes. Your Lord and I? Well, we're not on close terms." He clipped off the end of his last word, cutting his step short. They were only halfway around the lap.

Wordlessly, Leanne shifted their arms so that she held his elbow. He didn't allow himself to lean on her at first, but as they walked on, she felt him sink in slightly to the hold she had on him. It cost him something to do that, and his concession dissolved what was left of her annoyance. "I believe God yearns to be bothered with all our 'petty schemes,' as you call them," she said gently. "Every last one of them."

"He'd never have time to save the world if we bogged Him down with all that. God has a war to win out there. He's on our side, don't you know?"

In hospital rounds she'd had already, Leanne had seen enough meek and wounded soldiers to disagree. They were pale, shallow shadows, echoes of the men they must have once been. "God is in favor of justice, but I can't believe war does not grieve Him. Not as such costs to His children. Not when men…when *boys* come home like this."

"And what do you believe about the other side's boys? Are the enemy boys God's children, too?" He nodded to a slim young man grimacing through each step on a new prosthetic leg. John held the soldier's glare—for it was just that. Gripping two bars as a pair of burly orderlies coaxed him into awkward, painful steps, the look he gave John was sour. As if John had no right to parade his good fortune in front of such a pitiful existence. Leanne felt the air chill, felt John stiffen even as she did herself. "Did God's children do that to him? Why would God make His children wound each other in such horrible ways?"

The patient took one more dark look at John before allowing himself to be turned back the other way, and Leanne found herself grateful to have ended the exchange. It surprised her to realize not everybody admired Captain Gallows. As a matter of fact, based on the incident that just transpired, she was quite sure some men hated him. His golden achievements must seem to them like salt in their wounds. "God did not wound that man. A fallen world's ugly war did that. Hate and greed bring war, evil brings war." She tipped her chin in the direction of the amputee as they turned another corner. "God takes no pleasure in any man's pain and death. I believe God loves the enemy who did that as much as the patriot who endures it."

John was slowing, his gait growing more and more uneven as they went. "But one side is right and the other side is wrong. God cannot be on both sides. It wouldn't square."

She stopped and turned to face him, both to make her point and allow him rest. The effort of the smooth walk he'd just now manufactured had sweat dripping from his temples. His cavalier expression was only a neat mask over the pain in his eyes. "God is God, Captain Gallows. He's not required to 'square' with anything we think or do. I'm not convinced that we don't annoy Him so endlessly with our demands that He take sides."

John took a step away from her, pointing with new vigor. "Ah, so you *do* agree we annoy the Almighty?" He pivoted, as if to stride away in victory, momentarily forgetting his weak leg. The movement tripped him up, so that she had to catch his arm as he tipped against the wall of the gymnasium or he might have tumbled to the ground then and there. For a moment the cool mask was gone, replaced by a frustrated rage that stiffened him all over. For a split second he was hard and dark and dangerous, the kind of man who would smash something or put his fist through a wall. She almost let go of him, the glimpse frightened her so. Then, as if she'd imagined it all, he rearranged his body so that his leaning looked cavalier, lazy even, crossing his bad foot over the one now supporting his weight as if he hadn't a care in the world. "And here I thought courtesy would prove no distraction. Nurse Sample, you outdo yourself."

The way he said *distraction* had a steely knife's edge to it. A defensive blade brandished at her under a slick grin. Leanne didn't know what to do with that. Despite his gift at annoying her, she had found herself actually looking forward to having a serious conversation with the captain. Her boldness in broaching the subject of her faith surprised even her as they walked. Normally, Leanne shied away from spiritual discussions, preferring her passions to rise only around her knitting needles. Where had this eagerness to challenge John Gallows's faith—or lack of it—come from?

Even more surprising was that the captain allowed it—at least for a moment or two. Then matters went too deep, and he had yanked the conversation back under his control.

His statement was no compliment at all. "I…" No reply came to her.

She waited, expecting him to gloss over the moment with another of his smooth comments, but he did not speak, either. His look just now as he stood there with what she suspected others would find a cocky grin, only warned her never to trip him up like that again. As if she'd intentionally gone past his facade, as if it were her fault her beliefs wouldn't "square" with how he saw the world. As if the moment of weakness she'd just seen was an unforgivable sin—on his part and on hers.

Which it wasn't. A man of his influence—even a hardened soldier—wouldn't shy from showing true anger or appropriate fear. Yet, John Gallows kept his mask of dashing mastery up everywhere but with her. She seemed to see underneath the mask with far too much ease. Why was that?

Clearly he was wondering the same thing, if the hint of a glare behind his eyes said anything. And that was hardly fair. She'd not sought to deliberately expose the chinks in his armor. He had no right to blame her when she hadn't even asked for this assignment.

"If I am to walk you, Captain," she said as coolly as she could manage given the firestorm in his eyes, "you'll have to come off that wall." To her great shock, she then offered him her elbow and her best Charleston hospitality smile. "Shall we?"

## Chapter Nine

John hadn't slept well. Leanne's narrowed eyes, strong to the point of defiance, kept appearing behind his closed lids. He'd read her wrong, thought of her as an appealing, even engaging amusement while he worked to be well enough to return. He hadn't planned on her being such a challenge. His good looks and silver tongue never rendered women much of a trial, and while he was never so much of a cad as to abuse these gifts, he wasn't above leveraging them to his advantage. The fact that he didn't seem to have much of an advantage over Leanne Sample, that she pushed back on his ideas with challenging ideas of her own that stole his sleep, was making him prickly and irritable. It was the creamy quality of her voice that clouded his thinking, he decided as he made his way to the gymnasium the next day for his morning therapy.

Usually some form of weight-bearing torture came first, a half an hour or so of pain and sweat under the merciless hands of Nelson. Oh, he'd laugh and joke his way through it, but the truth of it was that the session hurt—a great deal—and the prospect of gentler therapy with the lovely Nurse Sample was the only enticement to keep his temper in check. Enduring laps around the track with her hurt just as much as Nelson's "ministrations," but they came with a far better view.

Resigned to yet another round of "useful pain" as Dr. Madison liked to call it, John pushed open the doors of the reconstruction room to find Leanne waiting for him. She wore a broad smile—no, a triumphant grin. She stood in front of an arrangement of horizontal bars, the banisters used to aid soldiers in walking therapies, grouped together to form a small square. Nelson was standing by with an equally mischievous grin—something that looked out of place on his brute features—and a phonograph.

"What have we here?"

"I've invented a way to make this morning's exercise much more pleasant."

John started to say something about her very presence accomplishing that already, but swallowed the remark as too flirtatious. That didn't stop him from thinking it. Being grateful for it. He managed a nondescript "Really?" as he took off his cap and coat, hanging it on the rack. At least the presence of a lady meant he'd not be required to work up a sweat in his undershirt, which seemed to be Nelson's methodology of choice.

"You mentioned yesterday how difficult it is for you to shift weight, particularly stepping from side to side."

All he'd told her during their endless final lap was that he no longer danced as well as he did before. "I don't recall putting it in such clinical terms." Suddenly the phonograph made a disturbing sort of sense. "You don't mean…?"

"I do indeed. Today—with the approval of Dr. Madison, of course—your therapy is the waltz. Suitably adapted, I daresay, for your particular condition." She ducked under the front banister to stand in the center of the small square, raising her hands in a presentational gesture that made him laugh. "Captain Gallows, may I have the honor of this dance?"

*Intriguing* didn't come close to covering what he felt about today's therapy. "You know, *I'm* the one who's supposed to do the asking."

"And when did you ever subscribe to convention?" She gestured him inside.

Laying down his cane, John ignored the pain that shot through his side as he ducked himself inside the tidy square of banisters. He'd have managed it even if it hurt ten times more than it did. "I take it Nelson and the phonograph serve as our dance band?"

"You catch on quickly." Hoping the smile on his face didn't match the shameless grin he felt, John raised his arms to assume the standard ballroom dance position. She dodged out of his reach. "We'll be going a bit more slowly than that at first. Arms on the railings, please."

"Well, that's hardly fun." He couldn't help himself. Genuine amusement hadn't buoyed him up like this in months.

"Oh, this is not about fun."

"Says *you*."

"Concentration will be required." She had her teacher voice on, the one she used in the Red Cross knitting classes, as she resolutely placed her hands on the railings to each side.

John cleared his voice in mock seriousness, calculating how close he could position his hands to hers and still keep his balance. Yesterday he'd hated these bars. Today he rather liked them. "Of course."

"Just side to side at first, please."

"But you said I was to *waltz*." It was childish to tease her like that, but she seemed to bring that out in him.

She shot him a look that all-too-clearly said *Would you like to return to pain with Nelson?* Then she nodded her head toward one side of the box. "To your right." She stepped to slide her foot and her body toward the bar on one side of the box. He did the same, despite the spike of pain it sent through his thigh. "Very good. Now your left." He did as she asked, grateful that side produced much less pain. "Again." They went through the clunky, side-to-side maneuver three more times until he could manage it with a bit of ease despite the pain. It took far longer than he would have liked.

"Whose idea was this, in any case?" he said as they began the fourth repetition.

"You may not like the answer to that question, Captain." They swayed together to the left.

"Surely you're not going to tell me Dr. Madison or Nelson hatched this scheme?" *Right.*

*Left.* "I asked God to send me an idea for some inventive way to help you other than those dull laps. The thought came to me in the middle of the night last night, and I was delighted when Dr. Madison found the idea—how did he put it?—'ideally suited to our good captain.'"

She'd prayed on his behalf. Or on her behalf toward the goal of helping him—and had kept him in her thoughts even in the middle of the night, no less. The idea of it worked its way under his skin like an itch. "I'm dancing on orders from the Almighty?" *Right.*

"I told you, you wouldn't like the answer." *Left.*

His leg was burning but wild horses would not stop him now. "On the contrary, I believe God has just gone up a notch in my admiration." A bolt of pain hobbled his right step and sent him lurching against the bar, wiping away whatever spark the moment held.

"Would you like to rest?" she asked quietly.

"I would like to *waltz,*" he replied in the most commanding voice he possessed. *With you, not with a fence.*

Leanne should have thought this through more carefully. So taken was she with the novelty of the idea that she completely forgot the necessity of touching while dancing. Truly she hadn't thought Captain Gallows would get much beyond swaying back and forth, given the extent of his injuries. She knew how much the motion pained him, how the repetition only made it worse. The phonograph next to them was really no more than an enticement—a carrot on a stick to help him get through the first difficult session.

And it had worked. Entirely too well. For now the square of railings fairly well boxed her in, fenced her in close quarters with John and his obvious determination. The man had been shown his target, and hurtled toward it at all costs. How ironic that she knew she could not distract him from her creative distraction. There was nothing for it, she supposed. This session must end in a waltz, so it would be best to ensure it was contrived, awkward and exceedingly short. "And waltz you shall," she pronounced in her best *this is exactly how I planned it* voice. "But not yet to music. I fear we'll need a slower tempo." Somehow the innocent accommodation sounded all too daring—most likely due to the triumphant look in John's eye.

"Only at first. I'm sure it will come back to me."

Hopeful, Leanne placed her hands elegantly on the banisters.

She might have known it wouldn't work. John shook his head, the gleam still in his gaze. He had her, and they both knew it. "Nurse Sample, may I have the honor of this dance?" He raised his left hand, palm up, nearly commanding her to place her hand in his. She did so, inwardly cursing how close the railings boxed them in, startled at how neatly her hand rested in his palm. Startled still more at the warmth of his right hand behind her shoulder blade. Of course he would have been an excellent dancer, preceding the injury—men of his social prominence always were.

Before she could count out the tempo, John chose to set it himself. "One…two…three. One…two…three," giving himself almost two full seconds to execute every shift of his weight without the support of the railings. She picked up the counting for him when it became clear the exertion clipped his words, eventually falling into a ponderously slow humming of the *Blue Danube*. She knew his leg must hurt him terribly, and yet she also understood his need for this victory. However slow, however painful, John could not leave this room halfway to a waltz. His spirit simply didn't allow for com-

promise—it was the best and the worst thing about him.
Here, haltingly sliding his feet to a beat more suited to a
funeral march than a Viennese waltz, he still possessed
a commanding dignity. Before she could stop it, her
mind conjured up the daydream of what it would have
been like to be spun around the ballroom by the John
Gallows of before his injury. He'd have been dashingly
elegant, strong and smooth in his steps. It took her a
moment to realize she'd stopped humming, and he'd
most definitely noticed.

"Yes," he said, smiling even though she noticed a
bead of sweat streaming down his temple, "I do think
our song is over. For now, at least. And you're right,
Nurse Sample, this is infinitely more enjoyable than
laps around the gymnasium." His smile doubled as
he pulled a handkerchief from his pocket—mono-
grammed, she noticed—and wiped his brow. "Do thank
that God of yours for His excellent initiative."

"I'd prefer you thank Him yourself."

"He and I aren't on speaking terms at the moment."
She took a breath to argue, but he held out a silencing
palm. "But you can add this item to your list of good
and worthy deeds, my dear—you've made a chink in
the wall."

## Chapter Ten

*Leave it to me,* John thought as he hobbled toward the hospital meeting room where Leanne held her knitting classes, *to be given the task of heroic knitting.* Bombing half of Germany would have been easier. Keeping the upper hand with Leanne Sample was hard enough without the complications of physical pain and ridiculous needlework. He'd made a whole two inches of progress on his sock—two inches in probably twice as many hours of work! This masquerade would have ended two minutes after the first photo shoot if Nurse Sample hadn't gleefully roped him into actually finishing the sock. As if any of that was nearly as important as his job recruiting soldiers. As burning as his need to get back *over there.*

No, there was nothing for this but to produce one stellar sock for auction and be done with it. "Behold, ladies," he declared as he pushed open the door to the classroom with his cane, "someday this will coddle the bravest calves in Europe."

John let fall the two inches of sock ribbing he'd been holding aloft and came to a dead halt. Expecting his attentive audience of Red Cross knitting nurses and their eager applause, John instead came face-to-face with Leanne and the wounded private from the other day's gymnasium session. Sitting in his wheelchair, grinning, with a ball of yarn and Leanne's full attention.

"If all my students had your enthusiasm, Captain, we'll have every brave calf coddled in no time," Leanne said, without looking up from her task, guiding the other man's hands on the knitting needles. The private made no effort to hide satisfaction at his current "teacher's favorite" status. "Private Carson, I believe you know Captain Gallows? My classes with soldiers don't start until next week, but the private was kind enough to join the nurses as my test male student."

Wasn't *he* her test male student? Carson merely nodded a cordial greeting, and John wondered why he felt outmaneuvered every time he was with Leanne Sample. "I've missed a stitch," he said, even though he promised himself never to point out the imperfections in his work, "I'll need you to help me fix it before it shows up in the photographs tomorrow." Leanne was supposed to be *his* teacher. Some other nurse could tend to the private and his newfound interest. Private Carson wasn't about to have his profile splashed all over the country's newsstands in the name of patriotic pride. Yes, the whole idea was to get boys to buy into the Red Cross campaign, but Leanne Sample was *not* supposed to achieve his job before he did.

Then again, Carson would give the wagging tongues in the barracks someone else to target with the teasing John endured for his "new hobby." Why hadn't *he* thought to drag another soldier in here with him? How hard would it be to get a bored soldier to sit in a roomful of pretty nurses? Most of them would sit through making hair ribbons for that kind of company, much less the kinds of incentives General Barnes had put at his disposal. But then, if John had the choosing of a soldier to share his work, he'd have picked one who smiled a bit less—especially at Nurse Sample.

"Of course, Captain," Leanne replied, although he didn't care one bit for the sparkle that lit up her eyes. "You are indeed my first priority. Mistakes happen even to the best of us. It's how we fix them that matters."

John was sure he'd just been lectured, but couldn't exactly say how. He shifted his gaze to the private, who despite his pale hair and bony face, looked sheepishly triumphant if a bit confused. "I'm sure, Private Carson, you can spare the good teacher?"

"Actually, I was just about to hand the private over to Ida's attention. She's mastered ribbing faster than anyone, and Private Carson is a quick learner."

Ida looked up from her socks. "Why thank you, Leanne." Her expression was pleased, but dubious. As though she, like John, hadn't quite figured out who had the upper hand. "My, but I am warming to the idea of coed knitting classes."

John tapped the canvas rucksack slung over his shoulder—the most masculine container he could find to hold his yarn and needles—and pointed out the door with his cane. With a wide smile, Leanne swept her knitting into the large basket at her feet and rose to follow him out the door. He hobbled halfway down the hall, not bothering to keep a slower, steadier gait, and then turned toward her. "What was that all about?"

She blinked at him. "I should think it's obvious. I asked Private Carson to join the class. You remember him from—"

"Yes, of course I know who he is," John cut in, the unpleasant memory of the man's glare pulling a knot up from the pit of his stomach.

"I do tend to other patients, Captain. Carson was on my shift yesterday afternoon, and I felt it a nice gesture given the…tensions…of the other day."

"And he said yes?" What a fool thing to say. Of course he said yes; he was sitting in the room, wasn't he?

"I would think you'd be pleased. The magazine hasn't even printed and already you've had results."

John sank into a bench at the end of the hallway, strain and fatigue getting the better of him. His leg was always failing him at the most inopportune moments. He tried—without much success—to remind himself that Carson's legs failed him continually. He should feel pity for the young man, and sympathy—nothing more. He had nothing to fear from the private. Fear? What exactly did he think Carson could take from him? Nurse Sample's attentions were hers to grant anywhere she pleased; he had no justification for his sudden envy. "Why on earth did you ask *him?*"

She sat down next to him. "He seemed so dreadfully sad and empty. So envious of you. I didn't really think about it, to be honest. I suppose I thought about how I knit when I'm sad. I'm rather stumped as to why it couldn't wait until the soldier classes start next week, but I believe that's how the Holy Spirit works."

John looked at her. "Holy Spirit or bad idea, he'll get a fair ribbing for it. Pun intended. I have, and he doesn't look to have a thick enough skin for it. I'm afraid it's not a popular idea. Soldiers aren't supposed to knit. They're supposed to fight in the war."

"Stanley Carson is not at war anymore. He has a new battle to fight now, even you can see that." She set her basket down at her feet. "And I'll remind you, my dear courageous Captain Gallows, that not all battles are fought with guns and ships."

She believed so strongly in what she was doing. He had to respect that, as ludicrous as he found the not-yet-a-sock in his canvas bag. "If you tell me you fight yours with yarn and needles," he said as he leaned his cane against the wall, "I shall have to moan. Really, save the slogan for the posters."

She pulled away from him on the bench, crossing her arms like a scolding schoolmarm. "Private Carson had nice things to say about you today. Whereas I suspect he would have called you all sorts of names had I left things as they were in the gymnasium."

"*I* can take it. And oh, I'm quite sure you saw to his appreciation." He regretted the jealous outburst the moment it left his mouth.

"*You* were late. Private Carson was not only on time, he was early." Her words were sharp, but her smile stole his annoyance.

"I had important appointments. I do have more pressing concerns that socks, you know." He wasn't about to let her know how miffed he'd grown at the press relations assistant who'd kept him twenty minutes over. Leanne Sample would not know that she had become the high point of his day. Not when she was so adept at stealing his upper hand.

"Speaking of which, I believe you said you needed my assistance? Mistakes to be fixed?" She held out her hand as if she'd find his errors endlessly entertaining.

He hoisted the bag over to her feeling like a pouting schoolboy turning in poor work. "Save me from this madness, for G—"

She raised her eyebrow, the sack still midair, her silent reproach stopping him in his tracks.

*"I declare,"* he said in a sugary tone, feeling the prissy language trip on his tongue, "but you are a challenge."

"Thank you." She reached into the bag. "I'm sure our Heavenly Father appreciates your efforts." She scowled at the short span of ribbing he'd so proudly displayed earlier. "Whatever did you do here?"

"Knit."

"Well, yes, I know it's *supposed* to be knitting, but it's rather a tangle." She peered closer at his yarn, and he leaned in as well, trying to see whatever it was that she saw. It brought their heads close. She smelled of lemon and something rather rosy. He didn't like the idea of Edward Carson getting a whiff of lemon and roses one bit, didn't want her bending over any man's hands but his. He parked his elbow on the bench back, his arm resting just inches from her shoulder. He watched while she poked at stitches and pulled at loops, her tongue peeking out over one rosy lip while she analyzed. When she turned to look at him, they were entirely too close, although she minded it much more than he. "You forgot to move the yarn from front to back." She flushed, and he felt the color in her checks ripple through a warm spot in his chest. "It has to go in between the needles like I showed you. You'll have to undo these two rows here or you'll end up with far too many stitches."

"Undo? We've got another photograph tomorrow." He applied his most persuasive smile. "Can't you just fix them for me so we can move on?"

"Captain Gallows, are you asking me to cheat?" Even her eyes were smiling, wide as they were.

"Can one even cheat at knitting? I'm merely drawing on your expertise. Your assistance. I've obviously made of muddle of it on my own. Please, or we'll have no real progress to show tomorrow. Can't disappoint the boys now, can we? Think of Private Carson." Actually, he didn't want her thinking of Private Carson at all.

She paused, her gaze flicking to his sock-in-progress and back. He was genuinely disturbed by how much he wanted her cooperation. He enjoyed getting his way, to be sure, but this was something altogether different. "I shall fix the first row for you." He felt himself smile. "But the second one will be yours to fix. I will stay and supervise if you find it necessary."

Normally John wasn't much for compromise. He'd make an exception in this case. Especially if it meant keeping her on this bench next to him. She began to undo the stitches, her small fingers working the yarn with an expertise he had to admire. "So tell me," he pressed, feeling victorious, "did you really ask Carson out of genuine concern for his welfare? Or just because you knew it would annoy me?"

"I had no way of knowing it would annoy you." That was true, technically, but he could tell that she suspected he'd be bothered, all the same. He could see the smile even with her face turned toward his sock. "I did think it might serve to cheer him up. He seemed so lost, sitting there as if there were no use left for him. God just popped the idea into my head and I knew it was the right thing to do."

"The Lord Almighty just pops things into your head, does He?" Faith seemed so simple, so effortless to her. As if it was like breathing. As if anyone could master it. And yet the idea of arranging for her to be his therapeutic assistant had just popped into his head with what might be called supernatural force. The notion that these thoughts might be connected made him decidedly uncomfortable.

She spared a glance up from the needlework. "My best ideas are always from Him." She paused, her eyes doing something he couldn't quite identify, before adding, "You were."

## Chapter Eleven

John stifled an impulse to gulp. "Me? Are you saying I am from God or that I was your best idea?"

John was glad this brought a hearty laugh from her. Things had taken on a strange tension in the past few moments. "I suppose I should say both. You must know I believe each man is God's creation. I'd have thought that would be clear enough, especially given that I am in nursing."

So she did feel it a calling. That didn't surprise him at all. She went so carefully, so completely about her work and she'd seen so much humanity in the private he'd so readily dismissed. He couldn't remember the last time anyone other than his father had made him feel even the slightest hint of shame. Most found his ego, his driven nature, a valuable commodity. But this woman reminded him that his responsibilities—as an officer, and as a man—meant showing consideration for others, something he was far too prone to forget. "And me?"

She held up the sock, the row she'd fixed now neatly rounding the needles in orderly ribbing. "Well, I sup-

pose the merit of that idea might have to wait until your
sock is finished. But it is a grand start, I must say. And
you've been a good sport."

He effected a general-worthy huff. "An average man
might break under such pressure."

Her laugh died down to a soft, fluffy sound he liked
very much. "And we all know that you, Captain Gallows, are decidedly exceptional." They stared at each
other, time as soft and gentle as her laugh. He realized,
with a start, that he felt physically different around her.
Pliable and light instead of heavy and rigid. He very
nearly forgot his pain. She handed the sock back to him,
and he shamelessly made sure their hands touched as
he took it. She had the most exquisite hands—porcelain pale yet strong as could be. He dropped his first
stitch as he tried to picture those creamy digits laced
between the calloused thickness of his own fingers,
quickly replacing the stitch while she pretended not
to notice. They worked in companionable silence for
a minute or two. He thought about asking her why she
hadn't requested they return to class, but decided he
didn't want to suggest any return whatsoever. Instead
he stopped his poor stitching and pulled out a slip of
newspaper from his coat. Dr. Madison had given this
to him yesterday, and its delivery was the real reason
he came to class today. He'd hoped for a personal delivery—more private than the full class, and most certainly more cozy than the company of Private Carson.
As such, now seemed the perfect time. "I have something for you."

She looked up, surprised. Good. He enjoyed surprising her.

"It's a poem from a Boston paper, from the War Between the States. Of course, those Yankees use a different name, but we won't hold that against them in this instance."

She smiled. "How very gracious of you." When he unfolded the paper and cleared his throat, her eyebrows arched further. "A recitation? Goodness, I am honored."

He started to say she was also beautiful, but stopped himself. She was the kind of woman more moved by poetry than easy compliments. And he could barely believe he was about to recite poetry for her. His father would cuff him and tell him he was soft, but his father was not staring into those stunning hazel eyes. He noticed, to his great pleasure, that she stopped knitting and gave him her full attention.

*"Faith and hope give strength to her sight,*
*She sees a red dawn after the night.*
*Oh, soldiers brave, will it brighten the day,*
*And shorten the march on the weary way,*
*To know that at home the loving and true*
*Are knitting and hoping and praying for you."*

Normally John would have said it was foolishly poetic to call a lady's eyes "glistening," but there was no other word for how she looked at him when he finished. A very tightly held piece of him flew out of his grasp as she did. He thought, at that moment, that he would do twenty painful laps around that horrid gymnasium if it meant she would look at him that way again. Or a while longer. He felt the curve of her smile deep in his chest, warm and disarming.

"You are a most amazing man, Captain Gallows."
She said it with something he dearly hoped was awe.

"John," he blurted out, not caring that they were in
a very public hallway where anyone could walk by.

"John," she said quietly. Her eyes flicked down, and
the delicacy of the gesture affected him just as surely
as if her eyelashes had brushed his cheek.

She looked up at him twice after that, and they both
pretended to go back to their work. By her third intake
of breath he gently pushed the hand holding her needles
down to still on her lap. "Go ahead."

"Pardon?"

"You're trying not to ask me something. Even someone with my alarming lack of subtlety could see that.
Leanne." He used her name, not wanting to lose the
closeness of the moment. "Ask me anything."

She hesitated again, carefully choosing words, tentative as a doe. "How did it change you? Your accident.
You speak so gallantly of it, and yet I can't help but
think it was a harrowing experience."

He saw the question hiding in so many eyes after his
speeches. *What's it like, to almost die?* Some were genuinely interested, others grotesquely fascinated. "How
did it change me?" He discarded his stock answer of
having been a better dancer before, knowing she deserved the truest answer he had. Trouble was, he wasn't
sure what that answer was. "I suppose," he started, no
idea where he was going, "that not much frightens me
now. Except, perhaps, the idea of not being worthy of
the second chance I've been given."

He needn't have worried she would find such words
foolish, for the comment only doubled the warmth in

her eyes. "I think that a very worthy thing to fear. Far too many soldiers have come home ready to squander their lives, as if they've suddenly inherited some grand fortune and must spend it immediately." She began stitching again, her fingers working without any attention or even a glance downward. Why was he so enthralled by Leanne's delicate hands? "Then there are those like Private Carson," she went on. "I think he fears he hasn't come home worth anything at all. I think it's good you recognize the gift you've been given." A small laugh ruffled around the edges of her words. "Even if you are dreadfully cheeky about it."

"I prefer to think I'm wonderfully cheeky about it." Her laugh was full and musical, as warm as her eyes and as clear as sunlight.

"Oh, I've no doubt. Pity the poor soul who can see through your bravado, my good captain."

Had she realized what she just said? "Can you?" Her laugh stilled, and even John was stunned by how dark his words had become without his realizing it. "What do you see?"

He watched her falter, then find her courage. He would wait. He wanted—needed—to hear her answer to this question. She finally looked straight at him, steady and honest. "I think that charming as you are, you are in more pain than you let on to anyone. I think what happened up there in the sky changed you even more than you know, and you are wise enough to be frightened of that fact. I think I amuse you, that you are used to getting your way far too much and..." she flushed, the needles in her hands finally stopping their movement "…that you have a very regrettable habit of making me say too much."

John ought to have had a clever comeback for a sermon like that, but his wit failed him. After far too long a pause, he resorted to the only superiority he could manage. "Well, now, you've given me no choice."

"I've misspoken. I'm sorry."

"On the contrary, I can't see how I can respond to that with anything but an invitation to the officers' ball Friday evening. You do in fact—" although he didn't really like her choice of words "—*amuse* me, far more than perhaps is good for either of us. And you're absolutely right, I always get my way so don't bother to decline. You do say far too much, but that should come greatly in handy at a ball, seeing as now I can't dance and I haven't any more poetry. And we've already seen you are a master of distraction."

"An officers' ball?"

"The *USS Charleston* crew is having a grand event thrown for them in New York. The ship earned its liberty flag."

"Surely you're not asking me to go to New York!"

John laughed to think she thought him capable of such celebrity. "Not at all. The general's throwing a much smaller ball here, though, as a twin celebration. I can't promise you the splendor of the Astor Hotel, but I suspect it will be a grand evening just the same. Besides, after our last session, I would think you'd find it in my medical interest. It was you who suggested I waltz, after all. To deny me is to deny my continued recovery."

She liked the idea. How could she not, when she herself had come up with the idea of a waltz to improve his movement? And truly, what woman can resist a ball? Yet she was trying. "I'm sure I'm not allowed to go."

"Anyone may come as a guest of an officer. And even if you weren't allowed, hasn't it yet become clear to you that I'm not much for rules? Aside from your therapeutic assistance, you and I constitute a community service. Barnes is giving the ball, he makes the rules—and he'll allow it if I ask him. I know that man. He will just see it as an extension of the publicity campaign—which it *isn't,*" he added quickly. "This is purely a social request."

She completed a stitch and eyed him. "Oh, no, it isn't. You've something up your sleeve."

"I'm crushed you would think so." She was right, of course; he did. "Have you peered into my soul and found me so deeply lacking?"

"It does not take much observation to know John Gallows is fond of schemes." She put down the stitching. "May I suggest a novel approach? Why don't you tell me the *real* reason why we're going, and I might surprise you by consenting. It will save us both time and considerable energy."

She meant it. That struck him as both disturbing and irresistible. At first he held back, hiding in a few botched stitches and clamping his mouth shut so hard his teeth nearly clacked.

"I would like to take you to the ball," he said, hoping the half-truth would suffice but rather sure it wouldn't. He looked up, expecting her to gloat, but found the most extraordinary expression on her face. Not victory, not amusement but genuine pleasure.

She waited. Glory, but that woman knew how to wield her silences. "And why," she said eventually, "would you like to take me to the ball?"

It had somehow become a game, a match of wits rather than some battle he must win. "There's no mystery there—men like to take women to balls. The dancing is so dreadfully dull if there are no women present."

"Ah, the *dancing*." Her eyes lit up. "You want to dance at the ball, is it? Jumping the gun a bit, aren't we?"

"Why? We danced the other day."

"It's just that you don't strike me as the kind of man to do things he doesn't do exceptionally well."

"I dance exceptionally well for a man of my...experiences." He started to say "limitations," which wasn't like him at all. A Gallows never bowed to limitations. "And yes, I want to be seen dancing."

Her eyes widened in understanding. "You want General Barnes to see you dancing, don't you? You want to show him how well your leg is so that he'll send you back."

He thought about denying it, but there really wasn't any use. "Partly."

"Entirely." She pushed out a sigh. "Why deceive him like that? You've made great strides, but your leg is not healed by any means. Certainly not enough to do what you're asking."

"I can accomplish one waltz, for goodness' sake. That is, if you help me."

"I'm sure you could find any number of women willing to aid you in this deception. As you said, men ask women to balls all the time."

He leaned in. "I need *you*." She knew how to let him lean on her, how to offer support in ways that weren't obvious. Any other woman would make him look— and feel—like an invalid. He had to look like the most capable man in the room. "Please do this for me." He'd sworn he wouldn't plead.

"I can't."

He gave her his best Gallows command. "You can. Just help me through one dance in front of Barnes. I shall be a model patient after that."

"You will not ever be a model patient. It will hurt, John."

"It hurts *now*. I'm no stranger to pain for a worthy goal."

She paused for an unbearable gap of silence until John was sure he'd burst. Then she began twirling the yarn around her finger the way she did when she worked out a problem, and he knew he'd prevailed. "I've nothing to wear."

A "thank-you" swelled in his heart, and for a frightening moment he wasn't sure if the gratitude was directed at her or Heaven. "I'll buy you a dress myself if I must call that bluff." He knew he would stop at nothing to get her acceptance—but if her arguments were on such trivial matters now, then victory was surely close at hand.

"Here is my proposition—if you get as far as the gusset on your sock, I'll waltz with you at the ball." She pointed to the bottom of her sock's cuff, the part where he imagined the heel began.

"That far? By Friday? You're mad."

"I could say the same of you, trying to make a show-place out of an officers' ball."

She had him. And he had her. He hadn't enjoyed anything this much since France. "Please ask God to stop popping ideas into your head. I fear I won't survive the next one."

## Chapter Twelve

Leanne turned slightly, watching how the fringe of the delicate champagne underskirt swished elegantly. It made the most delightful sound as it moved beneath the smooth rose overskirt. She was nearly ready for the officers' ball.

She'd owned the rose-and-white cameo for years, but it sat at her neck with a new regal air. Ida had loaned her some pearl ear bobs and pulled up Leanne's hair in a way that set them off beautifully. "I know Captain Gallows is a handsome fellow, but who knew it went deeper than that?" Ida said as she tucked a cream rose into Leanne's hair.

"Why do you say that?"

"Well, I'm no expert on such matters, but I do know it takes far more than a handsome face to catch your fancy. There must be a fair amount behind those gorgeous eyes."

It was unnerving to have someone else recognize the tumult going on inside her. "Pardon?"

Ida sat back on one hip. "You really think I didn't know? Honey, it's all over your face every time that man walks in the room. I know you try to hide it—he does, too—but neither of you are having much success. And tonight, why, you're fairly glowing."

Leanne felt her face flush. "I…"

Ida set down the hairbrush. "Relax. There's no shame in enjoying the attentions of a handsome man. Half of Columbia would line up to be in your place. I've never thought we had much choice in where our hearts landed, anyways."

Leanne turned to her friend. "My heart? He would not be the one my heart would choose. And yet, in the past few days I've seen…compelling things in his nature. It's as if I can't help it—I see too deeply into his character. And he into mine. But, Ida, why on earth would I have such a response to a man without faith? I can't have a future with such a man."

"How do you know he's got no faith?" When Leanne raised a dubious eyebrow, Ida continued, "Well, yes, I know he acts like a rollicking fellow on the outside, but if you say he goes deeper than that, why not straight-out ask him?"

Standing and straightening her skirts, Leanne eyed herself in the mirror. Her dress was stunning, her hair lovely, the evening air was perfect but none of these things explained why Leanne could not squelch the thrill she felt this evening. Like a princess. A princess with entirely the wrong prince. "I don't have to." She sighed, fingering the cameo. "We've spoken of it directly. I believe he admires my faith, that much is true, but he surely does not share it."

"Gracious, Leanne, it's a ball, not a marriage proposal. You said he asked for your help in something—"

for Leanne would not break John's confidence about the waltz "—and you're helping. What would he learn about God if you turned him down?" Ida helped Leanne into her shawl, sighing her approval as she cast her gaze from head to foot. "Perfection." She handed Leanne her evening bag. "Maybe it isn't the faith he *has* that's important here, but the faith he *could* have." Ida chuckled a bit. "Why, could you imagine what God could do with a fellow like that once He got through to him?"

She'd had the same thought dozens of times since meeting John Gallows, and it hadn't rendered her attraction any less dangerous.

It was the oddest thing to watch John turn as she entered the parlor. His entire countenance changed, as if someone had just sent an electric current through him. Most unnerving of all was the knowledge that the "current" had been the sight of her. She could understand the shock, however, for no less than twice the voltage seemed to shoot through her at the sight of him.

John was in the same dashing dress uniform he had worn for his presentation—hung with medals and strung with gold cords so that he looked every inch the hero—but it seemed to have double the effect on her this time. Maybe because now she knew more about the man under all those very fine trappings. He had his hat tucked under his elbow, so that the glossy curves of his hair picked up the flicker of the lights behind him. He looked at her stunned as if they'd never met, and yet smiling as though greeting a long-lost friend. She was sure she had the same expression on her own face, for John looked like the John Gallows she knew, and then again like the most handsome hero God ever created.

Ida sighed a swooning "My, my, my!" behind her. Some small part of her was glad they were friends, glad she'd been privy to his weaknesses, for had she met him in all his glory like this she would surely have been star-struck.

"I'd never have thought I'd be so happy to reach a gusset," he said, reaching into his pocket to show the nine inches of ribbing she'd required of him. In her fluster over the party, she'd completely forgotten the bargain she'd struck. John Gallows was very good at dissolving her sensibilities. "I'd have hated to miss this." He walked toward her, the cane making him look like some grand English lord. "You look absolutely lovely."

He truly meant it, she could see it in his eyes, but he paid the compliment with such oversize gallantry that Leanne was sure she was more pink than her dress. After the long moment it took to find her voice, she managed a "Thank you."

"Tonight will be a new experience for me," he began as he laid the sock on the hall table, donned his cap and extended his arm. "I'm not accustomed to everyone's eyes being on someone else. I find I can't decide if you've foiled my plan or helped it immensely."

She slipped her hand into the crook of his arm, feeling for all the world like Cinderella. "Captain Gallows, you overestimate my appeal."

"Oh, no," he said with a look that made Leanne's insides flutter in ten directions, "I don't believe I do." Ida opened the hall doors for them, grinning entirely too widely as she ushered them into the golden stillness of the fall evening. The weather was perfect beyond measure, and while they both paused at the top of the Red Cross House stairs to take in the glory of the evening, his gaze came to rest unapologetically on her. "I talked Nelson out of calisthenics today," he said as he gripped the railing to work his way carefully down the stairs. "I told him I'd shift my weight all afternoon and that you and I would walk to the Assembly Hall. In dress boots at that, so it ought to count for six laps if not seven."

He looked steeled for battle, so determined to reach the goal he'd set for himself that she felt guilty for her own doubts. It was a perfect evening for walking, but wouldn't that run the risk of taxing his leg in advance of the ball? "Are you sure you want to walk?"

"If you had any plans to push me in one of those horrid wheelchairs, I think I'd sooner crawl." He was trying to make a joke, but the edge of disdain in his words gave him away. He loathed this weakness. In many ways, John had no more made peace with his injuries than troubled Private Carson had. "Besides, why on earth would I want to lessen the time I get to spend alone with you?"

They'd reached the bottom of the stairs, and he rearranged his stance with a dramatic flair, as if they were stepping off into a parade. She half expected him to wave to a crowd she could not see. "Captain Gallows, do you ever come offstage?"

"Not if it can be helped." He twirled his cane before launching them forward. "And you will call me John for this entire lovely walk or we'll turn back right here. And don't get all worrisome about my stamina. I've already planned to stop and rest at least twice."

"A wise choice."

"Actually I'm telling myself it's simply because the sunset is so grand. I expect you to play along." He puffed up his decorated chest and did a spot-on imitation of Dr. Madison's Bostonian accent. "No use resisting. It's for my medical benefit and I am a hero you know."

"Does everyone always do your bidding?"

"Well—" his smile turned from the manufactured one to a grin of genuine warmth "—I am *knitting,* so what does that tell you?"

She laughed, once again enjoying the thought that she may have been among the first to best John Gallows at his own game. "That God is mighty indeed."

He did not offer one of his clever comebacks. They walked in companionable silence for a minute or so, and the glorious washes of amber painting the sky did indeed remind her of God's own glory. *"The Heavens declare the glory of God."* She sighed without thinking.

His own sigh held much less reverence. "Do you attribute everything to the Almighty?"

"I suppose I do. Does that bother you?" She watched in admiration as the breeze played with the fringe of her skirt. Finer ladies would have balked at the prospect of traveling to the party on foot, but she was glad for the chance. Walking—even their slow, laborious laps— had become part of their relationship. She believed they had their best conversations when walking or knitting. Truth or difficult subjects were always best conversed when there was some activity to focus one's attention.

"It baffles me, more like it." He looked at her with narrowed eyes.

She thought of Ida's comment about what feats God could accomplish if he ever got through to a man like John Gallows. Even if it were true, it was a precarious hook on which to hang her hope's affections. "I'm not likely to stop, even for you."

"It's not just preaching—you really see Him in everything, don't you?" *Baffled* truly did capture his expression.

"Even in you." She wanted to grab the words out of the air and shoo them away the minute they popped out of her mouth. Ida's fool notions had run away with her composure. Leanne stared down at her slippers, mortified, until John reached out and tilted her chin up to face him. It was far too private a gesture for such a public place, and her face tingled with heat.

Worst of all was the look on his face; the notion pleased him. Immensely, from the look of it. "I suspect that's why I find you so delightfully annoying. You do always look as if you've just unearthed some new virtue out of me. Have you any idea how disconcerting that is?"

Disconcerting was an apt description. John was disconcerting beyond measure. She began to wonder if tonight had been a mistake. With the fancy dress and the dashing hero in his dress uniform, she'd started to feel too much like Cinderella…and there was no happy ending to be had in this fairy tale. If John succeeded in this show of strength he planned in front of the general—and Leanne was fairly certain he would, since she knew him well enough now to know that John Gallows would reach his goals or die trying—then he might soon find himself sent back overseas as he'd planned.

The brief interlude between them would be over and forgotten.

*Guard yourself and your heart,* she told herself. *You aren't going to the ball to be wooed, or dazzled or swept off your feet. You are here as his friend—and his nurse—to help him because you said you would. That was all—all there was, and all there could be.*

They walked on for another block—the second of six, for the base was a large complex—and she could feel his gait stiffening. Pointing to a bench just ahead, she manufactured a wince and said, "Oh, bother, I've got a pebble in my slipper. Could we sit down over there?"

John stopped, speared by the transparency of what she was doing. "Don't do that!" he snapped at her.

"What?"

Did she actually think he couldn't see through her ruse? Didn't she know that he was absolutely sick to death of people trying to pamper him with weaknesses invented to nullify his?

"Don't coddle me." He barked it out far sharper than he would have liked; her eyes widened in a remorse he felt twisting under his ribs. "You've no more got a pebble in your shoe than I have a third leg." His wounded dignity wouldn't allow him to completely soften his words, but he tried. "I don't want that, most especially from you."

"I am sorry." She looked down, and he wanted desperately to put his hand to her chin and tip her gaze back up to him again. Her kindness was a welcome sting.

"I'd like to sit down, Leanne, but I'd like to sit because *I* need it, not because you've decided I should." Her honesty had become a precious commodity to him, refreshing in his posturing world of military hierarchies. "Will you grant me that? Grant me the honesty I like so much about you?" He gestured toward the bench, glad to have that over with.

"I suppose I could have just asked you if you were ready to sit down," she offered as she arranged herself on the bench.

"Better still, just don't concern yourself with it. I promise you, I'll tell you when I need to stop."

She gave him a sideways glance as her two rose slippers peeked out of her fringed skirt. Had she arranged them so evenly on purpose, or was she just that elegant in how she sat? "That's not what you do in the gymnasium."

"In the gymnasium, I'm under Madison's harsh thumb. Tonight is purely in my realm." Certainly she never dressed like this for the gymnasium. And while he thought she looked lovely even in her nurse's uniform, he couldn't help but be charmed by how transparently pleased she clearly was with how she looked in that dusty-rose color. A little smile would light on the corners of her face when she played with the lace at her sleeves. She reminded him of one of his little cousins, twirling in some new party frock. That had been part of his aim tonight, to spend time with her in his realm instead of under doctor's orders or the tyranny of Red Cross knitting. "I can't let you have the upper hand on every occasion, and you've no idea how skilled I am at punchbowl warfare."

"Oh, I can easily guess. I've no doubt the army has the right man for the job." She looked at him, one eye narrowed as if assessing a student's progress. "Actually, for both jobs. I have to say I found the knitting photographs a cockeyed scheme at first, but I've come to see the brilliance in it."

John wasn't quite sure he'd come to that level of endorsement yet. "So you're telling me it's worth the endless ribbing I take from the soldiers back in camp?" He'd heard every version of a knitting joke, many of which could never be repeated in polite company. No doubt Carson had heard even worse if he dared to knit in the barracks.

"The Red Cross officials tell me they're in dire straits. If you can convince young men to take up this cause and not feel like a—what was the word?—*sissy* about it, then you will have impacted the lives of thousands of brave soldiers. I watched those boys in the audience. They admire you. They want to be like you. Your gifts suit this challenge. God's placed you in just the right place at just the right time."

He laughed. "You make my sock sound like a noble crusade."

"It is."

Leanne was so straightforward, so refreshingly uncomplicated. Her socks really were a noble crusade to her. *Socks.* Who'd have ever thought he'd spend so much time thinking about socks? He angled himself to face her on the bench, not caring that it sent a pang through his hip. "Does the Red Cross realize what they've got in you?" When he'd first asked her that, he'd found her commitment—her passion—misdirected. Now he was coming to see why she dedicated herself the way she did.

"Oh, I suppose no more than the army realizes the secret weapon they have in you."

He settled for rising off the bench and extending his hand. "Let's go further convince them, shall we?"

"You're ready to go forward, then?" She placed her hand in his.

John helped her to her feet, tucking the hand into the crook of his elbow and liking very much how it felt as it nestled there. "Oh, my dear Leanne, I was born ready."

## Chapter Thirteen

Liberty bond sales were essential to the war effort, and General Barnes capitalized on anything crucial to the war. It may not have rivaled the Carolina Hall or anything at the State House across town, but the general had staged a respectable event. He'd been smart enough to invite several state capitol dignitaries and a few of Columbia's finest families as well. Barnes knew strategic allies on the home front were as necessary as those overseas.

Transformed from its daily duties as an assembly hall, the space sported bunting and flags, a serviceable army orchestra and as festive a selection of food and drink as could be had during wartime. Despite the affair being well underway—for it had taken a good deal of time to finish their journey here—most of the room turned to look at John and Leanne when they entered. John was clearly used to being at the center of attention. He seemed as at home in the spotlight as she was foreign to it.

"They're staring at you," he whispered as they circled around the reception.

"They're staring at *you*," she replied, wondering if the flush would ever leave her cheeks this evening. A waiter with a tray of punch cups appeared, and John selected one for her without taking one for himself. Of course, she realized, he needed one hand on his cane while the other leaned ever-so-slightly on her. She sipped it quietly as she watched John's eyes scan the room for General Barnes.

"He's not here."

"No, he won't appear for another half an hour or so. Probably holed up in some library with cigars and senators." When she raised an eyebrow, he added, "The man never throws a party just to throw a party. I'll know how many items he's ticked off his agenda just by the way he stands." When she finished her cup of punch, he offered, "Shall we mingle?"

The mayor of Columbia greeted her warmly, remarking on how the addition of Camp Jackson had invigorated the state capital.

"She's heading up several classes for the Red Cross knitting campaign, too," John offered, when the conversation turned to Leanne's activities as a nurse. "I'm her newest student, you know."

"So I hear, young man, so I hear," cooed the mayor's wife. "Well, if anyone can get our boys onto yarn and needles, I suspect it's you." The woman turned to Leanne. "You know, our ladies' guild might be able to supply you with more yarn, if that would help."

"It would indeed, thank you," Leanne replied. By the time they'd circled the room, John had maneuvered assorted conversations to no less than six offers of help for the Red Cross classes. He seemed to be able to draw assistance from people with uncanny ease. "You've not asked a single person for their help," she whispered with amusement, "and yet I find myself with half a dozen offers of much-needed assistance."

"I thought all good Charleston girls were taught the art of social commerce."

"Not in the way you employ it. I'm afraid I don't go about it with quite so much…" As she searched for the words, John's demeanor shifted dramatically. She did not need to see the general to know he had entered the room; John stared at him with an intensity that prickled her skin. Surely it was dangerous to place so much importance on one dance—she couldn't help thinking tonight would end very badly. John was already leaning heavily on her arm just to walk around. It didn't seem possible that his scheme could be achieved. Then again, hadn't he just achieved more than she'd ever bargained for in a handful of "innocent" conversations?

"He'll work his way over to that side of the room," John said, pointing to a series of windows that faced west. "We should do the same."

This would work. He'd convince the general of his leg's health without his even being aware of it. That's why this was so brilliant—anything so obvious as a physical test or exam would heighten the commander's awareness whereas this would sneak the idea in under his consciousness. Leanne had declared it "propaganda" in jest, but she wasn't that far off. Of course she didn't know he'd paid the band leader to ensure a slow waltz two numbers after General Barnes entered the room. When it arrived, John took a deep breath, laid his cane up against the chair railing and extended his hand as if this were the easiest thing in the world. She caught his eye with such an expression of encouragement that it felt as if ten pounds lifted off his frame.

She was delightful to hold. To truly hold, the way he used to hold a dancing partner. Leanne was light and airy on her feet, yet keenly aware of where and when he needed to lean on her. The sessions they'd had with the bars told her just which steps were most difficult for him.

*One, two, three*…it was the slight twist at the end of the third step that pained him, but not too badly at first.

One, two, three…they circled within yards of the general. Out of the corner of his eye before turning, John caught Dr. Madison pointing him out to the Barnes. Never mind the scowl on that pessimist Dr. Madison's face, he'd made it halfway around the room and he wasn't even sweating yet.

"Smile, my dear," John said as he caught Leanne peering around his shoulder to check if the general was watching. "This isn't supposed to be so serious. I'm charming, remem—" A wrong twist sent a spark of pain through his hip and he almost missed a step. He'd aggravated something, for the pain stayed through-out the steps now instead of waxing and waning. No matter; he could endure it.

"Are you all right?" She applied the smile he'd requested, but worry darkened her eyes.

"Delightful." He leaned on her a little harder as they made the difficult turn.

"You most certainly are not. Shall we stop? I could feign a turned ankle."

"I told you not to do such things. I'm fine." He cursed the traitorous rivulet of sweat he felt stealing down his temple. "Halfway around the room again so we pass in front of him."

"John, you're in pain. Stop this before you hurt yourself."

"Just let me put my weight on you on that third step and we'll be fine. And land sakes, try to look enthralled. I'm to be sweeping you off your feet, remember?"

"It is getting you off your feet that I'm most concerned with at the moment."

John's leg was on fire now, but he'd pass out before he'd pass up the chance to waltz past the general one more time. He tightened his grip on Leanne's shoulder and stared into the welcome distraction of her eyes. "Stay with me. Just a few measures more." He discovered he was gritting his teeth.

"John…"

The final measures of the waltz placed them right in front of the general, and John turned Leanne just enough to face her toward Barnes as they stood still at the song's conclusion and applauded the orchestra. He leaned in to catch her ear above the noise. "What's he doing?" he whispered, more breathless than he would have liked.

"He's talking to Dr. Madison."

"Laughing?"

"It looks rather more like a frown, I'm sorry to say."

"And Madison?" He needed just a few seconds more before he could turn and face Barnes convincingly.

"Scowling like a bear."

"Excellent. Now, I'll turn to face him, and if you'd be so kind, duck over to the side of the room and fetch my cane. It'd be lovely if you could be rather insistent that I use it, for I plan to refuse a time or two."

Leanne narrowed her eyes. "Really? This has become an exercise in playacting."

"You're my secret weapon, Leanne. Just a minute or two longer and then I shall be yours to command. I'll knit baby booties if it comes to that."

"Honestly." Her words were harsh, but the amusement hiding behind her glare did her no favors in making her seem stern. She turned in the direction of his cane, but not before he brought her hand to his lips and placed a lingering kiss there. She smelled of roses, and her eyes made the fire in his leg fade to embers.

A long hour later, Leanne raised an eyebrow as John turned to the car that had brought them back to the Red Cross House and barked at the driver not to wait. She said nothing as the car rumbled off down the street, just as John had said next to nothing as they'd driven home. She'd caught him looking at her a dozen times on the short trip, silent, a quizzical smile on his face.

"Did things turn out the way you wanted?"

"I'm not at all sure."

She didn't know how to respond to that. "What were you expecting?"

"I wasn't expecting anything. The point was to hand him an impression without him realizing it."

"I thought you did marvelously. I have no doubt you were a superb dancer in your day." She regretted the backhanded compliment the moment it left her lips.

They'd never discussed his full prognosis, whether Dr. Madison expected him to regain full use of the leg. John certainly seemed to brook no doubts on the issue. "You *are* a superb dancer now."

The correction was useless. He looked at her, and for the first time she saw the doubts he tried so very hard to kill. "I needed your help." He whispered it like a confession.

"You were smart enough to ask for it. I was glad to give it." She smiled at the memory of all the eyes upon her and John. "We were a very convincing pair, weren't we?"

John took a step closer, his hand on the house railing. "We were. I was the envy of every man there."

"Oh, I doubt that." He was the center of the attention, so handsome and charming people flocked around them when they left the dance floor. If anyone was an object of envy, it was her. She had little doubt that every single woman in the ballroom coveted her position on the captain's arm.

"I didn't dance with anyone else now, did I?" The way he said it let her know John was aware of how she'd noticed the attentions of other ladies at the ball.

She crossed her arms over her chest. "You couldn't have. No one else knew our system."

John stepped in again. "Our *secret*. But even if they did, I wouldn't have danced with anyone else." He'd downed several glasses of champagne after they'd danced, saying he needed it to dull the pain, and she suspected that was the reason his words took on such a dramatic flair. She also knew John used dramatic flair to get what he wanted.

His eyes were intense, as dark blue as the night sky behind him. It was becoming clear he wanted to be closer to her. Clearer yet was that she was beginning to want it, too, despite a hundred reasons to resist. He leaned in, and while she took a breath to stop him, no sound would come out of her mouth. He ran one finger down the length of her hand. The sensation made her head spin. "I can't dance with anyone else. Just you. Another of the Almighty's impressive ideas, I suppose."

Leanne was thankful he'd managed to say the one thing that would shake her senses back into place. "John."

"We're an excellent pair. Socks come in pairs." He let his finger feather against her wrist.

She removed her hand. "We are a mismatched pair."

He looked into her eyes, his voice silken. "I don't see it that way."

"You are looking for the conquest you did not gain tonight. And you have had too much champagne."

"It kills the pain."

"It kills the *senses*," she corrected. "We are a pair of friends, and that is how it must stay."

He stepped entirely too close. "Are you sure?"

Leanne pulled in a deep breath. "Not at all, but as Dr. Madison would say, 'there it is.' Good night, John."

John took her hand and kissed it dramatically. It was a showy kiss, not the delicate kind he'd placed on her hand at the end of their waltz at the ball. "Good night, my dear friend Nurse Sample."

Leanne was grateful she could almost laugh. "Do you even know how to be friends with a woman?"

"You'll find I can be the epitome of paternal civility."

Now she could laugh. "Don't you mean 'platonic'?"

He tipped his hat. "Perhaps I should not have downed that last glass. But it is a lovely thing not to have one's leg on fire every moment. So perhaps your friendship will allow you to forgive my indulgence."

"We are all in need of forgiveness." She stepped up onto the short flight of stairs that led into the house.

"Not you." He looked up at her with an unchecked, wide-eyed admiration. "You're perfect."

She fought the urge to lean down and kiss his cheek. Never in her life had she been so tempted to cross such a line—but it would do neither of them any good. She was his friend. She was his nurse. That was all she could ever be. "I most of all, Captain Gallows. Good night."

He put his hand on his heart, a theatrical wounding, before turning off to spin his cane as he disappeared into the night.

## Chapter Fourteen

Leanne was reconsidering her agreement to meet John today. Yes, they needed to prepare for Monday's photograph session, but she wasn't at all sure time alone with John was a good idea. Before the ball, they'd decided it would be smart to have John's sock heel nearly completed in the photographs. It would show off well, and most knitters knew turning a first sock heel was a significant accomplishment for the novice knitter. She wanted John's sense of victory to show up in the photographs, hoping to convince the intended young boys to see how challenging knitting could be. Still, it was a complicated lesson, requiring much more interaction and—regretfully—much more touching than she would have liked given how things had transpired after the ball. To cancel, however, felt like too much of an admission, and she needed to return the sock he'd left at the Red Cross House last night. She suspected John saw right through her insistence that they meet outside "for the good sunlight." The way he looked at her now, Leanne had little hopes of hiding how she fretted over the prospect of being in close quarters with him.

"I half worried you wouldn't show," he teased when she arrived at the bench they'd designated. Leanne felt like a walking battle—the conflict of "just fine" and "horrid" tumbling in her chest—whereas John looked as if nothing had transpired between them.

"You can't go forward without this," she ventured without too much cheer as she produced the unfinished sock, which only served as an unneeded reminder of the previous evening. "And I could never miss the great Captain Gallows turning his first sock heel." Leanne steeled her determination to get past this awkwardness and focus on the work to be done. She changed the subject by asking "Does your leg pain you much today?"

"It hurts twelve ways to Sunday this morning. You'd think I'd set the thing on fire last night for the way it's acting up. Not to mention my head. I hardly slept."

Leanne hadn't slept much, either, but for entirely different reasons. "I'm sorry."

"Dr. Madison seemed to take no end of pleasure in torturing me this morning. Lectured me like some rascal schoolboy about how I had no right 'gallivanting around like a circus pony' last night." John shifted uncomfortably on the bench. "A circus pony. The man's a monster who feeds on other men's pain."

She sat down cautiously next to him. One the one hand, John did strike her as a petulant child, sulking and thrashing about. On the other hand, it was clear Captain Gallows nearly always got his way and suffered obstacles with little grace indeed. "He is trying to keep your best interest at heart."

"My *best interest*," John barked back, "is waiting

for me back in France, if Barnes would stop listening to overcautious coddlers and just sign the orders."

"It's good we have such an engaging project to distract you. Sock heels are challenging."

John stretched out his stiff leg. "You're alone in your enthusiasm. I've been called 'a heel' so often in the barracks this morning, it's losing its appeal."

"Don't listen to them. A sock heel is a great personal victory. Just the sort of stuff warriors thrive upon." Now she was letting her nerves make her hopelessly wordy. Perhaps friendship with John Gallows wasn't possible after all.

Not with the way he stopped her hand when she pulled her knitting from her bag. "Leanne." It was unfair how the sound of his voice danced over her name.

"Yes?" It came out a tight, girlish gulp.

"I do know how to be friends with you. I'll be a perfect gentleman."

To know her discomfort lay so transparent to him just made things worse. His words were perfectly aimed at the very thing that troubled her most; John Gallows very rarely bothered to be a perfect gentleman. She'd heard the stories, she'd seen his full-blown charm unleashed. It would be so much easier to hate him, to dismiss him as a cad, if he behaved badly. If he pressed his cause, or even if he discarded her for some other, more permissive female, she could dismiss him as the overblown, cinema-worthy hero with secret feet of clay. To her dismay, he did not. In fact, today John seemed more natural, more "offstage" than she'd ever seen him. The effect only heightened her attraction. His efforts to be "friends"—and the knowledge those efforts were exclusively on her behalf—well, that was distracting beyond measure.

Leanne fled for the safety of the stitchwork. She pointed to his sock, determined to keep her hands from his for as long as possible. "Start across here, stopping three stitches from the end."

"Yes, ma'am."

He'd never "yes ma'am-ed" her in any of their previous sessions. How on earth did he manage the paradox of such a respectful twinkle in his eye? To keep going with this was risky indeed, playing with fire. Were this any other task, she would simply write down the directions and leave him to his own devices. Turning a sock heel, however, really was something that needed teaching face-to-face.

"Will you look at that?" John said when the heel began to cup, to take on the distinct curvature that turned a tube into a sock. At first she thought he was joking, but he was genuinely impressed. With himself, of course, but with the technique as well. He held it up, turning the work this way and that. "I'll never dismiss a sock as ordinary ever again."

What red-blooded American knitter could dismiss a man's respect for a well-turned heel? "It is extraordinary, isn't it?"

"Extraordinary," he said all-too-smoothly, dropping the knitting to look directly at her.

Leanne raised an eyebrow and applied a "please behave" expression to hide her inner smile.

"In the most platonic of ways, of course," he declared, not bothering to hide his grin one bit as he continued the required stitching. "You're right, this is going to be far more difficult than I thought." When she looked at him, he added, "The knitting, I mean. Tricky stuff, this."

Leanne began to wonder if her resolve would last an entire sock.

"Turn a little to your left, please, and hold the thing up a little higher." The photographer assistant's voice grated like a rusty hinge as the afternoon heat increased the friction. Leanne was trying hard to be pleasant, but the stiff starch of her nursing uniform—they'd asked her to come in uniform today—grated like Mr. Palmer's voice.

John had stopped trying to be nice twenty minutes ago. "It's called a *sock*, Palmer," he snapped at the young assistant. "I know it doesn't look much like one now, but that's the whole point of this, isn't it?"

"It is a rather fine ankle and gusset. It will photograph wonderfully, don't you think, Mr. Palmer?"

"Just *grand*, Miss Sample." Mr. Palmer droned as if rather be doing just about anything else.

John bristled. "You wouldn't take that tone if you'd just put your feet into a warm, dry sock after four days in the trenches."

Leanne hadn't the nerve to ask John how his morning session with Dr. Madison went, but it didn't take a cross examination to see John wasn't pleased. It made her grateful she'd had her first soldiers' class this morning and hadn't been in the gymnasium. John stalked through the photography session like a uniformed grizzly bear, smiling when called upon but otherwise dark and surly.

The photographer peered around his large camera. "Slide a little farther over on the chair, Captain Gallows. We don't need that much of Nurse Sample in the shot." Evidently photographers had little need to master social graces for he seemed to have no idea how dismissive his command sounded; as if she were a vase to be moved or a lamp casting an unwanted shadow.

John nearly growled. "Nurse Sample is in the shot or you'll have no captain to shoot. Do I make myself clear?"

The photographer's remark did sting a bit, but Leanne had no wish to become the center of a photographic squabble. "I assure you, Captain Gallows, it's not necessary that I be featured."

"These young boys aren't interested in learning knitting from their grandmothers. They want to know pretty young ladies like Nurse Sample will spend time with them if they sign up. They won't *know* that if you don't *show* it, now will they?"

The photographer's words may have been "Yes, of course," but his tone was much closer to *you stick to your job and I'll stick to mine.* By the end of the session, Leanne couldn't imagine how any of the images would do the Red Cross much good. *I don't know much about "red,"* she thought with a sour humor as she pulled her knitting from the prop basket they'd given her to use at these sessions and returned it to her usual canvas bag, *but "cross" certainly applied today.* John looked as if he would throw his cane across the room at the next person to ask him to smile. He dumped his sock on a table at the back of the room and hobbled out into the hallway at the first opportunity. She'd never seen anyone slam down a piece of knitting before.

She caught him in the hallway. "John…"

"I need to stop all this parading and get back to France. *Now*."

Leanne touched his elbow gently. "You have things to finish here, John."

He turned to her. "I've nothing to…" He caught himself, running one hand down his face while the other gripped his cane with white knuckles. "It's not that what you do isn't important. You wouldn't understand, I'm afraid."

"Perhaps you should try to explain it to me." She started to tell him to sit down, but remembered how poorly he took such orders. "Would you care to rest your leg on that bench over there?" she said in a deliberate tone meant to highlight it as a request, not a command or manipulation.

John didn't answer; he simply set off toward a bench in irritable, limping silence.

Leanne let him arrange himself to his comfort on the bench, then sat next to him, her knitting bag on her lap. He brooded wordlessly for a minute or two, clearly not ready for conversation. Deciding it was better to wait him out than try to draw him out, Leanne reached into her bag and began the process of stitching up the toe of the sock she'd used in the photographs. *If he needs to speak about it,* she prayed, genuinely stumped as to how to help the captain out of his bitter gloom, *let him do so to me. You know best what he needs—likely better than he knows himself.* The prayer calmed her, and she stitched on at peace with his prickly silence, trusting God knew when and where to start the conversation. She would show patience, even if he had none.

## Chapter Fifteen

"I am first and foremost a soldier," John opened up after they sat there awhile. "Not a spokesman. I wonder some days if the army sees me as anything more than a mouthpiece, a hired verbal gun."

He'd said as much other days. She started to remind him that his speaking was a true gift, but stopped herself. He was blind to that gift, at least for today. Instead she tried a different tactic. "It can't be a bad thing to respect your body's need to heal. What possible purpose could be served by going back before you're fully capable?"

John gave a bitter grunt. "Capable? Who's ever truly capable of facing battle? All men go to war with wounds, whether they are physical or otherwise. You think these boys, these young fellows funneled straight out of school onto ships, are *capable*?"

No, she didn't. Some of these boys looked so young and glory-hungry it made her heart break to know some of them would return with Private Carson's hollow shadows in their eyes. "You're an impatient man."

"You bet the…" She watched John swallow a curse.

"Yes, I am, but even a patient man would be tested by Barnes's dawdling."

She watched the way John's leg relaxed and regained a bit of its flexibility. Did he realize how much his temper tangled his healing? It made her wonder if the skewed importance he'd placed on that waltz hadn't been half the reason for his failure. He'd waltzed smoothly in the gymnasium. His gait always evened out when she got him talking. His pain seemed to disappear onstage. "I believe you will go back, John. Does that help?" It was true, but only half the truth. She believed he would go back whether it was wise for him to go or not. She was coming to realize that, wise or not, spiritually sound or not, a small part of her would leave with him when he left.

He turned to look at her, and Leanne feared that part of her would not remain small for long. The blue in those eyes conquered her reason all too easily. "I must go back. I don't know that I can explain it any more clearly than that. Honor comes close, I suppose, but I don't know that I could explain that to you, either."

She could see that. Despite the fact that all the scheming and persuasion might lead one to think otherwise, John Gallows was a warrior, a man driven by pride and honor. "Yes, I suppose honor comes close."

"Honor takes different shapes for different men. Don't you see? That's what makes a man into a soldier or a sailor, not the outcome of some physical test. Tomorrow is a foolish exercise in things that don't matter."

Tomorrow. John had an exam with Dr. Madison the next day to assess his physical progress, one he'd hoped to circumnavigate with his waltz in front of General

Barnes. Dr. Madison had told her it was a straight-forward enough exercise—timed completion of tasks, measurements of flexibility ranges, such things.

Such things as could not be manipulated. Facts even the cunning John Gallows could not bend to his liking, could not wield to serve his notion of honor.

She nearly gasped, so striking was her insight: John's body was at war with his honor. That's what drove him to try anything—even a waltz—to sidestep his phys-ical assessments. She instantly understood the basic struggle that drove him to do what he did. It had been there all the time in the steel edge in his eyes, the de-fiant way he brandished his cane, the cocky nature he hid behind: his honor would never, ever surrender to his body. The fact that he'd suffered a serious injury would never override his warrior nature—in fact, she was quite sure it would only feed the man's need to prove himself.

John hated when she looked at him like that. All too often in conversation with him her eyes would widen, her lips part in the most unsettling way and her face would alter as if hit by a ray of sunshine. It always gave him the nerve-racking sense that she was receiv-ing some sort of divine revelation—usually about him, which made it all the worse. He would have much pre-ferred God left him alone. "I think I understand," she said as though that was the last thing she expected.

It certainly was the last thing he'd expected. "Really? I rather thought I'd botched the explanation, myself." He waited for some speech of chastisement from her, the "be sensible," "you've suffered a serious injury" or worst of all "don't be such a selfish, ungrateful cad" sort he'd been expecting her to launch into any moment. Especially after the way he'd just behaved in that insufferable photographic session. He'd deserve every word of it if she did decide to scold.

She didn't. She just stared at him for a long moment, as if reading some startling new information in his face, and then resumed her knitting. With the most confounding smile on her face. She understood. How, he'd never guess, for he knew the thought was foreign to her. She was a creature of peace and comfort, he of pride and battle. He mostly just let her knit in silence because he was truly stumped at how to respond. Land sakes, when was the last time a woman stumped him?

A few minutes later she came to a decision of sorts, for she put down her knitting, sat upright and turned to looked him in the eye. "John, I should like to ask you something."

Did she have any idea how beautiful she looked when she got like that? Warm and effervescent as if she held the secret of life in her hands? "Anything."

"Well, actually, I would like to ask you to let me do something."

He couldn't help himself. "Why yes, *of course* you may kiss me." The resulting flame in her cheeks was entirely too irresistible, and he laughed until she did as well.

She covered her face in her hands like a schoolgirl. "You are incorrigible. Really. I am trying to be serious."

He'd known that, knew it would mortify her and had been helpless to rein in his impulses. Only half of him regretted it, which was a dubious sign indeed. "My apologies," he said, truly meaning it. "I made a promise to be a gentleman the other night, and I mean to keep it. Very well then, let us be serious. What is your request?"

She could not raise her eyes. "I cannot ask now. You've dashed my courage." He felt her words like a thorn, knowing he deserved the prick. She pushed her knitting back into the bag and went to rise.

John caught her elbow. He could not, would not let it go after she'd been so forgiving of his misbehavior after the ball. "Please," he pleaded, tugging her back toward the bench. "I am sorry. Truly. Please, Leanne, ask me anything you like. I can't imagine denying any request you have to make."

Leanne let her eyes fall closed for a second, mustering her nerve. What could possibly be so difficult for her to ask? "I should like to ask…if you would allow… I should like to pray for your leg. I don't see any other way for you to pass the exam as quickly as you feel you must save with God's help. If not for your peace of mind then for mine."

John didn't know what he'd expected, but this surely wasn't it. "You want to pray for my leg? For the test?"

She looked embarrassed by the thought. "Yes."

He blinked. It had been a long time since someone surprised him so. "For *your* peace of mind?"

"What you want seems terribly foolish and a waste of many of your gifts. And yet, somehow, I can see why you want to be there even when you are so needed here. I don't know which is right, so how can I do anything but leave it to God to decide? I cannot go on having no peace about it. And, quite frankly, neither can you.

When you are angry and frustrated your leg is only worse."

"Your prayers are yours to make, by all means."

Her face reddened further, and he felt heat prickle his own palms. "I meant here. Now. With you."

John's discomfort with the notion was nearly physical, and yet he found himself completely unable to launch any refusal. She was genuinely trying to help, and it clearly meant a great deal to her. "He's bound to know I don't...subscribe. Why assist someone who shows Him no regard?"

"Because we are all His children, and He delights in granting our requests—if they are for our good, of course."

Now it made sense to him. "So if you pray for my success and I achieve it, then you can be assured God considers it for my own good? And should I fail tomorrow's test, the same assurance holds?"

"That is rather putting it oddly, but I suppose, yes."

"Doesn't speak much for my role in the achievement, does it?" He shifted in his seat. "I suppose I should feel rather insignificant now that you put it that way."

She smiled. "I don't think you are capable of feeling insignificant."

He coughed, rattled beyond words. This was going to be awkward. He could already feel a sweat breaking out above his collar. The photographic crew had left, and they were essentially alone, but they were still in a *hallway*. In the middle of a *building*. Ought such things happen rather in churches, in private or on ancient mountaintops? Here seemed so—ordinary. Yet try as he might, he could not find it in his heart to deny

Leanne this request. "I'm not at all sure how one goes about such things." He sighed, trying not to sound put out. "Closing of the eyes and folding of hands, isn't it?"

A warm amusement replaced the flush on her features. "Nothing is required of you. You may close your eyes if you like—I always do—but you need not pray with me, only allow me to pray for you." A sparkle lit her eyes. "It won't hurt. I suspect you won't even feel a thing."

*I doubt that,* John thought, although he didn't know what on earth he'd do if he *did* feel something other than the acute uneasiness he currently suffered. God did not simply show up on army benches at the request of insistent young ladies. John realized he did not especially want God showing up in any of the everyday parts of his life, did not welcome the idea of the Almighty following close behind his ordinary undertakings, even at Leanne's insistence. He watched her fold her hands, fighting the urge to take a deep breath as she closed her eyes. He'd dived off high cliffs into unknown waters with less trepidation.

"Holy Father," she began in a tender voice, "I come to You on behalf of my friend John and his desire to serve." John shut his eyes, finding the moment too intimate to keep them open. "Cast Your hand over all that happens tomorrow. Let Your will be accomplished. If it is through the strength of his leg and the regard of General Barnes, then let it be so. Your will is to be trusted, so help us both to trust that tomorrow's outcome is as You wish. I thank You for the many who serve, for the comfort of all those who have lost—lost abilities, loved ones, dreams and health." John found her voice so peaceful and so full of grace, he had to open his eyes to confirm they had not amazingly transported to some sacred space. She was so changed when she prayed, and yet it came from her as easily as any common words she spoke. "All lives are precious to You, and I thank You for the price You paid for our lives in the sacrifice of Your Son, Jesus. May You guide my path and John's both tomorrow and always, in Jesus's name, amen."

After a second's hesitation, Leanne opened one eye to his startled gaze and whispered, "It is customary to say 'amen,' if you agree with the prayer."

John didn't know if he agreed with either the prayer itself or the woman who prayed it, but the "Amen" sounded full and satisfying as it slipped from his mouth.

## Chapter Sixteen

John had grown to hate the gymnasium. Without Leanne, it loomed as a drab battlefield on which he waged his personal war against the leg that had become his enemy.

"Gallows. Ready to show me what you can do?" Dr. Madison walked over with the clipboard and pen John had come to loathe almost more than his leg. The doctor was sly, always adjusting the paper so that John could not read whatever notes were being taken. To make matters worse, Madison had a habit of becoming disturbingly cheerful when a benchmark approached. The doctor's upbeat manner made John feel like a child about to take a school test. Some days he half expected to walk out of a session with a letter grade marked on his forehead. Today was the ultimate "pass" or "fail."

The exam consisted of several exercises to show his flexibility, two tests of strength and the dastardly test of stamina. "How far, how fast" haunted him every lap of this place, especially when Leanne was not by his side. And she was not by his side today—by his choice, not hers. The distraction of her presence was a risk he could not take. Today was John against pain, pure and simple. John would prevail, pure and simple.

"Weights first, shall we?" Dr. Madison's smile broadcast confidence as they walked over to the groupings of free weights, pulleys and dumbbells that occupied the north corner of the room. Some considerate soul had placed these benches next to the windows, so that soldiers had a view of a lovely patch of green as they endured therapy. "You worked eighty pounds easily on your left leg last week. If you can get to forty-five degrees with sixty pounds on your right leg, I think you'll have shown grand progress."

It was the angle that always posed the problem. Any brute could hoist a pile of iron. It was bending like a pretzel while one did it that always eluded him. "And we all know I'm nothing if not grand." John smiled as he removed his tan day uniform shirt and hung it on the series of pegs by the wall. He settled himself on the bench, breathing deeply while Nelson loaded the weights.

*Breathe in. Brace. Extend. Bend.* The healthy left leg complied with ease. Nelson removed half the weights so that John's right leg hoisted forty pounds. Some pain, but nothing to faze the likes of him. Fifty pounds hurt enough to silence his chatter, but still he managed it with the appearance of ease. Fifty-five stung. Nelson loaded the final five-pound weight and John focused every ounce of his being on the muscles in his right leg. The last six inches of the extension were nasty, but he made it not once but twice. Nelson smiled.

"And the flex next, please." Dr. Madison merely raised one eyebrow in appreciation as he made some mark on his paper. John rolled over as if in the comfiest of beds. The flex was much easier.

Three more exercises met the requirements John knew Dr. Madison placed on his return orders. "Range of motion, your specialty," the doctor joked as they moved to a wall marked with a large collection of arcs and lines.

"Where are my cameras?" John casually wiped the sweat from his brow with a rough towel.

"Ever the comedian. To the right, if you will." John held the bar bolted to the wall and swung his left leg to the right. While it was hard to hold his full weight on his bad leg, the move wasn't that challenging. It's opposite—moving his right leg to the left—produced some pain. It was the next exercise—side steps with his body weight involved, precisely the move Leanne was attempting to improve with her waltzing scheme—that proved difficult. He closed his eyes, imagining his careful twirls around the room with Leanne, grafting her image into his memories of easy dances and carefree parties before the war. His leg cramped up a bit with the second try, but he was able to meet the black mark on the wall he knew to be his goal. How irritating to have one's future hanging on a smudge of paint two inches out of reach.

"Nurse Sample's ingenuity agrees with you," Dr. Madison remarked with amusement. "Two inches greater range. Perhaps we should enlist more violinists."

"I'd prefer if you enlisted better cooks," John said as he turned to stand with his back against the wall, bending to the far left as instructed. "I've lost weight in the time I've been here. How is it the army managed better rations in France than on its own..." He caught a sight out of the corner of his eye that stole the end of his thought. Through one corner of one window, perhaps where she thought he could not see her, John saw Leanne. She was seated on a small bench by the corner of the yard outside the gymnasium—one of the many chairs set out for reconstruction patients to sit and take in the sun.

"Captain?" Dr. Madison pushed his clipboard into John's vision. "On its own what?"

"...soil," John finished, fishing the thought back up from the depths of his brain where the sight of Leanne had banished it. He'd asked Leanne not to attend today's examination, and yet there she was, sitting on the hill facing the gymnasium. "Soil," he repeated, fighting the urge to blink and shake his head as he performed the "touch your toes" movement he knew came next. "How is it the army can't cook on its own soil?"

"I expect it is the sheer number of mouths to feed now." It was true: Camp Jackson had swollen beyond capacity weeks ago, with men and facilities tucked into every conceivable corner. Dr. Madison peered down to see how close John's hands got to his boots. John pressed the extra two inches to brush the top of his laces, pretending the lightning bolt of pain currently shooting up his right leg wasn't really there. He returned to upright, half expecting to find Leanne gone, the image of her under the tree a figment of his imagination.

"Again, please." Dr. Madison's tone was dry, rather less impressed than John would have liked.

He started to say "Why?" but replaced it with "Certainly," making it sound as if reaching for his boots was the highlight of his dressing routine rather than one of the most painful parts of every morning. When he returned upright for the second time, he fixed his eyes on Leanne to block out his leg's complaint. Why would she come here when he'd asked her not to? The answer hit him when he recognized the particular fold of her hands. Why must he continually experience the sight and sound of Leanne Sample praying for him? That's what she was doing, he could tell. Hang her, she had to pick the one thing he'd find even more distracting than her presence! She had no way of knowing he'd catch sight of her, probably thought she was hidden, and if Dr. Madison had not asked him to bend to the left in this particular spot, he most likely would have missed her. Which begged the even more disturbing question of how "fate"—for it was much easier to consider it fate than Who he knew Leanne would credit for the coincidence—had lined up this glimpse at this particular moment. *She's praying for you. Right now. Your name is leaving her lips, flung toward the vault of Heaven to do something she doesn't even think is wise.*

"Gallows? Captain Gallows!"

John managed to wrench his attention back from Leanne's folded hands. "Pardon?"

"Are you finding your exam so dull as to daydream out the window?"

"It's so dreary without the pain," he lied, enjoying the disbelieving *"hrmph"* the remark drew from the doctor. "I'm all healed, thanks to you."

Dr. Madison gave him the look of weary toleration he gave all John's "I'm healed!" lies and pointed toward the track painted on the gymnasium floor. "You're much improved, I'll grant you that. Laps, please."

Laps, as they had always been, were the true test. John could gut through any measure of pain for the handful of seconds it took to produce a pose, but laps were his ultimate enemy. No matter what mental fortitude he possessed, he could not will his knee not to buckle. He could not persuade his tendons to unfreeze, could not fool his way through a final lap without the help of his cane. John could sway the muses of speech and appearance, but time and distance were two masters he could not best. He'd grown to hate the incessant tick of Dr. Madison's stopwatch and the battlefield of those cold green ovals with their merciless white borders.

"One mile, eighteen minutes?" John tried to make it sound as if he were selecting between steak or lobster entrees.

"Twenty will suffice."

In truth, John's best time at the mile had been twenty-three minutes, and they both knew it. In fact, they never talked as if any of this were ever half as painful and difficult as it truly was. That was the game they played. "Well, as I'll not be stalling for time with the lovely Nurse Sample on my arm, I expect that should pose no problem." With a wink and a salute, John set off.

She shouldn't be here. He'd told her not to come and she'd argued against it, until he'd told her she would prove too much of a distraction. Part of her told herself he was a soldier who needed to focus on the vital task at hand, but another, more rebellious part of her latched onto the look in his eyes when he'd asked her to stay "where that pretty face can't undermine the mission."

"I'm not blind." She'd sighed to Ida the evening before as they'd each sat on their beds after supper. She'd just related how she'd dared to pray over John's leg, and the dozen emotions of that encounter washed over her with new vigor. "I know my heart is beginning to wander toward him."

"He's mighty wander-able." Ida's West Virginia drawl languished over the words and she braided her hair into the thick plait she did every evening. "I can't blame you at all, but you'd best keep the eyes of your soul wide open, as my daddy would say."

"John has so many good qualities…" She'd told herself that over and over.

"But there are so many…considerations in his case."

"Considerably!" she joked. "He maneuvers people and situations to suit his own ends far too easily. He is a charmer in the best and worst sense of the word—a silver-tongued man if there ever was one." Leanne curled her toes up under her skirts and let her head fall back against the bedroom wall. "And he couldn't be further from any kind of faith. He's an unsuitable prospect on any number of levels."

"Were you picking a horse, I might agree. Matters of the heart don't come quite so clear-cut, I find. Even in horses, though, it's the yearling that makes the least sense on paper that just may well take the race by storm."

Leanne managed a chuckle. Ida often had the strangest way of looking at things, and yet they made their own kind of wise sense. "Are you calling Captain Gallows a long shot?"

"I'm just saying the finish line is a long ways off, and you'd best take this race one turn at a time." Ida tied her braid up in a silk ribbon—one of the few luxuries still within wartime reach. "You've put tomorrow in God's hands. How about you leave it there?"

Leanne had gone to sleep meaning to do just what Ida said, but couldn't now that the day was here. She'd made too many errors during her rounds this morning, to the point where the doctor had sent her home an hour early and told her to rest. Rest? How could she rest not being allowed to watch John's test? Unable to stay completely away, Leanne had hid herself on the hill where she could see just into the gymnasium but not in a spot where she'd see him in particular. From here she could watch over *where he was* without watching over him, and John would never catch sight of her.

She had brought her Bible, hoping to find comfort in the words, but found herself lost in fervent prayer instead. *I fear his leaving, Lord. I fear he means too much to me. I fear he'll never know You and that means we must never be together.* Thoughts and surges of concern washed up over her, disjointed as they were heartfelt. *Guard his leg from pain. Send strength to those wounded muscles. Send him calm, Lord. You know his fear won't serve him well today.* The prayer that barely formed itself into words, the one that covered all the others, was simply, *Do what's best for him. Save him from going if he ought to stay. Send him if he needs to go. He can't yet see what You want for him—spare his life until he sees You at work in it. Spare him. Spare me this storm I've tried so hard not let into my heart.*

Leanne hadn't even realized how much time had gone by—she'd been watching the lights in the tiny corner of the gymnasium she could see, foolishly thinking they'd shut off when John was finished. A tap on the bench back startled her, and she jumped in fright only to see the tip of John's cane resting on the seat beside her.

# Chapter Seventeen

"**Y**ou'd make a poor spy."

John, on the other hand, would make a very good spy, for while his voice sounded tired, nothing of the day's outcome showed on his face. There was no hope of hiding what she was doing, and she found she didn't really want to keep her concern a secret. "How was the testing?"

He eased himself down beside her, slowly, the way he did when his leg pained him most. "I don't know," he said. "I really don't know. It could go either way, I suppose. I met some of the standards, came close enough in three more that Madison could sign the orders today— if he chose to."

"That's good, isn't it?" She noticed his fist was clenched around the arm of the bench.

"I would rather have left him no room to choose."

That was John, always needing the world to turn on his own terms. No wonder his brush with mortality had rattled him so. "How do you feel about the results?"

"You mean other than the wrenching pain and the frustration?" He attempted a smile—the false one he applied to make light of his pain—and tapped his cane against the boot of his good leg. "I think Madison will send me off."

He said it so easily, as if he'd been asked to take the hallway on the left instead of the right. The part of her that tried to trust God with today's outcome fell prey to a surge of panic. He might really go back. "You do?" She nearly gulped it.

"Mostly because I told him I'd make his life a living nightmare if he kept me. It isn't wise to cross a Gallows, you know." The momentary dark flash in his eyes showed John for the warrior he was. It was probably a very dangerous thing indeed to wake the ire of such a man. Just as quickly, the darkness receded and he raised an amused eyebrow. "And you know I asked you not to come here."

"You asked me not to attend your testing and I did not. And, well, I thought I'd placed myself where you couldn't see me."

John looked as pleased to hear this as she was embarrassed to admit she couldn't stay away. "Had Dr. Madison not asked me to bend to the left, I wouldn't have. As it was, I happened to look up at just the right moment to see where you were…and what you were doing."

He knew! Leanne felt as if she were glass, her emotions laid plain to his insistent eyes.

"Isn't God everywhere? Still you had to be here, watching over me in the gymnasium?" His eyes fairly glowed. It wasn't fair that he was so handsome at this moment when she felt so vulnerable.

She wouldn't answer his question. He wasn't really

seeking an answer in any case. Leanne knew exactly
what he was doing, peeling away her excuses for needing to be here, forcing her to admit what they both already knew. What they'd brushed up against the night
of the ball.

John moved one hand to touch her arm. "I was angry
at first. You're a terrible distraction, and I did miss one
lift simply because you threw my concentration."

She looked down, but John ducked his head to catch
her eyes and return her gaze to him. "Then during
the laps, those horrid, endless laps when my leg was
screaming and I needed to walk faster, I thought of you.
Out here, doing…what I knew you were doing. And…"

She could see he was deciding how far to step out,
what to believe about the test he'd just endured. Had
God shown His face to John in those laps? Could it be
that simple? "And what?"

"And I gritted my teeth and walked faster than I've
ever walked before for longer than I thought possible.
Because I felt…pulled along. By you. Or by…well, I
don't know just yet, but I suspect you have several the-
ories."

It was the closest thing to a consideration of faith
she might ever get from him. A smile bubbled up from
the part of her heart she'd tried so hard to ignore. "No,
only one. I prayed exactly that. I prayed that God would
pull you mightily toward the outcome He had planned,
even if it wasn't what you or I wanted."

John stared at her, deeply, his eyes a mighty pull of
their own. "What is it you or I want?"

"Captain Gallows, you've never drawn a single
breath not knowing exactly what you wanted." She'd

meant it as a snappy retort, a way to stave off the warmth in his steady gaze, but they were the wrong words. He'd turn them on her, most certainly.

He did. "You're right. I do know exactly what I want." He reached for her hand. "If you didn't want it, you'd have been able to stay away from here."

What would be the point of denying it? It was so clear, so strong, resonating between them even now. She ought to pull her hand away, to resume her insistence that they couldn't be together. She couldn't draw the breath to do it. The heat of his hand on hers, the way his thumb followed the shape of her wrist dashed every sensible thought from her grasp. When he feathered one finger down the side of her cheek, Leanne felt as if she'd dissolved into thin air, mere breath and yearning. When he took her face in his hand and gazed at her as if the whole world were found in her eyes, everything else fell from existence. "You've undone me, Leanne. I don't know how, I don't know when, I don't even know what to do about it, except this."

His kiss was careful, reverent, unlike anything she'd expect from the dashing Captain Gallows. It wasn't Captain Gallows's kiss, she realized; it was John's kiss. A kiss filled with one young man's wonder, as though it were the first honest thing this hero had ever done. She'd read novels where men "claimed" their women with powerful kisses, but this wasn't anything like that. He'd surrendered to her in this kiss, surrendered to the pull between them neither of them seemed able to stop or control. He inhaled as though the scent of her could heal his pain, clung to her as though her touch flooded him with peace. It was as if the whole world shimmered, as if the war itself paused at the sudden gush of grace.

Every inch of John's body, every corner of his being burst out of some dull fog he'd not even realized was there. Leanne was the opposite of everything he sought in a woman and yet, that was just the point—he *hadn't* sought her. He hadn't set out to win her; rather, they'd been pulled steadily toward each other since that first day.

"Did you know," he said as he let his forehead fall against hers—a hopelessly romantic gesture he'd vowed never to do—"how easily I picked you out of the audience that day? Oh, I cast my eyes over the full crowd because that's what I've been trained to do, but it was as if all I could do was crave the sight of your wide eyes."

She made a little gasp that wrapped itself around his heart. "Then it wasn't just me? You really *were* staring right at me? I thought it just a trick of presentation, the acclaimed Gallows oratory technique."

It felt important—poetic, even—that their eyes had so locked in a crowd of hundreds of people. It lit a glow in his chest to know his gaze had affected her so strongly. "So you felt it, as well?"

She cast her eyes up to the tree limbs that shaded the bench. "Oh, I must admit it made you terribly intimidating. Had I not seen you bend over in the stage wings, I might never have thought you a mere mortal."

John liked to think no one caught him with his guard down. Not especially at an event like that. "You saw me in the wings?"

"Don't be upset. It was my first glimpse of the

person you really were. I think that's when I first began to…"

She couldn't even bring herself to finish that sentence. Were her feelings that strong? Or was she that much of an innocent? "I can't even tell you when or how I first 'began to.' Like I said, you snuck up on me." He kissed her forehead, finding the flutter of her lashes against his chin a most exquisite sensation. He moved to kiss her mouth again, wanting to cover her in a dozen tender touches.

Leanne pulled away slightly. "You are too persuasive, John."

He moved back in, grinning with a pure happiness he hadn't expected. "It is one of my many gifts."

She pulled farther away. "No, truly, John, I must ask you not to take advantage of how I feel. I'm…I'm not used to such strong attentions. In fact, I should never have let you kiss me."

She had an analytical look in her eyes, as if solving a thorny problem. Certainly not like any woman he'd just kissed so soundly ought to look. "I'm rather glad you did. I'd like to think you were glad I did, as well."

"That's just it. I can't think clearly with you so close, looking at me like that."

"It is a classic symptom, you know. I'm having a bit of trouble thinking myself."

She took a deep breath. "John, please. There are so many complications. How am I to deal with the truth that we ought not to be together? Not now. Not when… you're…leaving, perhaps."

How like Leanne to look straight at the thing he was

trying to deny. "But it is not also truth that I'm here, now, and feel what you feel?"

"Life is more than 'here, now,' John, even in wartime. And while it is true that I...feel what you feel, there's another truth. You don't share my faith, and even what I feel can't change what I believe about the match of hearts and souls. How can it be right to consider a future when we don't share the God who holds that future?"

He placed his hand over hers, and while she tried to pull it away, he wouldn't let her. "I don't believe that has to come between us."

"I do."

Her voice wavered. She turned to look at him, and he saw how he'd unraveled her resistance. The honorable part of him admired her all the more for clinging to her convictions, while a darker part of him wanted to pull them down one dishonorable kiss at a time. It stung the conscience he wasn't sure he still had. Where was the grace and mercy Leanne attributed to God in a tangle like this?

"You feel something for me, and I for you. If God creates us, then He surely creates what we feel. He must have known this would happen. He must know what you feel, what I felt when I kissed you."

"John, the choice is neither yours nor mine. I am under orders, just as you are. I am no more free to ignore God's instructions simply because I wish differently than you are to ignore the general's."

"But you *do* wish differently. That must matter for something."

"It makes little difference. Faith means I surrender

to God's will in my life, trusting He knows better than my foolish heart."

Her sad smile was a torturous enticement. She was velvet and porcelain and tenderness, and she was stealing his heart even now by refusing it. He couldn't recall wanting a woman more ever in his life. "What if I don't want to surrender you?"

She stood up, putting distance between them. "Please don't press me beyond my strength, John. If you do care for me, grant me that."

He hated the idea of her thinking of him like some advancing foe, something God must protect her from, something she must flee. Still, Leanne was right; he never stopped pushing until he got what he wanted, and now that he'd realized what—*who*—he wanted, he knew his own nature. Dark as it was to admit, John knew himself perfectly capable of charming her beyond her resistance, unforgivable as it was. "I can't not be near you. You can do no better, today's already proven that."

Leanne covered her face in her hands. "Perhaps it is God's wise kindness, then, that you do leave."

She'd done it. She'd found the one way to cause him greater pain than any of his wounds.

## Chapter Eighteen

"What on earth happened to you?"

Leanne had barely made it through the door of her bedroom before she sank to the bed and gave in to the tears. Everything was so mixed up inside, crying seemed like the only response she could manage.

Ida sat down beside her, putting an arm around Leanne's heaving shoulders. "John failed the exam?"

"No."

"He passed?"

"We don't know anything yet." Leanne let her head fall onto Ida's shoulder. She was so weary all of a sudden.

"Y'all do not look like someone who doesn't know anything. Y'all look like someone who knows too much. What is going on?"

"Oh, Ida, I do know too much. I've gone and lost my heart to John Gallows. It's awful. It's wonderful and terrible all at the same time." She took the handkerchief Ida produced from a pocket and sighed as more tears came. "He's the wrong kind of man and the timing couldn't be worse. Still, when he kissed me it felt like I'd fallen off the end of the earth. I can't think when he's around, and yet I can see some things so very clearly. He cannot be the one for me, I know that, but…"

"Hold on there, he kissed you?"

Leanne felt her cheeks burn at the memory of the way John had touched her face, the things she saw in those eyes before his tender kiss. "He did." New tears stole down her cheeks. "Why did it have to be so wonderful, Ida? Why couldn't it have been awful and easy to refuse instead of leaving me with the horrid way I feel right now?"

Ida's smile was nearer a smirk. "You've not been in love before, have you?"

"No." Leanne dabbed at her nose. "But I am not in love."

Ida chuckled. "I don't have loads of experience in this department, but once is enough to let you know it feels like…well, just like you're feeling now. And he kissed you, did he?"

"Wonderfully." Leanne fell back against the coverlet. "It made it so much worse."

"So we can assume the captain feels the same way about you?" Ida leaned back on one elbow.

"He said as much, and more. He said the dearest things to me, I thought my heart would pound right out of my chest." Leanne rolled to her side to face Ida. "I almost couldn't do it. I nearly couldn't tell him not to kiss me again. My thoughts were so tumbled, when he said the timing and our faith didn't need to come between us, an enormous part of me wanted to believe him. It still does." She covered her eyes with her hands, frustration mixed with her still-pounding pulse. "I know better than this, Ida. I know he's most likely leaving—I've known that from the first. And I know what I believe. Why must he test it so?"

Ida pulled her feet up to hug her knees. "Let me see. Two people who don't belong together but can't keep their hearts from locking on to each other. I ought to sketch you right now—you could illustrate two hundred novels. This story is as old as time."

Leanne moaned. Sometimes Ida's humor was a blessed light. Other times her wit was too sharp not to sting.

"I'm not making light of you how feel. A breaking heart is the worst pain there is. My mama told me love is the most awful wonderfulness a person can feel. Loving the wrong man—especially one that loves you back—is just about the most pain a soul can bear. But it begs the question—are you sure he's the wrong man?"

Leanne did not care to tangle the matter further. "What do you mean? Look at where we are, who he is. How could he not be the wrong man?"

"Well, what if he is the right man at the wrong time?"

"Ida, I don't…"

Ida put up a silencing hand. "I'm not saying you should deny your convictions—I don't think the Good Lord ever wants one of His daughters to do that for a man—but here and now can't be the whole story, can it?"

"That's just it. We've no future together, not unless lots of things change. It already hurts just to be near him. I cannot endure more of it on such a thin hope. I've asked God over and over to show Himself to John, to do something about this whole muddle. I prayed so hard over his test and how he strives beyond what's wise, but I don't see anything coming of it at all." She let out an enormous breath, feeling as if she could sleep a week and not lose this weariness pressing down on her. "In fact, it's all only gotten worse." Leanne looked up at Ida. "I want to wish he'd never kissed me. I *ought* to wish he'd never kissed me, but…" She knew no matter how much it hurt, she'd never regret John's kiss. It's what made it so "awfully wonderful" as Ida said.

"That, my dear friend, is a most hopeless cause. When will you know if he is shipping out?"

"Tomorrow, I suppose." Leanne pulled herself upright. "I can't imagine he'll let Dr. Madison and the general rest until they give him their decision."

"Well, then, our task is to get you through tomorrow. We'll deal with the outcome when we know what it is."

Leanne managed a weak smile. "Remind me— over and over—that God already knows what it is, will you?"

"Absolutely." Ida pulled her into a hug. "Over and over."

One of the great truths of military life was that morning came quickly—whether it was welcome or feared. John dressed for his 0900 meeting with General Barnes with a weary anxiety. There had been nothing to do after Leanne's declaration except walk away. He almost turned when he heard a small sound from her—a cry?—but did not trust himself to behave with any restraint if he went back to her at that moment. Still, he felt certain she'd slept no more last night than he had. Had his leg not been so sore, he might have gotten up in the middle of the night and walked over to the Red Cross House just to see if there was a light on in her window. More like some love-struck schoolboy than the decorated war hero who was about to win his return to the front.

John deliberately left his cane in the outer room and walked into the general's office unaided. It hurt, but he absolutely refused to submit to any limp whatsoever. His dramatic entrance was lost, for Dr. Madison and General Barnes were standing over a large piece of paper on the general's desk. John executed the customary salutes, after which Barnes held up the paper. It was a sample cover of *Era* magazine with John and Leanne in their first knitting photographs. "Outstanding work, Captain. You hit the newsstands in two weeks."

A month ago, John would have been thrilled to grace the cover of *Era,* even for something as ridiculous as the Red Cross knitting campaign.

This morning as he looked at the photograph, he didn't see his impending glory. All he could see were Leanne's and his eyes. Hadn't the photographer made some remark about "photographic chemistry"? Now with the clarity of hindsight, John recognized it as the first sparks of the flame that had been lit yesterday afternoon. A flame that singed far more than it warmed this morning. "Well, sir, it's mission accomplished, then." He'd have preferred to relish the victory more.

"The director of the Red Cross called me this morning. They're over the moon with the article, calling you their new 'Homefront Hero.'"

"Leave it to Captain Gallows to be declared a hero on two continents in as many months," said Dr. Madison.

"That's our Gallows." The general nodded, signaling John and the doctor to sit down. "No challenge too great, no job too hard."

"I did have a bit of help, sir. Had Nurse Sample been unable to teach a lug like me, I doubt the Red Cross would be so pleased."

"Nonsense. We know who we've got in you. You've got a star quality we need at the moment. Our battles at home are as big as the ones over there." John didn't like what Barnes was implying. It wasn't in his plans to be too valuable over here—it's why he'd resisted both the speeches and the photographs at first. He'd worked hard to turn both into leverage he could use to get back to France.

John pulled himself upright in his chair. "With all respect, sir, it's time for me to get back over to those battles. In two weeks I'll have finished all I can do for you here. I have big plans."

"The captain has too many big plans in my opinion," Dr. Madison interjected. "He works himself too hard. Encourage that, and he'll not heal that leg as he should."

"You have your results from yesterday?"

Madison handed Barnes a file, but the doctor's face was a frustrating blank. John felt his leg turn to knots as the rest of his body tensed with anxiety. He'd wanted to ace the exam, to give Madison no choice but to pass him through; the tiny window of doubt he'd left with those last two exercises was driving him mad. Leanne's prayers that God would grant the wisest outcome despite John's wishes was driving him madder still.

General Barnes opened the file and donned his glasses. John looked at Dr. Madison, but the man would not return his stare. Was that good or bad? Why were these men drawing this out so when they knew all that was hanging on their decision for him? *Please,* the silent groan echoed up from somewhere so deep inside John he was startled to think it might actually have been a prayer. Out of nowhere, he remembered the story Leanne told him on one of their insufferable laps about a Roman captain who asked Christ to heal his daughter. Out of respect for the Almighty's authority, the soldier didn't require a visit, just a command. *Fine then, I respect Your authority. Please, Sir, if You're all Leanne says, You know how much I need this.*

"A remarkably fast recovery," Barnes said without looking up.

"An alarmingly fast recovery," added Madison, and John glowered at him.

The general removed his glasses. "Madison here says that you do, in fact, meet the physical qualifications for being returned to active service. However, he's recommending against it."

"It's simply not wise to rush this." Dr. Madison pinched the bridge of his nose.

"Gallows, you've been working hard. I reward hard work when I see it. Even when someone else doesn't see it my way." Barnes smiled. "I'm overriding the doctor's recommendation and sending you back."

John shot up out of his chair, all pain forgotten. "Thank you, sir. Thank you!"

Barnes motioned him back down. "Don't thank me until you've heard it all. We still need your particular gifts on the home front. The truth is you're not done here yet."

How very like the army to offer something with one hand and snatch it back with the other. "Meaning?"

"John, I've got places you need to be." He pulled a slip of paper out of his coat pocket and handed it to John. "Those higher up like what you've done here. I've been asked to ship you to Chicago in a week. They heard our recruitment rate has doubled since your presentation and they need you to do what you did here."

"Chicago, sir?" Fully aware of the general's rank, John was still ready to argue. *"Chicago?"*

"Only for a week of speeches at Fort Sheridan. Oh, you'll thank me for this—it's the president's baby, that base, all big and fancy and they plan to give you quite the send-off before you ship out to air corps."

"Air corps? Pilot training?"

Barnes smile widened. "You didn't think we'd keep you on the ground after all that airborne heroism, did you?"

Pilot training. It was better than he'd hoped. He'd have a chance at the real future on a ship of speed. On battle aircraft. "Yes, sir, thank you, sir. You'll absolutely not regret this." He dared a look at Dr. Madison. *"Either* of you."

"I regret it already." Dr. Madison sighed.

John shook the general's hand. Pointing at the magazine cover mock-up, he said, "May I, sir?"

"By all means. I'll make sure a dozen of them go to your family when they hit the stands."

"Thank you again." John shook Madison's hand for good measure, even though the doctor looked sourly outranked. He saluted, snapping his heels together for emphasis even though it shot flames up his leg, and turned to go.

"Your cane, Gallows," the general called, the hint of a laugh in his voice showing how pleased he knew he'd just made John.

John turned with a smile wider than the commander's. "Left it outside, sir. Not needed."

Madison frowned even further, Barnes grinned and John ignored the fire in his leg as he nearly sauntered from the room.

# Chapter Nineteen

John stood outside the general's office, smelling victory in the fall air. The camp hummed with activity; new soldiers seemed to be pouring in daily. The overcrowding had bothered him before—every man was well aware things had gone far beyond capacity and even the officers were feeling crammed in like sardines—but not today. Today the bustle was music. He was going back. John spun his cane like Charlie Chaplin, whistling. There was far too much energy shooting through his body to be bothered with anything mortal like pain. They would send him back. His final chapter in the Great War would not be in the role of poster boy, but of soldier. He was leaving.

He was leaving Leanne.

It was for the best, he saw that. They were too different to share a lifetime, and war split even the truest of matches. He looked at the *Era* cover image Barnes had given him. Even in the stark black-and-white, her eyes pulled him in. Was it just his imagination, or was that spark already present between them back when this was taken? Had his annoyed amusement been something more all along? Did it matter now?

She could not hear about his leaving from anyone other than him. He knew that, but dreaded the conversation. They'd need to be together at least once more in order to finish the photographic sessions. He ran his hand over the paper and wondered what would show in their eyes on that final image. Would fate allow him a farewell kiss? Would Leanne? John thought of the single sock, nearly finished yet never to see a mate, and thought it would make a fitting parting gift. There would be nothing gained by waiting to deliver the news. It'd be best to tackle the task now, while he was still feeling the thrill of achievement.

The house matron no longer asked his name, merely gave him a pleasant-but-supervisory smile as she went up to Leanne's hallway on the second floor. The creak of the stairs cast his mind back to the dance, when she'd come down those same stairs, an absolute vision in rustling rose satin. That was the first time he'd wanted to kiss her—but that time was more about a man and a pretty girl than the far deeper stirrings of the previous day. Yesterday had told him he could love Leanne Sample, perhaps already did, but could not have her. John nearly laughed at his sorry lot. He knew her weaknesses, knew how to overthrow them, but was bowing to her request that he stand down. Nobility proved dismal company.

She knew the minute she saw him. He'd spent the past few minutes searching for the kindest words, only to realize they weren't needed.

"Captain." In a single, sad word, Leanne robbed his victory of satisfaction.

He took a careful step toward her, noticing the way her hand tightened on the banister as he approached. How her hands fascinated him. He'd see them for years when he closed his eyes at night—those hands, and the color of her eyes. "I'm not leaving for two weeks, but I am leaving." He did not want to have this conversation in a Red Cross House parlor. "Walk with me, please?"

Her grip tightened. "What more is there to say?"

"A great deal." He wasn't sure he could ever make her fully understand why he was going, but it was better to try than to spend this remaining time in such tension. "Please, Leanne, I beg of you." He'd never used that phrase with anyone, ever.

"I'll get my wrap." He hated the thin, fragile tone of her voice, hated knowing it was he who hurt her so. Leanne turned to go back up the stairs, only to meet Ida bringing a wrap down to her. Ida shot John a "don't you hurt her more" look and handed Leanne a handkerchief, as well.

They walked in silence. John led them purposely to the bench where she'd prayed over his leg. It felt a kindness to remind her that she'd prayed over the outcome of this test, prayed that God would allow the result best for all, not just the desire of either of their hearts. This was best for all concerned.

"I'll regret leaving you," he began, knowing it was a poor start. "Can you understand why I must go back? Why I can't leave it at dangling over the ocean? Only a fool with a piece of ribbon considers that bravery, not I."

"Is that how you see your honor?" Her words were sharp for the first time. He'd finally caused her enough pain to overpower her infinite grace.

"Yes," he replied. He never spoke of this to anyone, but he would not leave her without the truth. "I can paint the most valiant picture of my daring escapade when it's called for, you already know that version. It's nearly all fiction, Leanne. Yes, I saved lives, but do you know what that stunt up in the dirigible truly was? Pure fear of dying. Not bravery, nor honor, just fear. I didn't climb out onto those stay wires to save the crew or the mission, I went out because it was the only thing I could think of to do to keep from dying."

"You sought to keep everyone from dying."

"No, that's only how it looked. I gave no thought to anyone else on that ship, only to my own skin. There was no heroism in it, no nobility. And as for daring? Well, let us just say you'd be surprised at the lengths a man will go to stay alive." He looked out over the lawn, not wanting to see her reaction, feeling sharp and raw as if he'd just ripped the bloody bandage off a wound. "And you'd be surprised the lengths other men will go to make it look like something it never was, just for the sake of gaining a poster boy to acclaim."

Her silence drew his eyes back to her despite his own resistance. It was unfair, what her face could do to him. Even hurt and angry, the morning sun set sparkles in her eyes and spun a halo of light through her hair. She seemed as weary as he, yet the stillness made her seem ethereal.

"You lie even to yourself, John." Her sigh was so delicate, so full of regret that he felt her emotion ripple down his own spine. "God spared your life and you tell yourself you must throw it away in order to deserve what He's granted? He places you here and you run back to harm? Why must you thrash your life about like a battle-sword?"

She said every question except one, so he said it for her. "Why must I leave you?"

Leanne did not reply.

"Leanne, I've always had to leave you. We are at war. It has only been a matter of 'when,' never of 'if.' It's a wonder we met at all. Consider that God granted us the gift of some time together. Not much time, but some. We should make the most of it. I don't want to spend my final days here keeping clear of you when I would much rather spend them *with* you."

"I cannot stand pain as well as you can."

She couldn't have made her decision more clear. He'd promised to be a gentleman—he'd abide by her wishes. John stood, gathered his cane and pulled the magazine cover from his pocket. "I hope it is not too painful to have this." He handed it to her. "It's the eyes I like most. We'll do fabulously. General Barnes tells me the Red Cross is thrilled."

Leanne took it, running a delicate finger over the "Knit Your Bit" slogan that splashed across the top of the image in large red letters. She managed a shadow of a smile as she looked up at him.

"I'm not sorry for any of it, Leanne. Not one bit of it. You're..." He didn't even know what he wanted to say to her. There wasn't a word for what she was to him, so he chose the closest one he could find. "You're a gift."

\* \* \*

The final photo session was to show John stitching up the toe of the sock. John mastered the grafting stitch with ease, even though Leanne often found it the hardest skill to teach. She'd chosen to do this final step without rehearsal, not because it didn't need preparation, but because she couldn't endure any more time alone with John. He'd made it easy for her, sending word he was too busy with Chicago preparations to do anything but manage the photograph.

Things were indeed chaotic at the camp—soldiers were coming in at twice the rate they had been over the summer and an outbreak of a common flulike soldier ailment called "the grip" had taxed all the nursing shifts. Still, Leanne saw easily through John's ruse. He was avoiding her, plain and simple, and she was glad for it.

All of her prayers for peace and contentment dissolved at the sight of him in full uniform again. She'd thought it impossible for him to grow any more handsome in her eyes, and yet achievement of his goal lent him an even more commanding presence. Even the sock he displayed made things worse. The cuff spoke of their first lessons, their verbal sparring and his oversize persona. The ribbing of how they'd grown to know each other, the gusset of the waltzes that had opened her heart to him and now the toe would speak of the end. Complete and yet incomplete, for a single sock is insufficient unto itself.

"It's a pity there'll be no pair," he said as they sat down in front of the lights. Had he seen the same symbolism in what they'd done together?

"You know the skills now. I can send you with the yarn and needles to finish the job." She'd tried to make it sound like the banter of their earlier lessons, but it fell hopelessly short.

"It isn't to be," he'd replied. She couldn't understand how his eyes could hold such regret and satisfaction in the same gaze. Perhaps it was by God's design of male and female, how men could go to war and how women could wait at home. But there was no waiting here, just as there was no second sock.

"Come on, you two, you've no energy today," the photographer complained. "I need to see victory in those eyes, Captain Gallows. Show me victory!"

After a handful of exposures, the photographer came out from behind the camera. "Thank you for your tireless service," he said in poorly hidden frustration, looking directly at Leanne. "We'll only need the captain for these final shots." John balked, but Leanne was glad to stop trying to be something she wasn't under those hot lights. There was no hope of recapturing the spark of that first photograph. Not here, not today.

Dismissed as she was, Leanne still couldn't bring herself to leave the session. She watched from the back of the room as they shot the last exposures of John. His eyes found hers between shots, kept looking at her even though she could not always meet his gaze. Then the photographer would call for him to pose, and somehow John could instantly transform, could pull the charismatic presence up from some well she didn't possess. He was every inch the hero, tall and dashing. Every boy would want to be him.

"Should bring a pretty penny at the auction, Captain," the photographer's assistant admired when the final flash had gone off. "Carolina's most famous sock."

She'd forgotten about that. Somewhere in the letting go, she'd convinced herself he'd give the sock to her. That when all this was over, she'd have that one memento, the fitting but painful symbol of their time together.

"Not much else a single sadly knit sock can do, is there?" John replied. "It had better fetch a fortune—I doubt it's good for anything else."

It had better fetch a fortune indeed. That single sock had cost Leanne her heart.

## Chapter Twenty

❧

"But you told me to do that other stitch here." The soldier from Atlanta had every right to look annoyed. Leanne had given him completely wrong instructions. She'd been useless in today's knitting class. She'd been useless in most of her duties, her mind dangerously preoccupied with the one student she no longer taught.

"I'm sorry, soldier, you're absolutely right—the pattern does say to knit that row." No amount of prayer had banished John from her mind, no Psalm had replaced the loss with contentment or trust that God knew what He was doing. Her mind knew what was right but her heart refused to comply—and the tug between them had overthrown her concentration. Leanne looked around the classroom to realize she was missing a student. "Where is Private Carson?"

"I was wondering the same thing," Ida said. Whether Ida had come to the soldiers' class for moral support or for the view, Leanne was glad to have her. "He was going to turn his heel today, wasn't he? I'm surprised he isn't here."

Just the thought of turning a heel brought back

John's delightful admiration of the process. Why must everything remind her of him? She knew he most likely stayed away from the base hospital now, but Leanne found herself looking for him around every corner anyway. Was she searching for him, or watching out to make sure she didn't see him? She could not decide.

"Maybe he's got the grip," another soldier offered. "Poor fella, if he does."

"I do hope that's not the case. I'll check up on Private Carson this afternoon."

After class Leanne pointed herself in the direction of the barracks housing recuperating soldiers. Everyone at the base seemed to know the location of every soldier, so it shouldn't be too hard to find Private Carson and arrange for a makeup class if he chose. He was still so physically weak in many respects, and the grip was a nasty business even for the healthiest of soldiers. *Don't let that be what kept him from class, Father,* she prayed as she walked.

"A nurse!" One soldier standing near the barracks saluted with a wry smile. "They're sending you *to* us now? I hadn't realized it got so bad."

"I beg your pardon?"

"Those two barracks got dozens of men down with the grip. If you ain't here to help, you'd best keep your distance."

"Do you know if Stanley Carson's come down with it?"

The soldier took off his cap and gave her the strangest look. "Stanley Carson from Georgia? The one missing a leg?"

"Why yes, that's him. I'm worried that he didn't

show up for a class I teach." The man's expression grew alarmingly grim. "Has something happened to him?"

"You teach that sock class, don't you? I think Stan liked that. He talked about it a lot. When he talked, which wasn't much." The man offered his hand. "Roberts. Pleased to meet you, ma'am." He looked anything but pleased. As a matter of fact, he looked as if he'd have rather been anywhere but talking to her at the moment.

"Can you tell me where to find Private Carson? I've a training session in an hour and just wanted to check up on him."

Roberts motioned to a bench a few feet away. "Why don't you sit for a minute, Miss…"

Leanne reluctantly took a seat. "Sample. Leanne Sample." Roberts wrung his cap in his hands. "Mr. Roberts, what is it?"

Roberts sat on the edge of the bench. "I sure am sorry to be the one to tell you this, but he…well, they found him yesterday afternoon. He's gone, ma'am. Passed."

He'd never looked well, always so gray and sad. Still, the shock of it was one more blow to her frail composure. "I'm so sorry to hear that. I hadn't realized his injuries still posed such a threat."

Roberts gulped audibly. "Stan didn't die of his wounds, Miss Sample. You know how sad he was. Carson…well, ma'am…he done ended things on his own, if you understand my meaning. I really am sorry you had to hear it from me, but seeing as you seemed to know him and all, I thought you ought to know."

Leanne's throat went dry. "Private Carson…took

his own life?" It seemed too horrible to think. She'd thought her class a bit of hope for him, had been so proud of the tiny spark she could occasionally light in his eyes. To think it hadn't been enough, to think she'd been so busy with John, never taken the time to talk to the man about her faith, turned her throat from dry to burning with tears. She hadn't done enough.

"It happens. Sadder than anything it is, but Carson, well, he never could seem to find his place around here. He was proud of that sock, though. You ought to know that. The only joke he ever made was about how he'd only need one sock at a time."

One sock. Complete yet incomplete. And here Leanne thought her heart couldn't break further.

## Chapter Twenty-One

Something was wrong at the general's office.

John was used to the chaos behind the calm—he'd been involved in enough military promotional junkets to know that the appearance of control required frantic backstage maneuvers—but this was something altogether different. It had been brewing for days, now that he thought about it. Clerks buzzing about offices with frowns, higher-ups huddled in secretive meetings and a general undercurrent of alarm. Either the war had taken a turn no one wanted to publicize, or something else had reared its ugly head.

"Captain Gallows, you'll need to wait. I'm afraid the general is behind schedule." The clerk at the reception desk looked as if he'd been up all night. John felt the hairs on the back of his neck stand up. Barnes watched the clock with an obsessive punctuality—if he was behind schedule, something was most definitely amiss.

Feeling his leg respond to his body's tension, John chose a chair that offered him views into several offices. A group of officers, sleeves rolled up and ties loosened, bent over a table of documents. All three of the office's telegraph machines clacked without interruption, each telegram quickly scanned, ripped off the machine and rushed off to other offices. Whatever it was, it went well beyond Camp Jackson.

John caught the words *hundreds* and *Devens* as a pair of men in doctor's coats came out of the general's office. They halted conversation immediately upon exit. A minute later the door opened again, a weary General Barnes leaning out. "Taylor, get me a meeting with the mayor and the university president before three." He wiped his hands down his face. "And find more coffee and some sandwiches."

"Yes, sir."

Behind the general, John saw a handful of nervous men pacing in front of a United States map covered in lines, pins and numbers. This was no overseas crisis. Whatever was happening had pins placed up and down the Eastern Seaboard, with more than a few heading into the Midwest. Were they mobilizing troops? Preparing for the possibility of an air strike? Most of the push was to send men overseas right now—it was why the camp was teeming with bodies, all funneling in from elsewhere to board ships to the front. Soon enough he'd be one of those walking up the gangplank of a transport ship to walk down onto French soil. If they were gearing up to go faster, that'd be all the same to John, maybe save him this detour to Chicago, as well.

"Gallows." Barnes pointed at John, nodding back toward his office. Without further invitation, the general turned and walked back in, leaving the door open for John to make his own way inside.

John felt like he'd stepped inside a beehive. In the outer office, there was at least an effort to appear calm. Not in here. A doctor pushed past John without so much as a word, barking orders to two clerks about bed partitions. John heard the word *quarantine* twice in as many seconds. "Sir?"

"Influenza's run mad down the coast. Ships are coming in on skeleton crews with heaps of bodies. Philadelphia's a mess, Boston's a disaster. I want you on the train to Chicago tonight, but you're not to go to Fort Sheridan. You'll be met in Chicago and taken to an office downtown. It's time to keep everyone calm and we'll need your silver tongue to help do that. The *Era* cover couldn't be hitting at a better time—you'll have enough celebrity from that to get the attention we need." He stuffed a pile of papers in John's hand. "These'll get you off camp and anywhere you need to go."

"I need papers to get off camp?"

"This isn't an ordinary influenza. We're about to lock down in quarantine, Gallows. At least until we can figure out what's going on. As far as the public is concerned, this is just a bad case of the grip, understood? Under control and nothing to worry about."

"And what the public doesn't know is…?"

"We just heard from Devens, sir." A clerk walked in without even looking up from the telegraph he was reading. "Four hundred dead and still climbing as of 0900 hours this morning." Barnes growled and the poor lad looked up. "Oh. Sorry, sir." He handed the paper to one of the men standing in front of the board, and the sets of numbers pinned up all over took on a grisly importance.

John knew Devens was an army camp outside of Boston—Dr. Madison had talked about his time there. Half of Camp Jackson's new soldiers had just poured in from Philadelphia. America's military was evidently at war with a new enemy. And if the general had just asked to meet with the mayor and the university president, this wouldn't stop with men in uniforms. John's gut turned to ice while his leg began to burn.

With the gravest expression John had ever seen on the man, Barnes pointed to an envelope marked "Gallows" and a handful of gauze masks. "Whatever it is, it's killing soldiers and it's on its way here, if it's not here already. So pack your bags and wear these. Wire me from Chicago. Dismissed."

Private Carson was dead. John was leaving. The wondrous new world awaiting her at Camp Jackson seemed nothing more than heartache upon heartache as Leanne made her way back home. She hadn't realized that she'd expected her knitting to save Carson, to draw him back from his personal darkness, but she found herself devastated that it had not. *I know a pair of needles cannot mend a soul,* she cried out to God as she walked, *but couldn't it have made this one bit of difference? I can't understand why You placed a burden in my heart for the poor man when it did no good at all.*

The lament seemed to apply to more than just poor Private Carson.

Leanne couldn't fathom going to some training class. She couldn't eat or sleep, she could not talk to John—

although she yearned to—and it seemed unfair to cry on Ida's shoulder yet another time. Leanne did the one thing she always did when at the end of her rope: she knit. Grateful she'd brought her knitting bag to sit with Private Carson should he wish it, Leanne found a quiet spot in the sunshine and began stitching. Around and around, stitch after stitch, Leanne let the craft soothe her soul.

Her prayers could always find their way up out of the yarn when she knit in solitude, but peace eluded her today. Tired of her own complaints, Leanne tried to pray for the soldier who would receive the pair of socks she was working on, but it was no use. Her thoughts refused to focus. Instead of picturing some wet and tired soldier, her imagination only conjured up images of Carson alone and afraid, hopeless in the dark. Worse, her thoughts turned to John. She saw him clenching his teeth as he tried to run on his bad leg. Falling while scrambling over battlefields. John crawling in search of safety as gunfire pounded around him. John lying wounded on some foreign shore.

Leanne looked down at the sloppy stitches and sighed. Had it come to this, that she could not even knit? It seemed like every solace had been taken from her. She gathered her things and began walking toward home when she noticed a young man slumped on a nearby bench, bent over in a violent cough. She looked around for the man's companions but found no one. She hurried up to the poor lad and put a hand to his shoulder. He was shaking. Another grip case, to be sure. "You need help, soldier."

"No, I'll be all right. I was fine this morning…" A violent cough prevented further words.

The young man looked up, forcing Leanne to swallow a gasp. His color was dreadful. She hadn't hid her reaction well, and fear crept into his glassy eyes. "Well—" Leanne put on her calmest nursing voice "—you've obviously caught whatever they told me is going around the camp. We'd best get you back to the infirmary."

"I'm supposed to be on duty in fifteen minutes."

"I don't think that's going to happen. What's your name?" It was one of the first points of bedside manner; learn the patient's name and use it frequently.

"Harper. It hurts." He sounded painfully young, like a child moaning to his mama.

"I expect it does. You'll not make it in far that condition. The hospital's right around the corner, we'll head straight there. Can you stand, Mr. Harper?" He managed a tottering rise, hanging on to her for balance. She noticed small spots of red on the soldier's handkerchief. "Where are you from?"

"Boston. Shipped out—" another cough, this one worse than the last "—a week ago."

"The way boys are pouring in, I suppose it's unavoidable lots of you come down with something." She forced a conversational quality into her voice as they limped along, but inside she was wondering if he had the stamina to make even the short walk to the hospital.

Thankfully it wasn't long before more soldiers happened by and with their help, Leanne managed Harper through the hospital doors to discover the ordinary outbreak of grip on camp had turned into something far larger. Two dozen or so young men lay on beds in varying states of a similar illness. A nurse Leanne didn't recognize, looking like a white specter in her uniform and a surgical mask, thrust a mask at Leanne and her soldier companions. "Go wash," she barked as another nurse gathered a collapsing Harper from Leanne's grasp.

"What's happened?"

The nurse's eyes—the only real part of her face Leanne could see—darted anxiously. "Some sort of virus."

"Not the grip?"

"Does this look like the grip to you?"

Leanne hadn't seen enough of the malady to answer. Still, it was true: these boys looked far worse than those she'd seen earlier. There had been stories in the paper of "the Spanish sickness" hitting some of the forces in Europe. It was powerful enough to slow the German offensive, so perhaps some soldiers had brought back this new strain. She'd been taught influenza was highly treatable. Even the worst cases required not much more than a quarantine for a handful of ships as they docked. Her nursing teachers had spoken of it as an expected outcome of global combat, something to be managed with a clinical calm. The sort of thing a wartime nurse must expect to encounter.

There was no clinical calm here.

"Why are you hesitating?" Artie Shippens, John's only bunkmate at Camp Jackson before three more officers had moved in last night, tossed down the cloth he'd been using to polish his boots. "You've been itching to get out of here since your arrival. Barnes just handed you a golden ticket out of town. You should be running to catch that train."

"They're not even shipping me to Sheridan anymore, which tells me Sheridan's in worse shape than whatever's starting here. No matter where I go, I'll end up in the thick of it, if I'm not already. Besides, my family is here. What if this thing, whatever it is, gets into Charleston?"

"You act as if a soldier's never come down with the grip before. This bursts through a camp for a few weeks and then everyone gets better. That's all this is."

John put down the stack of masks Barnes had given him. "I know what I heard, Artie. That is not all this is. They're panicking up there at the headquarters, even if no one will tell you that. Telegrams are coming in with death tolls. Not men ill, men *dead*." He eased himself onto his cot, his leg throbbing. "There's a huge outbreak in Philadelphia, and we docked a ship from there just three days ago."

"I played cards with them the other night. Took 'em to the cleaners, those boys from Philly. They said there had been a load of sick boats, but the grip don't kill nobody. Pack your bags and hit the road."

John chose not to argue. He ought to be doing just what Artie said, but somehow he couldn't get himself moving.

Artie stood over John. "Aw, no, don't tell me. Do *not* tell me you've got second thoughts about leaving that knitting nurse. Shoot your own career in the foot on behalf of a woman? She's not worth it. Not with all you've got to gain."

Allie Pleiter                              183

"It's not that." She'd told him to leave. Leaving was best for all concerned. It couldn't be that, he was just stunned by the fact that he'd been handed an escape from the disaster evidently about to strike the camp. John looked at Artie, calculating how many of his card victims from the other night had already fallen ill. For all John knew, Artie might already be infected, and himself from sleeping four feet from the man. The trio that had arrived last night had done their fair share of coughing, too.

Artie snapped the tin of polish shut and tucked it into his locker. "If you tell me it's because you need to finish that confounded Sock Brigade of yours, I'll have to consider shooting you." Artie had taken to calling John's Red Cross photo campaign "The Sock Brigade" the day John brought the yarn back to camp and hadn't let up yet. Artie would have a field day once the issue of *Era* found its way to newsstands.

"We finished the final photographs. I'm sure it's the only reason the general is able to ship me out so quickly. When I'm gone, you'd best take those winnings and bid sky high for my sock at the Red Cross auction."

"Off to Chicago while they lock us down tight back here. There are twenty men if not fifty who'd line up to be in your shoes." Artie started to laugh, but finished it with a small cough.

John sat up. "You're all right? Feeling okay? You said you were playing cards with Philly boys."

"Fit as a fiddle. Honestly, John, this kind of panic doesn't suit you."

He was done trying to talk himself out of it. "I need to see Leanne before I go."

"Don't do it, John." Artie's eyes were serious. "You know it'll just make things worse."

John put his jacket on. It would only take him minutes to pack, anyhow. "I can't not say goodbye."

"You can, and you ought to. Chicago, John, put your mind on that big shiny city. Hey, maybe they'll snap you stitching with a movie starlet." Artie leaned against his locker, waved his polishing cloth like a lady's hankie. "Oh, Captain Gallows," he crooned in a high-pitched voice, "what fine, fine stitching you do." His poor imitation was cut short by another cough, causing John to freeze in the middle of his buttons.

"I'm fine, Gallows, stop it. Go make your mistakes with your knitting teacher and stop mothering me."

# Chapter Twenty-Two

Leanne washed her hands again as she went off her shift for a lunch break and tried not to think about the hollow fear in Mr. Harper's eyes. She'd seen plenty of sick men in her short time here. Some of the expressions worn by men in the reconstruction gymnasium could chill her blood. Private Carson often looked worn to the bone. Still, there was something deathly in Harper's gaze that simply would not leave her.

"I sure am sorry to hear about Private Carson," Ida said. Every nurse on camp had been scheduled into double shifts as sick boys kept pouring into the hospital. "Seems an awful shame, even as sad as he was. I was certain he was turning a corner as surely as he turned his sock heel."

"It's heartbreaking, Ida. He was someone's son. Someone's brother, perhaps. No one should feel that alone, no matter what their injuries. God rest his tortured soul."

"No one will feel alone now. We're packed in like sardines, and now they're talking about quarantine?" They'd announced it to the hospital staff not twenty minutes ago. Ida rolled her shoulders with a weary yawn. "The whole base? It can't be that bad, can it? It's just influenza."

"The head of medical department was rushed over to the capitol building a few hours ago. Perhaps that 'Spanish Flu' they talked about in the papers is worse than our usual influenza."

"I heard they're starting to get cases over at the university. Someone said they'd be asking some of us who took classes there to go over and help if things got troublesome."

Leanne thought getting away from Camp Jackson and John Gallows might be the best thing for her right now. "I'd go. Would you?"

"We always made a great team. I'll tell the head nurse when I go back on shift." Ida sighed, following Leanne's gaze out the window in the direction of the officers' quarters. "I'm sure he's fine."

"How can I know? What if he's already one of those sick?"

"You just saw him yesterday."

"That doesn't mean anything. Mr. Harper said he was fine in the morning, and he could hardly walk by the time I found him. No one knows how these things get transmitted. John spends lots of his time in crowds, with strangers from everywhere."

Ida's hand came on her shoulder. "You're not helping yourself thinking like this. He'd have been brought in here if he was sick, you know that. John would find a way to get word to you if something else had happened."

Leanne turned away from the window. "He might

not. I told him not to come find me before he left. I didn't think I could stand to be around him, but I find it's even worse not knowing if he's all right." Leanne held her forehead, willing away the headache she could feel coming on.

"When's the last time you had something to eat?" Ida asked.

"I can't remember. Breakfast, I think." It was already well past two.

"Well, there's half your troubles right there. We're supposed to be on a meal break, let's go get some food before they stop giving us breaks altogether."

"I do feel rather peaked from all this."

"Mama always said the world looks worse on an empty stomach." Ida held out her elbow to "escort" Leanne down to the dining hall.

She and Ida found a seat by the windows in the far end of the near-empty hall and shared a tuna fish sandwich, a peach and a pot of tea. The tuna didn't sit especially well in Leanne's stomach, but the tea felt wonderfully warm and comforting.

"A veritable high tea. Feel better?"

"You're a good friend to have in a tight spot, Ida."

Ida raised an eyebrow and hoisted her teacup. "Y'all remember that when that magazine cover comes out and you're famous."

The thought of being seen everywhere with John, now that they would never see each other again—or at least, not for a very long time—made Leanne put down her cup.

Ida sat back in the metal chair. "That will be hard, won't it? Having that picture all over the place, seeing his face paired right up with yours? I don't think anyone else will see it, but I sure see what went on between you in that photograph. Y'all only have eyes for each other."

Leanne rested her head in her hand, tired now that she'd eaten. "I was supposed to look at him with admiration."

"Oh, you're admiring him, that's for certain. He's admiring you, too, but nothing in that look has anything to do with knitting." Leanne squeezed her eyes shut, feeling physically, emotionally and now even photographically vulnerable. "Relax, no one who doesn't know can see it. To everyone else it'll just be grand publicity."

Grand publicity felt like the last thing Leanne wanted. Her stomach gave a sour little flip, and she let her gaze wander over the scattered chairs and tables, wondering when John had eaten last and if he had any good friends in a tight spot.

"Leanne!"

It was funny how she thought she heard his voice. Then she did see John. He was striding across the dining hall, ducking and dodging chairs and tables at a pace far too brisk for his comfort. He never limped if it could be helped, and he was visibly hobbling in his rush. She pushed back her chair and went straight to him.

He had her by the shoulders before she could even say hello. "Are you all right?"

"Yes, of course I'm fine."

"We're locking down in quarantine. Within hours if not already."

"They just told us. Is it really that bad?"

John kept his hands on her. "I had to see if you were all right."

"*Told* you," Ida said with a wry smile. "How about I just head on back upstairs and leave you two to talk?"

"Someone said you were at barracks fifteen today." John pulled her down to sit at a table. "Why on earth did you go there?"

"I went over there to see if Private Carson was all right. He didn't come to his knitting class. It's terrible, John. Stanley Carson is dead."

"Lots of men are dying. And not just here. Army and navy camps are reporting death tolls in the hundreds."

Rumors often exaggerated. "People don't die like that from influenza. And, John, Private Carson wasn't sick. He took his own life yesterday. I can't believe it. We were so sure he was gaining hope, so sure we'd managed to lift his spirits a bit."

"I'm sorry about Carson, but do you hear what I'm saying, Leanne? Men are dying from whatever this is, and quickly. If they haven't yet here, they will."

John fought down the surge of fear in his stomach that had continued to grow since his visit to Barnes's office. It was very likely he had been exposed. He'd wrestled with that, surprised that his primary reaction to this threat was one of regret. Not the regret of perhaps not making it back to the front—for that would have sent him on the next train to Chicago. No, his initial, gut-level response was that he regretted not fighting for Leanne. If he were to meet his end in one of those hospital beds, he did not want to leave things with Leanne the way he had. The only doubt in his coming here was that he might expose her somehow, but what kind of foolish thinking was that? She was a nurse in a hospital about to be locked down in quarantine. She was in more danger of exposure than he.

The moment he'd walked into that hospital cafeteria and seen her again, he knew. Not in a monumental, defiant kind of way, but the quiet certainty of truth: he would not be on that train tonight. He would not leave her to face this alone, nor did he want to face whatever was coming his way without her beside him. The last time God had dangled him above death his thoughts had been only for himself, and he was finding that truth very hard to live with. If God were to dangle him above death again, he would seize this second opportunity and be worthy of the medal he wore. He would not leave. Hang Barnes and his schemes; this captain was going to stand and fight.

John allowed himself the luxury of running a hand down her cheek, glowing at how her eyes fluttered as he did so. "You're not feeling ill—not at all?" She felt a bit warm to him.

"I'm upset and haven't eaten well, but not much more is wrong with me than that. John, please tell me what you know and why you're looking at me like that. Are you well? Surely you've been around some of the men who've fallen ill."

"Have they given you masks to wear?"

"Of course they have."

"Wear them. I managed to wring some facts out of one of the general's clerks, and what he said made my skin crawl. Leanne, influenza doesn't kill men off like this. Not by the hundreds as they say is happening. In bases up and down the seaboard. This is no ordinary virus, Leanne." He took her hand. "I heard one of the doctors use the word *epidemic*. I doubt they'll use that publicly, but I can tell you the word is being bandied about behind closed doors."

John stared into Leanne's eyes, struck by the sudden strong urge to kiss her, right there in the dining hall, no matter what she'd asked of him earlier. She could be lying in a bed fighting for breath before the sun set tomorrow, so could he for that matter, and here he was just holding her hand. She'd done something to him, something he both hated and craved at the same time, but something he needed to be near if the world was truly falling apart the way he believed it was. If they came after him in a few days to drag him to Chicago, he'd fight that battle then. For now he must do all he could to ensure Leanne's safety. He brought his hand up to her cheek again, pleased when she did not resist. "Do all you can to stay safe."

"And you, as well. I'll worry about you when you go. I'm going to pray for your safety every day."

"I'm not going."

"What?"

"Change of orders in all this chaos. I'm not going anywhere." He didn't like lying to her, but now wasn't the time to go into everything. "Don't ask me to stay away, Leanne. I can't. Not now."

The tender look in her eyes told him before her words consented. "I won't." He would have fought, worn her down until she consented for her own good, but was doubly pleased she'd agreed without persuasion.

He'd been defenseless against her prayers, now he

found he could almost welcome them. "Would God laugh at my prayers for your safety?"

Now it was her hand that found his cheek, and the sensation was like a homecoming. "Never," she said softly. "He would welcome them with more joy than you imagine."

John placed his hand over hers, wanting to do so much more. Had they been anywhere but where they were, John was sure he would have dared to kiss her. Instead Ida's voice came up behind them to break the spell.

"We're to go over to the university. It's starting over there, and they're turning one of the dormitories into a makeshift hospital. There's a truck leaving in ten minutes."

"More sick?" Leanne asked. "Students?"

"As bad as here, if not worse."

It took John two seconds to decide. He was already packed, after all. "I'm coming with you." Leanne offered no argument, only tucked her hand into his elbow as they set out.

As the truck bearing them and a handful of others pulled up to the university dormitory, all conversation stopped. A dozen campus medical staff streamed frantically in and out of the building like white ants. Around them a more gruesome parade of fifty or so students—mostly men in various states of illness—streamed into the building from all directions. Coughing filled the fall air. One man to their left was being carried on a chair by two companions, a bloody handkerchief clutched to his mouth. Two white ambulances, their red crosses standing out like warning beacons, were backed up to the dormitory. Maintenance men, also in masks and looking as if they'd rather be anywhere else, hauled dormitory beds into the medical building at the direction of several more masked nurses. John felt Leanne's hand tighten against his arm, and for a split second the urge to pull her away gripped him. Fear's instinctual desire to flee, to take his train ticket and somehow parlay it into an escape for the both of them, wrapped around his throat like a noose.

*Dear God, save us.*

He meant every word of this first prayer, and prayed it wouldn't be his last.

# Chapter Twenty-Three

Mere hours later Leanne slumped against the wall and wiped her forehead with one hand. It had become clear no one really knew what to do. They began by placing patients in neat rows separated by canvas screens to prevent transmission of the virus, but the number of patients exceeded the number of beds within two hours. Workers scrubbed down dormitory floors as fast as they could, but still could not keep up with the stream of new patients.

The sheer numbers of ill made Leanne's mind reel. The constant wave of moans, ebbing and flowing from rows upon rows of beds, was like a sea of misery. At first patients would be alarmed by the pain; influenza wasn't supposed to hurt like this. They'd panic, thrashing about or crying for relief no one knew how to bring. Then, as the illness wore them down, their panic would fade into the most miserable fatigue. Leanne had to lift more than one head for a patient as another nurse struggled to get drops of medicine down his throat. All within hours of her arrival on campus.

Sweat tainted the air, and the sharp scent of disinfectant often cut through the mixture of odors Leanne associated with any sickroom: blood, urine, vomit, sweat, all in volumes that gave the ward an air of disaster. It smelled like a battlefield. It *was* a battlefield, with bloody wounds born of no weapons the doctors had ever seen. It was the color that frightened most of all. Those sick would begin to take on a ghastly blue-gray tone, starting with a vague pallor at first and progressing to ghoulish blotches that spread as the disease progressed. No one knew stages or symptoms, new information would be passed from doctor to nurse as it arrived, but all of it felt futile in the face of the onslaught that kept coming.

They began laying patients on the floors between other patients, forcing Leanne and the other nurses to literally step over groaning men and women to move through the ward. At one point Leanne was darting back and forth between no less than eighteen people, struggling to stay abreast of the soiled sheets, cries of pain and doses of medicines that seemed to do no good. And the blood. The blood was worst of all, for it seemed to be everywhere, unstoppable, staining and spilling and casting its sign of catastrophe over anything left clean and white. Every hour less and less was left clean and white.

Near the end of her shift Leanne found a Charleston family friend, an agriculture student she'd known last year. She barely recognized Charles Holling as he moaned the most dreadful request she could imagine: Holling was begging to die. He was in the far corners of the first room, a horrid shadow of the handsome boy she'd known back home. His words sent a chill down

Leanne's aching spine, and she sank to his bedside to wrap one purple-blotched and swollen hand in a cool cloth and hold it tight. It was a wonder she recognized him at all, for his blue color and sunken face made him look barely human.

"Charles, it's Leanne Sample." The man's glassy eyes found her in their roaming and she glimpsed the soul still fighting inside. "Do you remember me? Your brother took me to the St. Cecilia's Ball." She pulled down her mask for one second, allowing him to see her familiar face before replacing it as he gave way to another round of blood-spattering coughs. Holling dissolved into pitiful tears when from somewhere in his incoherence he finally recognized her. "Let me die," he moaned. "It hurts too much."

"No, no, you must recover. You must fight and live." She mopped his discolored forehead.

"I want to die," he demanded loudly, as angrily as his racked body would allow. His howl changed the atmosphere of the room as if he'd thrown a shroud over the lot of them, inviting death to hover and prevail.

Leanne did the only thing she could do in the face of such horror. "May I pray for you?" What else to do or say in the face of such suffering? What other comfort could she give? He gave a whimpering nod despite his hopeless eyes, and Leanne began to pray aloud. It only served to calm his cries to wordless moans, but she was grateful for even that small relief. She mopped his brow again, spooned a bit of water into his foul-smelling mouth and begged God for the worst to be over. *If he was among the first to fall, Lord, then let him be the first to recover. Heal his...*

"Nurse!" A young woman gasped as she lay curled and retching two cots over. Holling rolled to his side, lost again to the fog of his now-quieter moaning. Leanne forced her weary body to rise, grab the last two sets of clean sheets left in the room and tend to her next patient.

Mr. Holling got his wish. Leanne returned to him not twenty minutes later to find his moans had been stilled not by the blessed escape of sleep but the arrival of death. Her first day of classes Leanne had learned to take hold of a wrist to find a pulse. She felt hollow and frail as her fingers told her no pulse was there to find. The room swayed slightly around her as she took the stained sheet and pulled it over the young, lifeless face.

She knew his family. She knew his name. She wrote it in slow, careful letters onto the tag she affixed to his foot to declare Charles Dayton Holling the first official influenza death on the University of South Carolina campus.

As he stared at the dormitory, watching the patients stream in and knowing Leanne was inside, John battled a wave of helplessness. He preferred his destiny be in no one's hands but his own. And yet as he watched the chaos swirl around him, John couldn't help feeling as though he'd been swept up in something far larger than his own will. Really, it was the only explanation. What had he hoped to accomplish by coming to the campus in the first place? Self-determined men didn't do nonsensical things like disobey orders and throw themselves directly in harm's way for sentimental reasons. Were

Barnes to find him right now and demand to know the motives behind his actions, John wasn't sure he could give any explanation at all.

"You there!"

John turned to find a burly-looking man pulling several boxes on a wheeled cart. "Yes?"

"We need help here. Can y'all lend a hand?"

Pointing to his leg with his cane, John was forced to concede, "Bad leg. Afraid I'm not much for pulling and pushing."

"All I need's a man who can cut open a box with a knife. Reckon you can do that?"

John needed something to do, and the prospect of something with his hands, something physical, fit the bill. "I can."

"Mighty grateful. We're as shorthanded as they come today. Head on over here.

"Dan Colton, of the Chattanooga Coltons," he said with a wry grin after giving John's elegant cane a once-over. He set John up with a small knife and what seemed like an endless stack of bandage boxes in need of opening.

"Nothing to it. Cut this open, put the bandages in this here cart and Travers—" he pointed to another skinny lad "—will wheel it into the building." He nodded back to the set of delivery doors behind him. "Better to do it out here than in there with all them sick folk."

The pace required didn't offer much chance for conversation, and John and the two men settled into a quiet, efficient rhythm until the first cart had been unloaded. It was a frantic but simple business, the sort of hard labor John had known back in his father's textile mill, the kind that cleared a man's head for thinking. He found himself grateful for the activity, for the chance to feel as if he were contributing in some way other than making pretty speeches. The chaos lent him anonymity; when he took off his captain's jacket, he was just a willing pair of hands like any other.

When Colton returned with another cart, his expression had darkened. "It's getting worse by the hour. Mercy, but I never seen anything like what's going on in there. No wonder they done locked the campus up tight. Ain't nobody coming or leaving till this thing is done, whatever it is."

"The university is under quarantine?" John shouldn't have been so surprised, not with Camp Jackson already under lockdown.

"Well, sure." Colton wiped his face with a grimy handkerchief. "I figured it was the only reason you were still here and not back with all the other soldiers at camp."

John let the gravity of his circumstance sink in for a moment. The university was quarantined. There was no going back on his decision now. Quarantine meant no help in, no release out. He was here, and he was going to stay "till this thing is done." Somewhere in the back of his mind, John had known the irrevocability of his choice all along. He'd known he was throwing away his one chance of escape when he walked onto campus, electing to see Leanne safe rather than board that train. He waited for the panic to hit him, the consequence of his decision to rise up and frighten him.

It didn't.

Instead John couldn't shake the feeling that as frightening as things were, he was *meant* to be here. Not just here cutting boxes, but here at the center of this "plague"—and the word was being used all around him now—and with Leanne. There wasn't any other reason for the inexplicable stillness at the center of his very real fear. He'd never felt such surety giving speeches, even if Leanne thought it a fine use of his "gifts." He was a cool head on the battlefield, but this was a different sort of focus. Any man with half a bit of sense would have taken the golden ticket General Barnes had given him and escaped all this, but he hadn't, and he knew he *ought not to have.*

This, he realized, must be what valor feels like. This brand of courage was the way the man everyone thought he was would have felt up on that airship. The man who deserved that medal wouldn't have been scrambling for his life, desperate and terrified, but solid and centered the way John felt right now. Surely there was no less danger—in fact, John would have wagered he stood less chance of getting out of the university alive than he did of surviving that airship's crash. He knew he could not leave Leanne to face this alone, and whether he succumbed to the virus or not was…

John stopped his own thinking, realizing he was about to finish his thought with the words, "…in God's hands." The surprising realization froze him for a moment, knife midair. He didn't really believe that, did he?

"You okay?" Travers was staring at him. "You sick?"

"No," John said, "I'm well. Just—" he fished for a word "—startled."

Travers wiped his sweating forehead with his sleeve. "Ain't we all?"

Was he calm about being here because he was where God wanted him? It seemed a foreign thought—one Leanne might have, but not him. Still, the words had a ring of truth to them. He would not have been able to leave the base with the other medical personnel if he didn't possess those travel orders General Barnes had given him. He would not have those travel orders if he hadn't passed the physical exam. And somewhere inside John knew, disconcerting as it was, that he would not have accomplished those laps had he not spied Leanne sitting on the hill praying for him. The fact that he'd seen her at all—and at the precise moment he most needed to see her—seemed too much of a coincidence to put down to luck, for he'd expressly asked her to stay away and Leanne was not the sort of woman to defy a specific request like that. His mind seemed pulled inextricably back to her prayer that afternoon on the bench, the one where she'd prayed over his leg to "Let Your will be accomplished."

As he cut open the next box, John found himself entertaining the impossible notion that God's will had, in fact, been done. In him.

He was here with Leanne.

He was in peril but alive.

And he was amazingly content with all of it.

## Chapter Twenty-Four

Leanne had never seen a man die before. The waste of it all, the sheer mass of life draining out of bodies in that building seemed to crush the air from her lungs. Or worse, as if she were breathing in death itself, as if the flimsy, suffocating mask were not keeping the virus out but forcing it down her throat. She stumbled out of the ward, feeling she'd spent three days in there instead of three hours. Despite orders, she pulled off her mask to gulp in fresh air. How alive the world looked, with sunlight and green grass. How thankful she was to leave behind that desperate place of stark white, bloodred and deathly gray.

How thankful she was to see John waiting for her.

She had no strength to draw lines of faith or sense, she merely fell into his open arms and let him hold her up. How many times had she been his support? Today he was the strong one, and she was glad of it to her weary bones. "It's awful in there. Ghastly. There are so many of them, all so sick. We haven't enough of anything."

He didn't say anything. What was there to say? He

had no words for such a calamity any more than she. She clung to his shoulder, letting the soothing rhythm of his healthy breath and the steadiness of his heartbeat return her to the outside world. "Let's get you inside," he suggested after a moment or two.

"No, please, not yet. I need to be outside for just a little while, to feel the breeze and see the sun." Today felt a hundred years long, and although the sun was low in the sky, she needed every last scrap of it she could find. "There's a garden over behind that building. I used to go there when I was a student."

"Of course," he said, following her.

His limp was pronounced as they set off, and Leanne was glad it wasn't far. "It hurts, doesn't it?" She ached everywhere; she could hardly imagine how John's leg must pain him after a day like today.

"Hardly seems to matter in all this, does it?" He assessed her face as they walked. "You are all right? Not feeling ill?"

"I can't feel anything. And yet I feel too much of everything. Charles Holling, someone I knew back in Charleston, he died. Practically right in front of me. He begged for death, he was in so much pain. I couldn't…"

John tightened his grip on her arm. "Don't. Try not to dwell on it, try to be here, now, not back there."

"How? How do I do that?"

John's shrug reminded her that he had been in battle, had seen landscapes strewn with bodies worse than what she had just seen. "You force your mind to stay where you need it to be. You tell yourself over and over you're here and alive. Over and over until you start to believe it."

"I can't."

He stopped and turned to her, taking each of her shoulders in his grasp so that she felt the cool of his cane press up against one arm. "You can. You must. Look into my eyes and say it—'I'm here, I'm alive.'"

"I'm here, I'm alive." Her words had no strength.

"We're here, we're alive," he repeated, eyes locked on hers.

"We're here, we're alive. Thank God, we're here, we're alive." She brought her hands up to clutch his arms, craving the feel of his strength.

"I do, you know," John said softly. "I don't know how to begin to explain what had happened to me this afternoon, but I do thank God we're here and alive. I realize God kept you safe and kept me with you."

"John." She exhaled. Was he saying what she thought he was saying? "You shouldn't be here. You could have saved yourself from all this. You're too important."

John's hand came up to cup her chin. "I couldn't leave you. I needed to be here. I ought to be here."

Her breath caught as he ran his thumb across the curve of her cheek. "You ought to be safe." She fought the surge of feelings his words sent over her. "They'll need you back at Jackson. You ought to leave." She was trying hard to mean it.

"I cannot. You know the quarantine order, no one can come or go until it is lifted." He said it with a complete lack of panic, when Leanne thought he ought to be feeling as though he'd hung himself by his own choice.

"No." She turned her head away. "Now you're trapped here because of me."

"Everything has lined up to such order. Don't you

see it all fits only one way? You prayed for me, prayed that the outcome would be not what either of us wanted, but God's will. This is. I see that now."

Astonishment filled her heart to overflowing. "John?"

"You've done the inconceivable, Leanne." He almost laughed, his astonishment evidently no less than her own. "You've saved the last soul on earth I would have ever thought possible."

Her eyes welled up, and John smiled as he wiped the single tear that stole down her cheek. To know such joy, now, seemed impossible. "Surely you don't think yourself so unworthy?"

Leanne placed a hand on John's chest and felt his heartbeat pounding under her palm. Alive. Here. Now. The darkness that had always lurked in the corners of his eyes had vanished, an unlikely, irrational peace of in its place. "To be frank, I don't know what I think." He pulled her closer. She did not resist. "I'm quite sure, however, what I feel."

Leanne could scarcely draw breath. The world had unhinged itself in a single day, coming apart at the very seams, and yet here was this wonder unfolding at the very same time. It seemed unthinkable that God's will had been done, and yet John could believe that answer to her prayer more swiftly than she. To think that he had walked knowingly into danger, for her. It was a heroism too great to bear. "I've no words…"

None were needed. He bent his head and kissed her softly, and she felt life blooming back into her. Then his kiss was not so soft, and she found herself returning the urgency in his kiss with a vitality she thought all but

gone. His embrace pushed back the despair, blocked
out the sick ward's horrors. When John pulled back to
look at her, his eyes burned fiercely with the sense of
"here now and alive" she desperately needed.

What a splendid strength John had; how grateful
she was for his presence. The wonder of his fresh faith
offered deep encouragement—had she really been so
weary just moments before? John pulled her tightly to
him, and she marveled how perfectly her shoulders
tucked under his, how her head fell naturally against
his shoulder. "I've still no words," she said against the
warmth of his chest.

"Rendered you speechless, have I?" His tone was
almost a laugh, and she felt herself smile. To smile, in
the face of all this. What a gift that was.

She looked out at the fading daylight, thinking today's tragedies would only double with the coming
darkness. It seemed as if dawn could only bring worse
news. "Whatever is to become of us?"

John's chest expanded with a sigh as large as her
own. "God only knows," he said. Kissing the top of her
head, he added, "And goodness, I actually mean that
when I say it now. It's going to take me a little while to
get used to all this."

He did not say what she knew they both were thinking: a little while might be all they had.


The next day became a surreal, catastrophic struggle of life and death. John continued his work with
the supply effort while Leanne and the other medical
staff fought for life inside. He caught glimpses of her
as they worked through the day, but rarely had time

to say much more than a few words. Now, grateful for the dusk that marked the end of a long day, John and Leanne found half an hour to sit on the steps of a nearby building and share what meager food either could roust up for dinner.

John had coaxed some priceless meat—a pair of sausages—out of the cook in an effort to restore Leanne's appetite. He'd planned to let her eat both of them if he could, despite the fact that they smelled wonderful enough to set his own mouth watering. All of his world had the most awful smells these days, but he would gladly forsake the savory meat if he thought he could convince her to eat it. Leanne's color gave him pause. "Eat, my dear." Her shy smile, the one that always appeared now when he used the term "my dear," tickled him. He put the tin plate on her lap and stretched out his leg.

His confounded leg. He'd overused it in the worst way today. The thing ached to the point of distraction now, but all his pain medicine was still back at Jackson and anything they had here must be saved for patients. "This long day's end is only the beginning." He pointed to the plate. "You must eat more."

Her gaze was on the horizon, the purple dusk now barely visible through the trees. "Is this what war is like, John?"

He'd had the same thought dozens of times today— that this was a war. "Yes." He found himself hard-pressed to elaborate on such a drastic declaration, but her silence worried him. "This morning I couldn't help thinking I didn't need to go back to the battlefield because the battlefield has been brought to me."

When she still offered no reply, he took her hand. "You'd think that would be an awful thought, but it's not. I know I ought to be here. I've had my eyes opened in so many ways. I'm seeing God's hand in places I always put down to luck and self-importance." He put his arm around her shoulder, drawing her to him. She felt too thin, too void of the vitality that had charmed him back before the world fell apart. "That's you. That's you in my life and I wouldn't trade that for twelve shiny medals."

Leanne softened against his shoulder. The structure's thick wooden front columns, still warm from the strong fall sun, baked his aching back. The soreness in his leg eased up the smallest bit. He offered up a word of thanks for the moment's peace in a day of struggle, and the prayer came as easy as his breath.

He felt her sigh against his ribs. "I fought so hard to resist you. I suppose you know that."

Her admission made him chuckle. Was she unaware how hard he'd fought to resist *her?* "Well, I have often heard how irresistible I am. And here I am bearing sausages. It took six compliments to lure these out of the kitchen, so we're feasting thanks to my legendary charm." He tipped her chin toward him. "But you are not eating nearly as well as you should. I am worried about you. Let me care for you, Leanne." John swallowed, realizing he was dancing around what he really wanted to say. "For I do care for you. A great deal." He kissed her forehead and thanked God again, grateful to be granted this time with Leanne. "We must be the only two people in the world to have any reason to be thankful for this."

"And hate it at the same time. John, I feel too much all at once. I'm so happy, and yet so tired and so sad. And frightened. And worried. How can I feel hungry on top of all that?"

"Every soldier knows a body needs to eat, hungry or not. Your strength is important." He broke off a bit of sausage and held it in front of her as one would a small child, tucking it inside with a smile when she relented and opened her mouth. She consumed the luxury dutifully, without enjoyment, but she ate two more bites besides.

They sat without conversing. Around them the sound of hammers pierced the gathering dusk alongside birds and crickets. Mere months ago the constant hammers at Jackson had meant building—barracks and structures that sprang up in astonishing speed as Camp Jackson burst into being. Now the hammers were building only one thing: coffins. Twenty in the past four hours alone. Eventually, Leanne looked up at him. "I do wonder if we are at the end of the world."

He could hardly blame her. He'd had the thought himself walking past the outbuilding they'd set up as a morgue two hours ago. Still, it bothered him to see her optimism failing, so he attempted a jest. "Are you saying my faith is a sign of the apocalypse? I had no idea I was so influential."

She didn't laugh, merely pulled a telegraph paper from her pocket. "Dr. Madison dropped this off earlier."

"Madison's here?"

"He was on campus lecturing an orthopedics class when the quarantine order came. He chose to stay and help however he could."

John found his presence oddly comforting—a small piece of his past that had traveled with him to this surreal present.

"John, he told me one hundred and thirty men have died at Jackson. How many will die here?"

John cast his eyes down to the yellow half sheet Leanne held out. It was a wire statement from Army Surgeon General Victor Vaughan. While John might conclude it was Vaughan's job to size up threats in the worst possible light, this exceeded the staunchest pessimism. "If the epidemic continues its mathematical rate of acceleration," the smudged type declared, "civilization could easily disappear from the face of the earth within a few weeks."

It wasn't that hard to believe. Death felt as if it lurked around every corner, hid in every sunken set of eyes. According to the velvet box back somewhere in the bottom of his rucksack, John had faced death down, had "saved lives at the risk of his own." Still, John could not escape the truth that he'd felt terror at that episode and mostly peace here. Is that what faith did? Gave one peace in what might be the end of the world?

"I'll admit to very little knowledge of God, but I cannot think He would grant me you and then not give me the world to enjoy with you. Does it look like the end of the world? I've seen battlefields that show nothing but devastation, so yes, I suppose it does. But it does not feel like the end of the world, at least not to me. It feels like war." He gazed into Leanne's eyes, willing her his battle nerves. "I know war, Leanne. I know what to do in war. In the one out there and the one right here. Victory isn't out of reach. You hold on to that thought. I've far too many things I want to show you to consider anything else. I plan to take you up in a plane and show you the sky from God's point of view. Would you like that?"

She smiled for the first time this evening, and popped another bite of sausage into her mouth. "It sounds wonderful."

## Chapter Twenty-Five

"I ought to have you shot!"

John pulled his head away from the phone receiver and Barnes's tinny bellow. It was funny; he'd endowed the general with so much power over his life before, and now his anger didn't faze John at all. "It was very foolish, I agree. Still, I'd do it again given the chance."

The general's sigh was closer to a growl. "Your father will have my head for not getting you out of here."

Ah, so it was true. John had long suspected it was the Gallows name, rather than his silver tongue, that earned him a spot on that train. Father's leverage was still as powerful, his connections still strong if his father knew of the epidemic as fast as Barnes. "Father knows me well enough to know I'm not much for orders. One doesn't get the medals for being a good boy, but rather a brave soldier. Amazing how often that involves ignoring wise advice, isn't it?"

John could almost hear Barnes pinch the bridge of his nose. "Son, what good are you to anyone if you die over there?"

"Begging your pardon, General, but I could have died just as easily in Chicago and I'm tremendously useful over here." John had raised the recruitment rates in three states, had driven auditoriums of young men to their feet in cheers but had never felt more useful than he had in the past twenty-four hours. "I'm a soldier, and I don't have to tell you, this is war." Whatever it was he was seeking in his return to the front, he had already found it. The stand he'd taken here, holding the line against this deadly enemy, had settled his soul in more ways than one.

"Captain Gallows," Travers called from the hallway, "we got four less boxes than we thought. What do we do now?" Late last night someone had recognized him, and his anonymity was gone, but it hadn't mattered. Influenza had little respect for rank or status.

"What's going on?" Barnes asked through the line.

"Five minutes," John called to Travers, then returned to the receiver. "Enough of the staff has fallen ill that I've been drafted into figuring out how to make five loaves and two fishes feed the five thousand." Leanne had drawn the Biblical comparison, saying they'd need one of Jesus's miracles to make the meager supplies meet the herculean need. She'd also kissed him and told him she thought no one short of Christ more suitable to attempt the feat. He'd grinned; evidently his spiritual awakening had yet to squelch the legendary Gallows ego.

"What?" Barnes sounded duly baffled.

"Instead of getting me out, sir, can you wield that leverage to get supplies in?" They'd created a self-contained "no contact zone" around the dormitory

and two adjacent halls—a quarantine within a quarantine—and John had worked out a non-contact drop
system in the dormitory's west door. He found it no coincidence that the idea sprang from a cloister of French
nuns whom he'd frequented for excellent chocolates.
"We're in dire straits for bandages, medical alcohol and
chloroform."

The general made a gruff sound. "You and half the
Eastern Seaboard."

Travers shifted in the doorway. "Captain Gallows,
sir?"

"You do what you can from out there, I'll do what I
must from in here," he said to the general.

"Bandages, medical alcohol and chloroform?"

"That's what they tell me. At least today. Tomorrow
is anyone's guess." If anyone could throw his weight
around in Columbia, it was General Barnes. As fearful as the general's wrath might be once this was over,
it was better to have the man as an ally for the present
battle.

"Anything else?"

John couldn't resist. "A good steak might help. And
some yarn."

Leanne mopped another puddle of drying blood from
the floor. Every square inch of the room was occupied
by moaning bodies. Doctors darted between catastro-
phes, barking orders at nurses, all so tired themselves
that civility had been abandoned.

A young woman to Leanne's left gave out a raspy
cry, clawing at her chest. She'd torn open her blouse,
for the supply of hospital gowns had disappeared along

with the civility and clean linens. "There now—" Leanne grabbed the woman's hand and laid it back down on the cot "—they'll bring more medicine soon." It seemed the kindest of lies, for in truth Leanne had no idea how long supplies would hold out. "Try to rest." She redid the young woman's buttons, and wiped her brow. There were no sheets to tuck her under. Leanne smoothed her tangled hair, for there were no pillows to place beneath her head. Kindness was the only treatment she had to offer.

The woman quieted some, and Leanne rose to arch her back against the growing ache. She needed to leave the din of moans and cries, just for a minute or two to catch her breath. She found Ida in the ladies' washroom, catching her weary glance as they ducked over the line of sinks. "I'm worn to the bone and then some," Ida said, splashing water on her face and then leaning back against the wall. Towels had disappeared from the washroom, if they were ever there at all.

"I hurt everywhere," Leanne replied, using a wet hand to wipe the grime from her neck. The suffocating smells spun her senses and tumbled her stomach if she moved too fast. Her tongue dragged inside a parched, pasty mouth for the sheer mass of bodies had baked the room to a suffocating heat.

"Did you hear that doctor when he came in yesterday?" Ida asked, flexing one wrist in slow circles. "Took two steps in the door and pronounced it 'the very cradle of death.' As if we'd all somehow benefit from the description."

Leanne didn't find it much of an overstatement.

"That's the worst part, isn't it? How hard they're trying to hide that they don't know what to do?"

Ida's sour laugh echoed against the tile, bloodstained even in here. "Do we do any less? Telling patients medicine is on the way, that relief is coming?"

Leanne looked at the blood caking her fingernails, unable to recall the last time those fingers had touched yarn and needles. "It's a horrid false kindness, isn't it?" She scraped her hands against the slivers of soap left by the sink and washed again, the cracks in her knuckles stinging from the harsh lye. "Still," she said as she rinsed, "it calms most of them, and that's help enough." She cupped her hands and drank, the bitter trace of soap sending her into a fit of coughing. Even a decent drink of water had become a luxury in the ward. She coughed again, shut her eyes against the ache that doubled in her chest and wiped her hands on her skirts for lack of any hand towels.

Ida stared.

"Nasty soap." Leanne had tried not to give in to complaints, but she felt too battered to keep this one in. "I'm fine." She cleared her throat again, feeling as if she'd swallowed gauze bandages instead of poor water.

Ida made no reply, but stood there with dull shock written all over her face as Leanne grabbed the counter with one hand while the other went to her throat. Coughing again, Leanne followed Ida's gaze to her own skirts, damp from her hands.

Two bright red smudges.

Leanne looked at her hands and saw not the dried brownish-red smears of the ward's endless blood, but lines of fresh red in the creases of her palms. She fought the urge to cough again as she forced herself to look in the dingy mirror above the sink.

Red spots, bright as alarms, spattered one cheek. The edges of the room began to spin out of her vision, and she clutched the edge of the sink as another cough tore up out of her chest to shower tiny red drops across her clenched fist.

*I'm to die, then,* Leanne thought as she slumped against the wall, the tile cool and soothing against her flushed cheek. She heard Ida's cry for help and the squeaky bang of the washroom door as if it were a thousand miles away. She closed her eyes, feeling something in her core begin to unwind, like a snagged thread unraveling a sweater's knitting. *I've come undone.*

John was standing over a telegraph machine someone had brought in from the university's administrative offices, working with a clerk to wire calls for favors to every family member or family friend he could list. If the Gallows name held any weight, now was surely the time to wield it. Still, even a pedigree like his couldn't produce linens out of thin air, nor medicine when no one knew what drugs worked. Travers had begun to wear a bag of camphor pellets around his neck and brought one for John to use, but he declined. He suspected the smelly folk-remedy held about as much credence as the Gallows moniker against their invisible foe. Still, he sent out the next telegraph to a textile mill down the river from his family estate, asking for any help they could give.

Thanks to his new curative, John smelled Travers before he saw him. "Hank," John called, not looking up from the buzzing metal box, "I'd always thought the term 'I can smell you from a mile away' to be an exaggeration, but in your case…"

The look in Travers's eyes stopped him midsentence. The man clearly bore bad news. John wasn't sure he could stomach another shortage of anything, given how dire circumstances already were. He straightened up slowly, feeling sparks shoot down his leg as he reached for his cane. "What isn't coming now?"

Hank looked down, twisting his cap in one hand. John hated how the masks made everyone's face so difficult to read. Hank shifted his weight. "It's Miss Sample, sir. They told me to come fetch you."

John grabbed the back of a nearby chair. The words came slowly, thickly out of his mouth. "What about Miss Sample, Hank?"

Hank said nothing. Which said everything.

"Where is she?" He whacked the chair away with his cane, betrayal rising in his throat like bile. *"Where is she?"*

"Down in the second building with some of the other nurses that done got sick this afternoon."

John pushed past him into the hallway, his cane banging over and over on the wooden floor as he tumbled into something close to a run. Leanne could not fall ill. It was as simple as that. God would not give him her heart for two meager days and then tear it away. Everything else could fall to pieces, he could lose everything else but he could not, *would* not lose her. Not this way.

"Leanne!" he called as he rounded the corner to the ward Travers had indicated. He'd pulled his mask down, not caring what lay in the air he swallowed with each stinging breath. The burning in his leg had already lodged in his lungs and his heart, what was a mask to him now? John wanted to hit something, to punch through a wall or bellow curses into the wind, but he skidded to a stop in the doorway where Ida stood with apologetic eyes.

Panting from his dash, his leg absolutely screaming, John locked his gaze onto Leanne's face. She lay in the third of four cots, curled on her side and clutching her stomach, eyes narrowed in pain above a mask smattered in the bloody droplets that announced her fate. "Leanne." It was almost a cry, a howl rather than her name. "No."

He lurched toward her, but Ida caught his shoulder, pointing silently to the mask hanging around his neck. He couldn't care less about that useless square of cloth now, but Leanne managed a "John, please," that only served to send her into a wave of gurgling coughs. Her skin was the pale gray he'd come to hate, her brow beaded from fever so that damp curls of hair framed her face. It was agony to sink down beside her, the burning in his leg still no match for the shot-through sensation in his chest. He'd fallen from heights and not felt the wind so knocked out of him as when he clutched her hand. It was cold, dry and clenched tight with suffering.

"I'm not so bad," she lied with hopeless eyes.

"Leanne," he said, any other words beyond him. "My dear."

No shy smile greeted his endearment. "John."

"You're in pain." He grabbed the towel from its basin

on the floor beside her and mopped her brow. Even though he was no stranger to pain, the thought of her suffering made him crazy. She was too sweet, too fragile to be wracked in the fever's agony.

Her eyes fluttered shut as he cooled her forehead. "Not much yet."

That was the worst of it; she knew what was coming. They both did. He returned the cloth to its place and took her hand. It felt wrong; it was too cool and stiff, rigid but without life. The hideous purple spots had already begun to form on her wrist, and a cold coil of helplessness began to wind its way around his spine. "You won't die." The words were foolish. Nurses had begun affixing postmortem identification toe tags to patients upon arrival, not having time to wait until they'd passed. No one had yet recovered. No one. "You'll be spared, you'll see."

"Wouldn't that be lovely." Her head rolled listlessly to one side.

John hated the surrender in her voice. He had no intention of surrendering Leanne to this evil beast. Had it been a visible foe, he would have run straight at it, roaring with his bayonet lunging. But there was nothing to plunge his bayonet into, no target to shoot. He could not blow up the bridge to the next life before she crossed it. He couldn't do anything, and that was worse than any pain.

"I'm so very hot," she whispered, and John brought the cloth to her brow again. He folded it across her forehead, and she sighed. Any tiny bit of comfort felt better than the resignation clawing at his heels. She shifted, wincing as she did, and he rearranged the thin scraggly pillow beneath her head. She was lucky in that; despite the university laundry running nonstop, pillows and clean linen were becoming more scarce every day. And he was thankful she wasn't in that sea of near-corpses on the first floor, but here with a small number of nurses who had fallen ill. She stood half a chance that way, he told himself. "I'll sleep," she said, her eyes finding him again. "It's better when I sleep."

John ran a lock of her hair through his fingers. "You need your rest. You need it because you're going to live. Those students? Those socks? They need you."

Her eyes fell closed, but she smiled.

"I need you." His voice broke with the power of that truth. Self-sufficient, self-important, self-absorbed John Gallows needed. Perhaps it really was the end of the world.

"But you've finished your first sock," she said, speaking with such a thin calm that he wondered if she was still awake. "You'll be surprised. The second one is so much easier."

"I still need you." He wasn't talking about socks at all.

# Chapter Twenty-Six

It burned. Parts of her burned, then cooled, then burned again. The air had grown thick and hard to breathe, hot and liquid against her throat. The scents around her were familiar, yet some part of her knew they were cause for alarm. There were times—hours? days?—when her stomach would feel hollow and still. All of her felt hollow and still, like a water glass emptied out. Then there were the insufferable spaces where time twisted over on itself in pain, where every breath felt like it took hours and filled nothing. Voices and faces would ebb in and out of her awareness. Sometimes she conversed with them, knowing they were friends and yet not being able to place them in her life outside the heat and pain. Other times they were only noises she could not understand.

Days were hard. The bright sunshine hurt her eyes, made the sights and sounds too sharp. For a little while each day, however, the storm would subside and she could be in the world. Feel the cool gauze on her forehead, taste the salty broth someone held to her lips. She was very sick, she knew that, although she wasn't sure how. Every once in a while, especially when light returned to the room, Leanne would feel something tell her not to fight, not to strive. An inner voice assuring her that whatever this was, it was out of her hands.

She was sure the voice came in the growing light because the dark was so awful. Sleep and wakefulness wove together without clear lines, so that she never knew if her eyes would open to dark or light. In the light there were shapes and movement, but the dark held only sound and space. Once she thought Charles Holling came to her in the darkness, as pale and hollow as she felt. He didn't plead to die like she remembered, only asked very politely as if he were a gentleman asking a lady to dance. She would tell him she didn't want to dance, or to die, that John was here somewhere, and then she would turn and look for John in the darkness. She would push her hands out of the fog draped over her, and find the solid warmth of his hand. It was as if she floated, wandered, but his hand would anchor her back whenever she touched it. She'd call his name into the fog, and often his answer would come back like a lighthouse beacon. He held her to this place, to this time, even to this pain. It made her think of John's accident, hanging over the sea by the dirigible stay wires that both tore him and saved him at the same time. How did she know that? Had she been there to see it? She couldn't remember. Nothing made sense.

Nothing except God. God made the only sense there was. He was here. She heard His voice, only not in true words. God spoke to her thoughts and breaths, in colors and sensations. All her senses seemed to weave together—sometimes tight and coarse, other times loose and billowy. When the world was tight and coarse, she would feel God beside her, holding, protecting. When the world was loose and billowy, she would feel Him underneath her like the wind under a seagull. The Lord of Time whirled her in and out of time's grip, the Author of Life pushed and pulled at her breath, the Lamb of God cradled her in her suffering. One set of words kept coming to her, over and over. She knew it to be truth, but couldn't remember where she'd learned it. *In life or in death I belong to Christ.*

## Chapter Twenty-Seven

John startled awake to a hand on his shoulder, every joint of his body reminding him of the hard floor that had been his bed for two nights. His head turned quickly toward the cot beside him where Leanne lay with her back to him. Was she all right? Had someone woken him to deliver bad news?

The hand squeezed his shoulder in assurance, and John squinted in the sunlight to see Dr. Madison pulling up a metal chair. He looked as tired as John felt.

"She's still with us," he whispered, handing John a tin mug of mercilessly strong coffee. "I just checked and her pulse is weak, but steady."

Hearing their voices Leanne gave a soft moan and shifted a bit, but did not wake. "Even in her sleep," John said, looking at the too-sharp angle of her shoulder, "she's in too much pain. She's barely woken in two days."

"And you've barely slept in two days." Madison nodded to him over his own cup. "She'll have my hide if I don't keep you well enough to celebrate her recov-

ery." He winced as he swallowed. "This is dreadful.
I'm trying to be grateful it's hot."

"Thank you." John gulped down the hot brew with
gratitude. Leanne sighed softly. "It's hard to be grateful for her prolonged pain, but I'm glad she's still with
us."

"Pain is an odd companion, but try to think of it as
the body's way of fighting to stay alive. They say you
never feel a mortal wound, only the one that won't kill
you."

It was funny how Madison, who had once been the
only thing standing in his way, the enemy to be conquered, had become a friend. Unable to sleep, John
had talked for an hour to Leanne's sleeping form in the
middle of the night last night about this strange world
they now occupied. "You wouldn't recognize it," John
had said as he wiped Leanne's hands—still paler by
moonlight than their ashen color by day. "Our Dr. Madison, my chief inflictor of therapeutic pain, has become
a source of comfort. A friend, if you can believe it."

He liked talking to her when the room was dark.
Sleep eluded him anyway, and he hoped his monologue
kept Leanne anchored to this world where he needed
her to stay. "I hardly know what to do with this topsy-
turvy exchange of blessings and curses. They seem to
turn my world upside down and set it to rights all at the
same time. If this is the world with your faith, I almost
think I'd rather have something more constant and pre-
dictable." He'd fallen asleep fingering the gold cross
they'd taken from her neck, now his constant companion in his pocket. It was still in his hand now as he
stared bleary-eyed at Madison.

"I have news, John." Madison had never called him John in all their time together. "Boston has reported a survivor."

John sat up straight, for this was news indeed. There had been no reports of anything but fatalities from any of the camps. John had stopped watching patients being brought into the hospital, unable to stomach the fear in their eyes. Every person believed the trip through those doors ran only one way. The only variable so far was the rate of death—some died shockingly fast, others lingered cruelly for days. "Someone has lived?"

Madison took off his glasses and pinched his nose. "It is perhaps more accurate to say someone has not died. A single soldier. His fever has resolved. It's not much, but it's more than we've had to go on before."

Someone had not died. It was far more than anything they had before. John let his head fall back against the wall, glad to grasp even a thin hope of relief. "Thank God above."

"I thought you'd want to know." He managed a weary smile. "I thought it might convince you to actually sleep. I am still your doctor, you know." Madison drained the tin mug with a groan of displeasure. "I'll sit with her if you like."

"You'll do no such thing from the looks of both of you," came Ida's voice from the doorway. "I've a mind to ship the both of you off to some pantry and lock the door." She crossed her arms like a scolding school-marm. "When's the last time either of you ate?"

"I think I just chewed this coffee." John surprised himself with his first joke in ages. Someone hadn't died. The hourglass could be turned.

"I thought as much. Besides, I'm going to give Leanne a bit of a bath so you're to be gentlemen and flee the room. Off with the pair of you."

"Bacon and eggs," Madison wished aloud as he rose slowly from his chair. "Four of them, with hash browns and fresh strawberries." He extended a hand to John, who was still propped up against the wall on the floor.

"Eggs Benedict," John managed through gritted teeth as his leg—and the rest of him—loudly protested the night's sleeping quarters. "With perfect toast—" a wince cut through his words "—and orange marmalade. And ham. And real coffee, not whatever *that* was." John fetched his cane but left the cup of murky black liquid on the floor. He looked at Ida's barely amused face. "They've a survivor up in Boston, you know. Madison just told me."

"It's all over campus already."

John leaned over Leanne's discolored face, saddened to see her eyes seemed to have sunk farther into their hollows overnight. She was thinner still, ashen where she wasn't the harrowing purple that marked this disease. She had quieted overnight—he preferred to think of it that way, simply as a quieting, rather than entertain the notion she was weakening. Still, her brow wrinkled in discomfort, and her body lacked the peaceful ease of true sleep. He smoothed a damp lock of hair off her forehead, saddened to find it still warmer than it should be. "There's a survivor up in Boston, my dear. Someone can survive. Someone *has* survived. Stay right here with us where you belong." He kissed her cheek before pulling his mask back up, then nodded to Ida. "Find her some yarn. She'll want it for when she wakes up."

After a breakfast that rivaled any half-edible gruel John had endured in the battle trenches, he ignored the rock settling in his stomach and settled down for a stretch of real sleep. An hour in an actual bed, horizontal, on something that wasn't a floor, felt like a luxury. After that he was up, shaven and back at work in the small room in one of the adjacent inner quarantine buildings he'd commandeered as his "office."

Colton walked in halfway through the morning. John hadn't seen the man in almost a full day, since Travers had fallen ill shortly after Leanne. To see such a hardworking young man laid low was bad enough, but it served to make Colton and John doubly anxious about the state of the contagion.

Colton looked calm enough, so John ventured, "How's Hank?"

The big man shook his head. "Not good. Fella's just a whip of a thing, so it's hit him hard. They got him in the 'big room.'"

The "big room," as Colton called it, was a sea of misery on the first floor of the "hospital" dormitory, a vast ward of bodies in various states of the disease. Every time John walked by it he offered up a prayer of thanks that Leanne was tucked away in a ward on the upper floors. He wouldn't state it now, but to him the "big room" seemed like it smothered its occupants in a sheer mass of death.

"Hank's a tough fellow," John offered.

"And your Miss Sample?" The romance between John and Leanne had become common knowledge. It was hard to have any privacy in such close quarters, and the urgency of their world right now wouldn't allow for much subtlety. John took a novel pride in claiming her as "his," through a look, a quick touch of her hand in public places, the use of endearments. It was an odd thing: John used to pride himself on his ability to woo the most desirable lady in any crowd, often seeking her out for the mere challenge of besting other gentlemen. Now, as his mother would have put it, he "only had eyes for one."

"She's still with us," he quoted Dr. Madison with a deep gratitude. "With plans to stay that way. Boston is reporting a survivor, did you hear?"

Colton smiled. "I did. Camp Devens has just one so far?"

"That's all I've heard, but that's all I need to hear." John had shared the news with every ear that would listen, but he knew Colton held Travers as a friend. "Madison's sent word for more information from the doctors at Devens, but nothing's come through yet."

"Maybe there ain't nothing to tell. Some things just *is,* you know." John wasn't sure if Colton was offering encouragement or kindly caution. The big man didn't elaborate, just looked at the pile of pipes and mattresses at John's feet and raised an eyebrow. "What have you got going here?"

Fortified by food, sleep and hopeful news, John was attempting something that felt no less miraculous than Christ's loaves and fishes. "I'm attempting to see if one bed can somehow be reassembled into two. Or even two into three."

He pulled apart the mattress he'd unstitched into two layers of batting. "Maybe we can just put these on boards nailed to a pair of desks." The dormitory mattresses were thin to begin with, but no one was seeking luxury here. "I think we can split the wire mesh up into two, but I'm not sure it will hold."

"Won't hold me." Colton chuckled. "Then again, you could fit some of them boys in each of my pant legs, they's coming in here so thin."

John could only agree. Each day the incoming patients looked more ill—and more frightened than the last. "Philadelphia was fool enough to hold a liberty bond parade and they ended up with hundreds of cases. Here, hold this," he said, pointing to wire mesh he'd just unwoven from a disassembled bed.

"Locking us up tight was the smart thing to do then. Only it don't feel so smart from the inside, does it? My heart jumps through my mouth every time I cough even just a little."

John, Colton and every healthy person inside "the line," as it had come to be called, lived in the same state of watch: Have I caught it? Is this the first sign? The constant vigil had worn John's mind down to a near numbness, but in sleep, his imagination roused again, in the worst of ways. "I dreamed of being chased by a huge tiger, nipping at my heels while I ran through a jungle." He began threading a screw through a hole in a pipe.

"A tiger?" Waters chuckled. "Not a little bird?"

News wires reported a day ago that as alarm had been raised in the general public, children had begun jumping rope to a macabre little rhyme:

I had a little bird
Her name was Enza

I opened the window
*And In-Flu-Enza*


It was amusing and horribly sad at the same time.

"No, a big snarly tiger. You'd think I'd enjoy a dream of running, the way I hobble around."

Colton picked up one corner of John's new invention, inspecting the thing. "Did you outrun the tiger in your dream?"

"Woke up in a cold sweat before I could find out." While the sensation of running should have felt wonderful, John would have gladly passed it over to skip bolting upright out of the nap with his heart pounding.

"Well, then, how's about we say you outran that nasty tiger and saved your pretty girl, too? Sounds like a mighty fine dream to me when you put it that way."

John had to smile. "I thought you said some things 'just is'?"

"Well," said Colton as he handed the wrench to John to tighten the bolt, "I didn't say 'all things.' Well, now, looky here. This just might work." John showed him how the two salvaged sides came together to hold a mattress. "You are pretty smart for a war hero, Captain Gallows."

John smiled at his contraption. "If you can't outrun the tiger, you'd best outsmart him."

# Chapter Twenty-Eight

Once he'd devised the frame of the bed, John took a mattress down to send off to a ward of Red Cross volunteers to see if the ticking could be easily halved. Beds—even poor ones—were a commodity. Ill patients were actually placed on the floor beside near-dying ones to wait for the bed. John had made two attempts before coming up with a successful design, mostly because he couldn't stomach the thought of finding himself on a floor waiting for someone above him to breathe their last.

He went to see if Leanne was awake, hoping to share all his good news. What he found stole every ounce of optimism.

She'd lapsed into delirium again, weakly thrashing and succumbing to coughs that sounded as if her body was attempting to turn itself inside out.

"Been like that about an hour," Ida said, not bothering to hide the concern in her voice. "A bit more and I was going to send for you. She calms to your voice, and I'm afraid she's going to hurt herself."

"How's her fever?"

She winced as she answered. "Worse."

"How?" It was a foolish question—the disease seemed to take a unique course with every victim. Madison regularly bemoaned the sheer vacuum of protocol at every doctor's disposal. No one knew why one patient died within hours while others hung on for days, why one showed symptoms another did not. "She was improving. She ate something. I watched her."

"Perhaps it's just a minor setback." Ida's eyes betrayed the thin lacquer of optimism she'd applied.

"Surely." Liars, the pair of them. John peered at Leanne's too-gray face, willing himself to find some new source of color though he knew he would not. "She'll improve again, and keep improving." The ominous black hole in his gut grew deeper as he noticed one of the room's six beds was now empty. John looked up at Ida, who turned away to some pretended detail. Death had visited the room during the night.

The ghoul would not be allowed to stay. "I'll stay with her tonight." He spoke with all the command he could muster, brooking no refusal. If Leanne was going to leave him, he would not miss the goodbye for all the world.

Ida took a breath to argue, but simply shut her mouth again. "She'll be glad of the company, I'm sure." She gave the unreadable smile he'd come to call her "nursing mask," the one he'd heard Leanne describe as a way to keep what she called "unkind news" from worried patients.

A feathery touch on his arm drew his attention, and he turned to see Leanne's gaze wander in disjointed alarm around the room. "My dear," he said softly, angling himself down to her level despite the pain it caused him. Ida was right; the sound of his voice seemed to anchor her. Leanne's gaze found his and held it, if weakly.

She licked her dry, crackled lips, and he held a wet cloth to them for her to drink a few drops. "You should drink." She obeyed, wincing as she swallowed— many of the patients complained of throats so sore they seemed as if they were on fire. "I know it hurts, but you must." Dr. Madison had warned him that the most feared enemy was dehydration, even if it did feel like asking patients to swallow knives when they drank. He put the wet cloth to her brow, smoothing back her hair, noticing with horror that strands of Leanne's beautiful yellow hair fell out easily at his touch.

"John?" His name was not much more than a gasp of breath, and yet it was everything.

"Yes."

"John?" she said again, soft but less weak.

"Right here." He took her hand as it seemed to hover off the bed in search of his. Her eyes fell closed for a second at his touch. Her hand felt like bones inside thin paper. Too small, too thin, too lifeless to be Leanne's vibrant fingers. After an instant she opened them again and found his face, as if she were creeping toward him through the fog of her illness. "I'm right here and I'm not leaving until you waltz out of this hospital on my arm." A foolish, overdramatic statement.

She knew it, too. Even in her distress, Leanne could see through his facade. It took her a moment to find the energy to speak again, but she wore the vaguest hint of a smile as she did.

"I'm dying, aren't I?" The words came in simple innocence, childlike in its fearlessness. Or its faithfulness—he couldn't tell.

"You most certainly are not," he said sharply, despising and needing the deception at the same time. He wanted to say something else, something confident and hopeful, but couldn't manage it.

A fit of coughing seemed to snatch away what little energy she had. "So much pain."

"It will pass." But would it? Was he selfish enough to wish her lingering if all it meant was more suffering for Leanne? His greedy answer showed him for the faulty man he was, not the hero others thought him to be.

"I'm not afraid." The clear statement seemed as if it could not possibly come from the frail body beside him.

"That's because you're not going to die, so there's no reason for fear." Panic lodged a cold finger in John's spine and began to follow along his ribs, squeezing. He clasped her hand instead.

"No." She shut her eyes, reaching for words. "Faith."

"God can't have you yet." The petulant demand of a child's tantrum, but it was how he felt.

"And you should choose?"

He adjusted the flimsy pillow, thinking of all the fine linens he had at home and what he would give to couch her in them at this moment. "You said it yourself, I'm accustomed to getting my way and in no mind to tolerate obstacles."

"God's will is no obstacle. He is the only path."

"Then I shall insist He carve that path back to life and health."

She made to turn, and he helped her shift to her side, hating the way her thinness now shaved cruel angles into the curves he'd once so admired. She fell asleep for a second, drifting in and out of slumber the way she did lately. John took the moment's respite to lean against the wall, his head falling back to stare at the ceiling.

*You cannot have her,* he declared to Heaven, as if Leanne were ever his to possess in any case. The foolishness of his thoughts did nothing to stem the strength of his feeling. *I'll not let You take her from me.* Followed, almost instantly, with the more truthful, more disturbing, *I fear what I'll be if You do.*

He looked down to find her staring at him. "So much fear," she whispered. It made John wonder if his silent shouts at God had really found their way into spoken words. "There's no need."

The tear he saw wind its way down her ashen cheek was his undoing. "Do not leave me, Leanne."

"You'll not be alone. Not now."

John did not want to hear about God's comfort in loss. He'd heard Leanne give the speech too many times not to know the words nearly by heart, but such belief wasn't his. Not yet, perhaps not ever. "I've not the faith to believe without you beside me."

She smiled, and he saw the first glimpse of the Leanne he knew under the waxen figure before him. "Silly John. Still thinking faith is something you've earned."

"I sought it. You pointed me toward it." He was delighted to see her talking, engaging, coming back to him from the brink of wherever she was.

"Yes, but God gives us…" her breath seemed to falter "…our faith." Another fit of coughing seemed to steal all the progress she'd made toward life, vaulting her back to the limp slip of a thing that seemed to melt into the sheets. John reached out for the bowl and wiped her drained face. Every touch seemed precious, fleeting, and he refused to let his mind caution him that this might be their last time together. She seemed to have left this world already, as if she were more spirit and less solid than even an hour ago. John was somehow sure that if he failed to keep touching her, talking to her, anchoring her to this place, she would slip away to hide from the pain under God's wings. Colton came by to say that he was needed elsewhere, but John refused. Seeing Leanne's precarious state, Colton pressed it no further. John would have gone to fists if it had come to it: no duty was more important than the vigil before him.

He was only vaguely aware of the daylight slipping away around him. At some point he must have slept, for he woke to the feeble whisper of her voice in the light-less room. "John? John?"

"Beside you, my love." There, in the dark, the endearment slipped out of him unchecked. The shadows and disease seemed like beasts waiting to devour this woman who had stolen in to become the center of his heart. John realized he wanted her to know of his feelings, and he was too tired and too anxious to resist the urge. Calling her his love was the truth, after all, for he did love her. "And I do love you, Leanne." He looked for a response, but she seemed to be slipping away from his very fingertips, as if his next touch of her would pass his hand through her ghostly image to touch an empty bed. "I tried not to, you know. It seemed irrational, painful even, to love you, but in the end I had no defenses to resist. I love you." He pressed a kiss to her fevered cheek.

She tried to say something, but it left her lips as not much more than a struggling sigh. Had she understood what he'd just said? She seemed to be in so much pain, it almost seemed cruel to wish her awake and aware. Could not God grant her a peaceful end if she must leave him? Must it be in anguish, without the most important words he would ever speak to her? "I love you," he whispered close to her ear, even while hating the heat of her fever radiating against his face. "Come back to me so I can tell you properly. Stay with us, Leanne, please."

Her only reply was a thin, wheezing cough. A better man wouldn't be so greedy for her response, but he could not help himself. John selfishly yearned to see the look in her eyes when she heard he loved her. He craved a life with her too much to surrender her, even to her eternal peace. He didn't deserve her, knew the rage he felt at God right now made him no partner to a faithful woman like Leanne, but still he wanted her. For a few moments to look into her clear eyes and declare his love, John was sure he would have pulled the lethal fire consuming her onto himself. Despite a chest full of medals and the admiration of so many, John was sure of one truth: Leanne would bring far more good to the world than he ever could.

He would hold her. If she couldn't recognize his words, surely even in her state she would know the comfort of his arms. As he went to pick her up, it shocked him how light she was, how easily he slipped her delicate body from the bed to rest on his lap as he sat on the floor. Were he whole and healthy, he would carry her outside to the cool air, to the place where they'd sat in each other's arms and he'd felt the first of his heart slip away. But he wasn't whole and healthy, he could not walk with her in his arms. He could only offer what broken comfort was possible here and now. He handled her as though she were glass, some mythical vial with only the last drops of elixir left. He fought his urge to enfold her fiercely, to fend off all foes and somehow press his life into her fragile form.

In the distance he heard the ceaseless pounding of the casket crews as if they were banging down the door beside him, demanding entrance into the tiny sanctuary he shared with her. *I cannot let You have her,* he raged silently to the God she'd brought into his life. *I've not the faith to let her go.* He felt her heartbeat, light and skittish against his shirt. Her hands were cold, yet her face and chest glistened with fever. Even in the shadows, he could see the influenza's telltale blue-black imprint, stark and angry against her pale cheeks. Marred and thin as she was, Leanne was still the most beautiful woman God ever created. *Don't You love her enough to spare her?* He silently shouted the accusation to God through the helpless darkness that seemed to swallow them whole.

The answer came back to him with startling clarity: *Don't you?*

Unbidden, John's mind threw itself back in time to a stable when he was twelve. He was standing over his beloved mare, Huntress, the animal as bathed in sweat and suffering as Leanne was now. He was pleading the exact same case to his father, who had silently walked to the house and returned with a pistol. John had cried openly to his father that night—something a Gallows was never allowed to do—begging for the animal's life. He had never forgotten the sound of that pistol as it split the night, how even the sight of Huntress's final peaceful breaths had not soothed the wound of loss he carried in his chest for weeks. The memory overlaid itself on John's current pain, cinching around John's heart until he wanted to weep again, here, now. He had howled the same refusal to let Huntress go then as he had done to God tonight. It had been selfish and wrong then, it was selfish and wrong now.

John knew, then, that the memory was no accident. His father's words that night were his Holy Father's words to him tonight. It was not love to plead for more suffering. Leanne was more fit for Heaven than he could ever hope to be. "I don't know how to let You have her," he whispered to the darkness, praying as much for himself as for her. He looked into her face, limp against his arm with eyes sweetly closed. "How do I get to 'Thy will be done' as You would have me? I'm miles from being that man."

As the hours passed, the miles became a smaller and smaller distance to travel. Ida came in once, stopped to look at the sight of Leanne gathered against John's chest there on the floor, and silently let them be as she tended the other patients. As her fever soaked his shirt, as her winces of pain singed his ears and her spasms of coughing shook his own heart, John relinquished inch by inch. Broken, exhausted, perhaps already infected and in his own last days, John laid down what was left of his life. It seemed impossible that he and Leanne would wake tomorrow. Should he wake to find her gone, John felt sure he would stumble through life only as the hollow shell of a man who had loved and lost.

With what felt like his final thoughts, John surrendered to God this woman they both loved. "Take her even as I beg You not to," he whispered, a tear of his own falling onto Leanne's cheek as he held her near. He told her "I love you" over and over, hoping each of her shallow breaths was not her last. If he never heard the words from her, the hundreds of times she heard it from him would have to do.

## Chapter Twenty-Nine

Gray.

Vague gray and a strange coolness.

Leanne felt foreign inside her own skin, as if she were outside her body looking in from a curious distance. She felt pain, and yet the sensation wasn't nearly as sharp as before. It was a hollow ache, a dry and dusty feeling as though she'd blow away in the slightest breeze.

Papa was holding her. She was cradled in his arms, a little girl again. She could sense the steady rise and fall of his chest, feel the warm linen of his shirt against her cheek. Only her feet weren't curled onto the brown velvet of his sitting chair, they were on something cool and smooth. She thought about moving, about lifting her head to look around her because the sounds were all wrong, but her body seemed disconnected from her thoughts. She didn't seem to have any strength, not even to open her eyes. *Am I dreaming?* And then the more confusing thought: *Am I dead?* She felt like only a soul, surely, all thought and feeling but without substance. And then again, far too heavy to move.

The scent was wrong. This was not Papa, but still familiar, still comforting. The shoulder was not Papa's, but yet strong and trustworthy. It came to her like a single candle lit in a dark room, a tiny circle of light changing the darkness.

*John.*

She had been sick. Blurry impressions of light and pain and struggle floated past her awareness. She had been very sick. Yes, that explained why she felt too weak and thirsty, why her skin felt as if it would crack open if she moved too quickly.

*John.*

This was John's shoulder against her cheek, his chin resting above her head. His arm encircling her. She wasn't sure how she knew, only that it couldn't be anyone but him.

The hospital. She remembered that much now. The image of her blood spattered on the dormitory sink came back to her. Influenza. With enormous effort she forced her cracked lips open and asked her body to breathe. Both her chest and throat felt ripped and raw, yet she could feel the air slipping in and out. She was breathing.

She was alive. Some part of her recognized the impossibility of that fact, recalled enough of her circumstance to know it shouldn't be. *Lord,* she reached out in prayer, movement still beyond her ability, *have You spared me? Do I live?* Leanne let out a small gasp, the marvel of her survival sending a surge of joy through her fragile limbs.

The sound made John shift slightly in his sleep, a soft and weary groan tickling her ears. She was alive.

Leanne forced her eyes open, willed them to stay so until the swimming images before her gained clarity. Her first sight was the stubbled curve of John's chin, tilted back against the wall. Even in his rumpled state, he was without a doubt the most handsome man in all the world. They were on the floor of some small room with a handful of other beds. She remembered being here, gazing out the window and wishing for death to take away the pain. The memory returned the large ward's horrors to her mind, the rows upon rows of ill and dying, how she understood now why they begged for death. The image of Charles Holling's lifeless eyes just before she'd pulled the sheet up over his face washed over her vision, making her frightened and dizzy until she returned her gaze to John's sleeping face.

He must have taken her in his arms and held her there on the floor—for hours or minutes she couldn't say. He had been beside her, had cared for her. Fleeting images of his face and voice came back to her, blurred by fever and pain so that she could not remember the words, only the tone and how much comfort it had brought to her. She had a vague memory of him singing—which made no sense at all—but a very clear memory of him pleading for her to stay, to fight, to live.

And she had. She had survived, and she would survive. A tiny, powerful core of truth pulsed somewhere under her ribs like a heartbeat, telling her that her life was no longer in danger. Leanne wet her lips again, pulled another burning breath into her lungs, and pushed one word out into the morning air, "John."

He started, jolting to a bleary consciousness with

another groan. It seemed to take him as long as it had taken her to remember where he was, to pull his head from its propped angle against the wall and look down. When he did, it was as if the sun rose in the blue sky of his wide eyes. He blinked with disbelief, his face melted into an expression of such joy and relief that Leanne felt tears sting her eyes. He pulled a hand across his eyes, as if to wipe away a dream, then looked at her again. He worked to form a word, producing only a tender sound; the eloquent John Gallows rendered speechless. Instead he bent his forehead to hers, and she felt the warmth of his tears steal between the rough stubble of his unshaven cheek. "You're here. Thank You, Lord. Thank You. Thank You." He rocked her gently, his chest heaving in a way that made her wish she had the strength to throw her arms around him. "You're here. You've lived. You're here."

Leanne closed her eyes for a moment, letting the pure joy push away the aching weakness.

He pulled back and touched every part of her face, cherishing her existence with eager fingers. "I'm not dreaming? You are really here?"

"Yes." She remembered, looking at his eyes, saying goodbye to him in her heart as she felt the darkness pulling her down. "I'm here."

"I was sure I'd lost you." His voice broke as he pulled her carefully closer. She felt her heart pound in her chest, wonderfully alive despite her still-frail state.

"I love you," he whispered close to her ear, and she felt it flood her soul like warm sunshine. "I told you over and over last night when I feared…" She was glad he didn't finish the thought. "I yelled at God that He couldn't have you because I loved you too much to lose you now that I've just found you. And then you worsened, and I couldn't ask Him to keep you in such suffering, so I..." He pulled back again and stared into her eyes. "I love you and you've survived. What else matters now?"

He was actually rambling, running words together like an excited schoolboy, and she let his joy flow over into her. John's exuberance radiated life and hope, and she gulped it in with every trembling breath. "Love?" Of course he loved her, for she loved him. She loved him. The fire in his eyes kindled the clearest truth—that she had always loved him.

"Yes." His smile was brilliant beyond anything she'd remembered. "Love. I would have suffered through loving you and losing you, but it seems God is kinder than that." He kissed her forehead, and it spread throughout her body as though it filled her with light and sparkles. "I'll thank Him every day forever, I think."

"You stayed with me. How I love you for that. How I love you." It took so much effort to lift her arm, and the thin gray hand that stroked his unshaven cheek seemed to belong to an old woman. He placed his hand atop hers, the way he had done on the hilltop back before all the darkness, and Leanne reveled in the warmth and strength of his touch. She yearned to give him grand words, to shout her feelings from the rooftops, but her body was still far weaker than her spirit. She was filled with too many emotions to hold back the tears.

"Are you all right? Do you hurt? You're still so frail." How could she feel so weak and so alive at the same time? The room seemed to spin around her, and she was grateful for the anchor of John's embrace. "I'm terribly thirsty," she admitted. John tried to grasp something behind her—a glass, perhaps, on the small metal table she knew the hospital kept beside some of the cots— but couldn't reach it. He couldn't hope to get up with her in his arms. It would be difficult for a man with two healthy legs, much less his troublesome injury.

"You trapped yourself with me," she noted. He'd made the choice to stay no matter what happened when he'd pulled her onto his lap. There was something lovingly noble in the gesture. "My hero." Her smile was worth twice the effort it took.

"My damsel. My lovely, living damsel." He chuckled, attempting the rise they both knew was impossible. They were indeed stuck together on the floor, and while she could not manage a laugh, one bubbled forth from him. "Miss Landway!" he called, splitting the quiet dawn and waking the other patients in the room. "Madison!"

Ida burst into the room, the alarm on her face melting as she sagged against the doorway in relief and joy.

"Look what I have to contend with. Look at my splendid problem, Miss Landway!"

Ida's hands flew to her chest, then to her mouth, a tearful little whimper escaping her smiling expression. "She lives!" She rushed over to place an assessing hand on Leanne's cheek. "Her fever's broken. Mercy on us all, we've a survivor. You've survived, Leanne. You're the first one here."

"I have," Leanne said, letting her head return to the

support of John's shoulder. Truly, he had the most wonderful shoulders.

"She has indeed." She felt John's jovial laugh tumble through his chest in little shakes that made her smile. "And I'd waltz her around the room…if I could get off the floor. Which I can't."

Grinning, Ida broke her own rule of quiet by shouting "Dr. Madison, come quickly!"

He must have been close by, for within seconds the doctor dashed in the door to show the same shock of pleasure Ida had. "Land sakes, she's still with us."

"No fever," Ida pronounced, stepping away as she gestured Dr. Madison over. "She's come through it, Doctor."

Madison squatted down to check her pulse, clasping a hand to John's shoulder with a smile. Something had changed between those two, Leanne could see it in the way their eyes met. The enmity between them had dissolved, replaced by what seemed to be a deep friendship. What all had God wrought while she slept?

"Not yet strong, but delightfully steady. You've turned the corner indeed, Miss Sample, and I couldn't be happier."

"I was wondering," John said with a stiff groan, "if we couldn't all be happier *off* the floor. I fear at the moment it'll be a week before I walk steady." He stole a look at Leanne, giving her a tentative squeeze, "but I'll be the happiest limping man east of Chicago."

Madison laughed. "You will at that."

It took considerable effort—and pain—to untangle Leanne from the circle of John's arms and get her laid out onto the fresh sheets Ida had managed to find and set on the bed. No one cared at the bother—it was far more celebration than anyone at the hospital had seen in too long. Every inch of Leanne felt cracked and dry, and yet still she smiled. John made glorious protests as Dr. Madison eased his stiffened body from the floor. "You'll pay for that night under her weight." He laughed, giving John's shoulder a friendly shake.

"Gladly," John said, fixing his gaze on Leanne again with dazzling warmth. She marveled again at his vigil over her. She loved him dearly, every boisterous, defiant bit of this man God had sent to her side. Surely God was laughing this morning at all doubts she'd expressed at the Almighty ever getting through to a soul the likes of John Gallows's.

Ida had managed to somehow find a second pillow, and she propped Leanne up, fussing about her like a queen's handmaiden. She brought a chair from the other side of the cot and handed John a tin mug of water. "You can tend to your damsel in distress for ten more minutes," she clucked like a proud mother hen, "then it's time for the both of you to get cleaned and rested."

There were still people in the room as John leaned over her to help her sip the water, but she forgot all of them in the depths of his eyes. "Drink, my love." His voice held a new, tender quality that spoke to the deepest parts of her heart. The water was bliss to her throat, cool and wet and wondrous. John looked at her as though he couldn't help but do so, as though she were a treasure instead of the rumpled sight she suspected she was. Still, he was doubly handsome to her in his unkempt, unshaven state, so perhaps the same was true of him as he looked at her. She felt herself blushing under the directness of his eyes, that dashing regard that had won far lovelier hearts than hers. He fingered a lock of her hair as he yawned. "Now rest."

"You, too," she replied, yawning, as well. She was so very tired, so grateful to be enduring a dull ache instead of the stabs of pain she'd known before. "Sleep well..." and with a boost of courage she added, "my love." She drifted into sleep recalling the sparkle in John's eyes that followed her words. She loved him. He loved her. They lived. Tomorrow could bring anything, and she would have enough.

## Chapter Thirty

Dr. Madison looked at John from over the top of his glasses as they sat the next day in the tiny room that had become the doctor's quarters. "You've pushed yourself too far, but I suppose you don't need me to tell you that."

John leaned back against the room's single chair. It hurt to stand. It hurt to do anything anymore. "You know what I'm looking for."

Madison took off his glasses and pinched the bridge of his nose. "I've hardly the right equipment to make an assessment, especially under these circumstances."

John had given enough speeches to know propaganda when he saw it. "I'm long past pretending, Charles. Out with it."

There was a long pause before Madison answered. "No, I don't think you'll heal. Not properly. Not enough."

John felt the world tilt a bit and grabbed the arm of the chair for support. He'd prepared himself for this, had known on some level that this was coming, but it still felt like a punch to the stomach to hear it aloud. "I'm done, then."

"In service, yes. Honorable discharge, decorated I'm sure, but—" he gave John a steady, direct look "—flying is out of the question." Madison took a deep breath before adding, "If you'd have gone…"

"Who can say what would have happened if I'd gone to Chicago and France?" John stood up and turned toward the room's only window. He hated how the sound of casket-builders' hammers still punctuated the air. "Not that I haven't turned it over in my mind a dozen times. I could have gotten what I thought I wanted." He turned and looked back at the doctor, wincing at the pang that accompanied the move. "Then again, I could have gotten what I deserved."

"Who can say what any man deserves? I've conferred with doctors from seven other bases, and I still can't explain why Leanne and the others live while hundreds more do not." Madison dropped his gaze. "We're not done here, John. Not by a long shot."

The randomness of influenza, the jarring lack of logic in who fell ill and who escaped, gave heavy weight to such questions. It was why Leanne had spent so much time talking about God's grace to her patients. To him. John returned his eyes to the window and the clear blue sky framed within. "I'm not fit to rejoin the service."

Madison came up behind him. "Do you regret it? Staying?"

"No." John didn't even have to think about it.

"You'd be all-too-human if you did." Madison tucked his hands in his pockets and rocked back on his heels.

"To admit your regret doesn't belittle the act. It may even make it more heroic, if you ask me."

"I think I loved her even then," John explained, amazed at how easily the words came. "In the way I made the choice to stay so easily, with such certainty. I knew, somehow, that my place was here. No, I don't regret it, Charles. I'm alive, and so is Leanne."

"And two more besides," Madison added. "But not enough live. We'll not be able to lift the quarantine for days, perhaps even weeks."

John managed a smile. "What matter is that? My battle and my prize are already here."

A week later Leanne sat in a chair for the first time since she'd fallen ill. Ida and Dr. Madison had contrived a room for her in a corner of an upper floor, away from the still-infected patients. Eventually the other survivors would join her when they became well enough to move, but for now Leanne enjoyed the ultimate luxury of privacy.

This afternoon as she dressed for the first time, privacy felt too lonely. She felt lost in the large room and large clothes—her blouse and skirt looked as if they belonged to someone else, hanging loose and awkward on her bony figure. She was gazing in a hand mirror Ida had brought with a hairbrush and a small length of ribbon. It was as if a stranger's reflection returned her gaze. While only shadows now, Leanne felt as if she could still see influenza's horrid dark spots on her own face. It unnerved her to know she had borne the purple blotches she'd found so ghoulish on her patients. She was a survivor, yes, but she was also a victim. Would she always see the spots, imagined in the mirror even when her face was full and flush with health? She still looked and felt so sickly. So weak and scarred.

It almost made it worse that Dr. Madison and the rest of the hospital staff reveled in her survival. She did not know how to be this wondrous "first survivor," or what that meant. John was the one at home in the spotlight, not her, and she had not done anything worthy to earn her newfound significance. John had once said his only heroism was "not dying." How funny that she now felt the same sentiment.

"I am glad to be alive, Lord," she preached to the sallow face in the mirror, "but I've not the grace to ignore how much of my hair is gone." Leanne could do nothing with the thinned and lifeless locks influenza had bequeathed her. She'd learned about hair thinning out during a high fever, but it was another, humbling thing to live with the symptom. "How vain I am despite all my reasons for gratitude." Where was the lovely, pretty-feeling Leanne who'd gazed at John from her place beside him on the magazine cover? She looked at her sunken cheeks and moaned at how far she was from that woman now. "I look old. A crone."

"You are the most beautiful woman in the world to me." John's voice came from behind her. Leanne turned, expecting to see his "charm and flattery" face, the one she'd seen him use during his speeches. Instead, she saw a precious genuine affection fill his features. He meant his words.

John's appearance was sometimes hard to bear. While pain darkened his expression more often than not, he still possessed the handsome features of his war-hero past. He hadn't really changed, whereas she felt like a walking war-wound. She leaned back against him as she considered herself again in the mirror. "I see far too much of Private Carson when I look in this mirror," she admitted, trying once again to force her limp hair to twist up artfully over her pale forehead.

"Shh." John placed a kiss on the spot where Leanne had affixed the thin curl. "Carson had lost his appetite for life. That's not something you catch like a disease. It's something that festers inside a man until disease or wound sets it loose." He plucked the mirror from her grasp, taking both of her hands and turning her to face him. "You are a true beauty. I look at you and I see a warrior. Someone who has waged a mighty battle and earned her victory."

She turned away from him. "That's just it, John, I've earned nothing. Don't you see? You told me once you felt your medal was for nothing, that you were celebrated for merely staying alive. I feel like that. I don't know why I lived and others died. I've nothing to teach or share or contribute. I'm just *here*. It will be weeks until I'm strong enough to serve on the nursing staff again. What am I?"

"You, my love, are the most important thing we have right now—you are God's gift of hope. You and every other soul who manages to pull through." His winced as standing began to bother him, so he pulled a chair close to where she sat. It seemed like John couldn't stand for more than a few minutes lately, and while he was doing his best to gloss it over, she could tell it bothered him immensely. "Can't you feel how the atmosphere has changed since you've healed? Hopelessness doesn't sour the wards any longer. People don't come in here with a slaughterhouse fear in their eyes, because they know now that it's possible to live. Every healthy breath you take, every day you improve, is God's gift to everyone."

Leanne rested her chin in her hand. "Goodness, one would think you know how to give a speech."

"I know the power of inspiration. But yes, I do know what it's like to feel like more of a symbol than a person." John kneaded his thigh. "It wears on a soul to know others think you larger than you are. I do understand what you feel." He smiled. "God was wise to put us together, don't you think? Together. Us. The very idea still astounds me." He leaned in and kissed her.

It began as a soft and tender kiss, but deepened to a lingering, delighting, lover's kiss. The kind of rapturous kiss a handsome man would give to a beautiful woman. He made her feel so loved. His regard, the clear affection in his touch, was a balm to the sting of her unhealthiness. There they sat, sitting because neither of them were able to truly stand, but feeling they were strong together. She knew, *knew* John loved her, even now. Not in spite of her scars, but perhaps even because of them. Didn't she feel the same way about him, about his wounds? Could she have loved the unwounded John, the arrogant dashing hero too large for life? He wasn't the same man without the thorn of his lame leg. The way he coped with his injury, with her illness, was so very much a part of how she loved him now. How perfectly suited they truly were for each other. "Very wise," she whispered when she finally pulled away, breathless from his kiss.

"Oh," John said, reaching for a small bag he'd set

down near his cane. "You had me so spellbound I nearly forgot. I've a gift for you. I know you've been far too idle for your liking, but I'm in no hurry to see you push yourself too soon."

"You," she teased, "preaching to me about the wisdom of respecting one's physical limitations? Perhaps the world really is coming to an end."

"You don't want to force me to take back this yarn now, do you?"

"Yarn! You brought me yarn?" She grabbed at the bag even as John held it playfully out of her reach. "I can't think of anything I'd rather do right now than to be knitting."

John leaned in, holding the bag behind him. "Anything?" His eyes sparkled with cinema-star charm.

"You're dreadful." She leaned in and kissed him, deftly snatching the bag in his resulting distraction. "Anything productive, I mean. I'm hardly well enough to do much else, and my hands have been itching for yarn and needles." The bag held the current set of socks she'd been working on. "How did you manage to get these sent over?"

"You said yourself, I'm very persuasive. Look in the bottom of the bag."

Leanne dug deeper to find two of the softest, plushest hanks of yellow cashmere she'd seen in months. An absolute decadence in wartime, much less during a quarantine. "John!"

"And as you also said yourself, I'm rather fond of breaking rules."

She fingered the luxurious fiber, soft as clouds and bright as sunshine. "Oh, John, I can't."

"You can and you ought to. My secret source says it's just enough to make a bed jacket or whatever it is you call such frilly things. And I shall have Dr. Madison write out a prescription if you refuse. You're to be pampered, and that's the end of it."

"A yellow cashmere bed jacket? It's scandalous."

John's smile was perhaps even wider than her own. "It's therapeutic. Look at you. Your color's improved already." He picked up the mirror and moved behind her as she sat on the chair. He bent so that they could both see her reflection and held one of the hanks to her neck. Its fuzzy fibers tickled her chin. "Mmm. I've always liked you in yellow."

"I trust," she nearly gasped as his murmur tingled down the back of her neck, "you were able to secure the sock *you* were working on, as well?"

"Alas, no." His eyes suggested he hadn't even attempted to do so.

"Oh, but Captain Gallows, you promised me a sock for the charity auction." She pulled a strand of the cashmere from its twist in the hank, wrapping it around one finger with nothing short of glee. To knit something for herself, something so extravagant, something from John, filled her with a radiant energy.

"My duties as makeshift quartermaster don't allow for such luxuries." He straightened with a groan and returned himself stiffly to the chair opposite her. "I may not be able to walk far, but I'm a champion of stretching supplies for miles."

Leanne put down the yarn to lay a hand on John's knee. "How is your leg? It seems worse."

John's sigh told more than his words. "It is. Madison said..." He stopped himself. "No bother about that. What shall you knit first? The olive or yellow?"

"Yes, I *will* bother about that. What did Dr. Madison say? Has he been treating you?"

John shifted his weight, as if the leg ached more at the subject. "Nothing to treat, nor anything to treat with. Fevers need ice more than sore legs, pain medicine is more luxury than your yarn there, and...some things just...don't heal." He busied himself with the olive army sock, inspecting it with false curiosity. "Impressive heel, my dear. Such neat stitches."

The John Gallows she'd known didn't use tones of resignation. She pulled the sock from his hands. "John, stop avoiding the subject. What has Dr. Madison told you?"

John pushed up off the chair, turning away from her and yet leaving his cane on the floor where they had sat. "There's no point in discussing it."

"There is every point in discussing it. Don't keep this from me. Not this."

John faced out the window, leaning against the sill for a long moment before he spoke. "Madison said I've abused it beyond repair. The leg is lame. Permanently. He couldn't sign off on active service for me now even if he wanted to, even if Barnes demanded it. Which I doubt Barnes will do, as I suspect the general's hunting for my head as it is."

Returning to service had been everything to John. He'd sacrificed everything, pushed himself, broken rules and called in favors to make it happen. He'd been on the brink of achieving that goal. The influenza outbreak was supposed to be a detour, not the end. "I am so sorry," she said, even though the words hardly did his pain justice. "I know how hard that is for you." And here she was pitying herself because she looked sickly. She had every chance to recover, and now John did not. It seemed unjust.

The second part of his statement struck her just then. "And why is General Barnes after your head?" John still had not moved. It dawned on her that John hadn't told her everything. "What did you do?"

# Chapter Thirty-One

John avoided her gaze. "I did nothing out of character for me."

"That leaves a fair amount of room to wonder. What did you do?"

He propped his hands against the sides of the window and slowly stretched his leg, an attempt at casual movement she knew could not be true. "I suppose it's more about what I didn't do. The general doesn't take to having his direct orders disobeyed."

Leanne had seen enough to know John disobeying orders couldn't be news to the commander. This had to be larger than that. She put down the yarn and mirror on the table beside her and sat up straight. "And which disregarded orders are so important as to have General Barnes up in arms?" When John didn't respond, she added, "John, please. Whatever it is you think I ought not to hear, tell me."

John turned slowly, leaning against the wall next to the window. He spoke slowly, reluctantly. "I was supposed to have left the base the day we came to campus. Barnes knew what was coming. The base in Boston had already been hit and ships coming into Philadelphia were falling fast. He gave me a train ticket and orders to ship off to Chicago that night so I'd escape the outbreak. He said it was for promotional purposes but I knew better. I suspect it was my father's doing. Why else should I be swept out of harm's way while everyone else sits like targets?"

"Because you are valuable and important." Then the true weight of what he had said began to hit her. "You defied the order to leave? Knowing what was coming? Chicago and France were what you wanted, John. Why on earth did you stay?"

He looked surprised she needed to ask. "For you."

She felt his words like physical force. Tight and clenching. It was suffocating enough to be the survivor on which an entire hospital pinned its hopes. But to be the reason a man had forsaken his goal? Placed himself in harm's way? Destroyed his chance at achieving his dreams? Especially if it was a man she loved. The weight choked her. "Me?"

John limped over to the chair again, grabbing her hands. "You. And not you. Me. Everything. I looked at that ticket and I knew I couldn't use it. Knew I ought to be here. Beside you."

"John…"

"And not only beside you, but here, fighting this battle. I didn't choose what happened on that airship, but I could choose this. I knew whatever I was running back to France to find was already right in front of me."

"That makes no sense."

"It does to me. I don't know that I can explain it any better than that but I don't regret it. I didn't want you to know because I didn't want you to feel like this." He shook her hands, his voice fierce. "I don't regret it. Not for a second, do you hear me? I'll limp until I'm eighty and not look back."

"It's not just your leg. You knew the outbreak was coming. You could have fallen ill just as easily as I. Either or both of us could have…" She didn't want to finish that sentence, nor did she have to. Every single person in this building was aware that every cough held the possibility of death. "Could still…"

John pulled her to her feet and held her. "None of that. I'm invincible, remember?"

She wrapped her arms around him, and they wobbled a bit as if the unsteadiness confirmed that lie. "You most certainly are not." She had not, for one second, ignored the possibility that John could still fall ill. "We don't know how it's contracted. I pray every day you won't start coughing. I couldn't stand it if I'd infected you."

"You heard Madison. He thinks that those exposed either succumb or don't. I haven't yet, so I'm unlikely to." He tightened his embrace. "And I've been very close to an infected patient."

"They're only guessing, John. Dr. Madison says he still can't say why I survived. There's so much they still don't understand."

She swayed a bit, and John pulled them both back to the seats. He tipped her chin up to look at him. "Look at me. There's only one thing to understand here, and it is that we *are* here. Not altogether perfect, but alive, and with each other. This is where I am meant to be, where God means us to be. I know you know that. Have some of that faith you boasted to me about. The quarantine will be lifted soon and we'll trust God with the days after that."

Leanne let her forehead fall to touch John's. She could only marvel at how the disaster had changed him, what God had done. "When did you become such a wise and faithful soul?"

"One very long night not too long ago. You fought influenza while I did battle with…other things." He pulled back to trace what must be the shadows under her eyes. "You've been up long enough, as have I. Rest." He nodded toward the room's one bed. It made her wonder if John's leg let him sleep in any comfort at all. "Dream of fluffy yellow yarn." He yawned.

"I love you," she said, cupping his poorly shaven chin. She felt too full of emotion and fatigue to say anything less. "I am so very, desperately glad you are here."

"We may be the only two souls on earth thankful for an influenza quarantine. God certainly works in mysterious ways." He kissed her again, and she thought she could never tire of his tender touch. "I love you." He touched her face, then slowly moved to pull himself out of the chair.

Leanne pulled her own self upright, handing him his cane. "I shall buy you the grandest silver cane ever for your eightieth birthday. It will be so huge and impressive, little boys will fear it and little girls will think you a king. Dream of that."

"Goodness, no." He laughed weakly. "I prefer to dream of steak."

John offered Leanne a smile as he helped her into one of the parlor chairs at the Red Cross House. It was a victory, moving her back to Jackson. Yes, Dr. Madison approved it half for the benefit of Leanne's parents—who were coming despite numerous requests to hold off. Madison also approved it for purely practical reasons: the small "recovery ward" she'd "launched" was filling with patients. The quarantines at Jackson and the university had been lifted. An end to the calamity seemed to be in sight.

"I'm well, you know. In fact, I'm quite sure I could have walked." He'd borrowed an army wheelchair to ferry her from the transport car to the Red Cross House steps.

"Strolled up those steps *and* fended off your parents on arrival? You overstate your recuperative powers, lauded as they are." Her "recuperative powers" had become a joke of sorts between them, for doctors and nurses everywhere wanted to know how Leanne had survived. He felt an urge to protect her from such attentions, knowing how he felt when people asked him how he'd dared to go out on the stay wires of the dirigible. People wanted an answer where no answer was to be had.

Leanne arranged her skirts on the chair. She'd gained back a bit of weight, looking less like a scarecrow in her own clothes. Her color was better but still not what it had once been, and she tired easily. More than once he'd come up to her room in the dormitory to find her fast asleep with her knitting needles and what she called his "scandalous yellow yarn" still held in her fingers. She held that yarn in her lap now, and he felt the surge of satisfaction he always did when he'd found some way to please or pamper her. "Will you stay and meet them?" she asked.

"I don't think today is the day for such an introduction, and…I've a dreaded commitment."

She raised an eyebrow at his terminology. "Dreaded?"

"General Barnes." Horrific as it was, the quarantine had cocooned him and Leanne in a bubble of their own, shielded from the war, the outside world and all such consequences. In truth John was sure fear of infection was the only thing that had kept Barnes from storming onto campus the moment the quarantine had been lifted and hauling John personally into whatever punishment generals devised for valuable liabilities such as himself. Now John found himself with the daunting task of testing his new faith in the realities of ordinary life. If life ever became ordinary in love and at war.

Leanne reached for John's hand. "What will he do?" He was glad she hadn't asked the more accurate "What will he do to you?"

"God only knows." Such phrases used to annoy Leanne, but now he loved using it because now he knew he truly meant it. He ran his hand over the back of her palm delighted he could no longer trace the outline of her veins through paper-pale skin. "We've prayed over this, I ought to be calmer."

"The timing seems dreadful. How can I keep my mind on Mama and Papa knowing you're with General Barnes?"

"How can I keep my mind on General Barnes knowing you're with your mama and papa without me to protect you?"

The joke roused the laugh he'd intended. "They're

my parents, John, not some angry monsters. They'll fuss and demand to take me home, I'm sure—" she took his hand in both of hers "—but I'm stronger now. So many things are different. I only hope I can make them see. I'll admit I do wish I had some of your persuasive abilities today."

John leaned in and kissed her. "There. I've transferred the lot of them, my mouth to yours. Now I wish I had your faith in unknown outcomes. I'm nothing near calm enough."

She returned his kiss. "There. I've transferred the lot of it, my mouth to yours."

John managed a smile. "If only it worked that way."

She caught his collar before he pulled back. "I love you, no matter what."

Her words managed what her kiss had not. Should all of the United States Army come crashing down around his ankles in the next hour, he had the love of a Sovereign God and the only woman that mattered. He let his fingers grace the perfect line of her chin. "Then I have all I need, my love. Be well, charm your parents and I'll come back when…when it's done."


"I'm well," Leanne repeated, trying to convince her parents' fearful eyes. "Really, I've improved a great deal, and I get stronger every day." She couldn't bear to tell them she looked much better than just a few days earlier, for Mama clutched her gauze mask in a white-knuckled fist.

"You should come home with us. Right now," Papa pronounced as he paced the room. She couldn't blame their apprehension on being inside Camp Jackson. Everyone was afraid of everything, for the air was the enemy, and the enemy was everywhere. Only the fiercest of worries could have pulled Mama and Papa from the protection of their home in such a crisis. Papa was clearly here to collect his little girl and take her home to safety.

"Dr. Madison says I'm not yet strong enough to travel." It was true, but only half the truth. She couldn't bear the thought of leaving Camp Jackson, not now. Her world had turned upside down and righted itself in a completely new way. To go back to who she was six months ago—which was exactly what would happen if she went home now—seemed terribly wrong. It made her thankful for Dr. Madison's medical excuse. She couldn't conceive of how to make Mama and Papa understand she wasn't anything close to the young woman who'd left them on the station platform just a few months ago. "It's best I stay here." After summoning her courage, she amended her statement. "And, Papa, I want to stay here."

"Nonsense. Military camps are the most dangerous places of all right now. We can easily take care of you at home where it's safe." Mama said the words as if defying the world to breach the sanctuary of the Sample family threshold.

The reality was that no place was truly "safe." The quarantine had been lifted, but cases were still coming in. The base hospital was still full to overflowing, as were both of Columbia's hospitals. Some were surviving, but many were still dying. The last report predicted that the number of cases here would peak near three thousand, and other cities were just coming under the wave of infection Columbia had crested. Safe? *Safe* couldn't mean a lack of danger anymore. *Safe* had come to mean simply wherever John was. Wherever God watched over the pair of them together. "I am safe here, Mama. I'm healing, and when I'm well enough I'll need to return to my post."

Mama's wide eyes showed she didn't believe a word of it, and that she didn't much care for her daughter's newfound independence. "You're so very thin and pale. Are you eating? Is everyone wearing masks?"

*I've watched men die behind their masks,* Leanne wanted to say. "Yes, they're very careful here. And now that the quarantine is lifted, the camp is eating quite well." Her words brought back the memory of John feeding her sausage on the front steps, and she hoped Mama would mistake the flush it brought to her cheeks as the radiance of health.

John stood before General Barnes's desk, at attention despite how much it hurt. The general had not invited him to sit as he normally did when they met. This was no normal meeting.

The general ran his hands down his face, the weary gesture a revelation of how difficult life under quarantine had been. "Do you know what the worst part of my job is, Gallows?"

"No, sir."

Barnes pointed to a stack of letters on his desk. "Signing these. Orders for telegrams bringing the worst possible news to some poor mother or father, or wife. I've signed nearly three hundred of these, and I'm sick to death of ugly, pointless deaths. Influenza isn't supposed to kill, Gallows, it makes no sense."

John couldn't argue with that. "It doesn't, sir."

"The last thing I need—" Barnes took off his glasses and looked at John for the first time since he'd entered the room "—is one of my best weapons doing something even more senseless. I needed you in Chicago. I tried to save you from what I knew was coming, and you disobeyed a direct order and went A.W.O.L. The thing I can't work out is why."

John gave the only answer that came to him. "I doubt you'd believe me if I told you, sir."

The general leaned back in his chair. "Try me."

John had prayed all morning that Barnes would simply reprimand him and not demand an explanation. He was sure any attempt to convey all that had happened to him recently would fail miserably. Barnes didn't look like the kind of man who'd embrace either a spiritual or a romantic motive, and John had no other explanation.

"You might as well sit down, Gallows," Barnes interjected at John's hesitation. "It looks to me like this is a long story and frankly I could use the diversion."

John wondered if God wasn't smiling somewhere. He'd prayed specifically for a short meeting, afraid that his passions would run away with his mouth if asked too many questions. Today his father was right when he called John "a man of too many words." The simplest explanation seemed the best place to start. "A woman, sir."

"I beg your pardon?"

"It wasn't hard to glean what was coming from my last visit to your office. I found I couldn't leave a particular woman to face it alone. Well, without me. Or rather, I suppose I couldn't bear the thought of her falling ill and not being here." The words sounded far more ridiculous than romantic.

General Barnes crossed his arms over his chest. "Surely you're not telling me Nurse Sample survived because of your illustrious presence?"

John raised an eyebrow. He'd hoped not to name names.

"Captain Gallows, you're anything but subtle and camp gossip is faster than the telegraph. I have one clerk drafting a list of charges to bring you up on while another is suggesting we should call *Era* magazine and give them the exclusive update."

For once, John was speechless, his wobbly smile feeling foolish. "I'd rather you did neither."

"I ought to do anything I please at the moment, rather than taking suggestions from the likes of you. How do I explain what you've done? I can't very well let a highly visible, recently publicized soldier—an officer at that—get away with disobeying direct, self-preserving orders for *love*. You've got to give me another reason."

God's smile must have broadened. There was only one other reason, and it wouldn't sit any better with the general than John's first explanation. "You'll like it less," he quipped, swallowing the feeling he was facing a firing squad.

"There's not much 'less' left in me, Gallows." He leaned forward on his elbows with the expression of a man bracing for a hit to the stomach.

## Chapter Thirty-Two

John recalled the Bible passage about Paul defending his refusal to obey orders of silence to Roman officials. He felt a particular affinity, the helplessness of trying to explain the relentlessness of God to someone who'd never experienced it. He couldn't blame the general; two months ago, had someone given him the answer he was about to give Barnes, he would be balking, as well.

"Well, sir, I looked at those tickets, I knew what they represented, and all I can say is that I knew at that moment that God had led me to Columbia and I wasn't supposed to leave it."

Barnes looked understandably shocked.

"No one expected it less than me, sir. And I'll be the first to admit that it makes no sense to anyone else. But that's the honest truth. I knew, as much as I've known anything in my life—and certainly more than I knew on that dirigible—that I needed to stay. That the place I most needed to be was where God asked me to be, and that wasn't Chicago. Or France."

"God?" Barnes clearly would have preferred just about any other answer. "I ask you for a logical expla-

nation to keep you from Courts-Martial and the best
you can give me is *God* and *love?*" He squinted his eyes
shut in frustration. "I don't know why I'm surprised
at this nonsense. I can't fathom a *sensible* explanation
for what you did." He gave John an incredulous look.
"You've put me in a hard place, Gallows. Of course
you're not the first soldier to have his head turned by
a pretty nurse, and I suppose you're not the first man
to turn to his Maker in a foxhole, but you've done so
*with the press watching.* Land sakes, son, the two of
you were on the cover of *Era.* I can't let it go, nor can it
ever be known that you disobeyed direct orders without
consequences. Miss Sample was the first South Caro-
linian to survive the influenza. I can't just sweep y'all
under a rug."

"I understand your position, sir. I don't regret what
I did, though. Not for a moment." After a pause, John
asked, "Are you married, sir?"

Barnes managed an annoyed smirk. "Contrary to
legend, I was young once. Your father introduced me
to my wife, as a matter of fact. Mrs. Barnes was a great
beauty and I made a bit of a fool of myself to catch her
eye. I'm no heartless beast, John, but you're no fool,
either. You know what's at stake here."

"I do." His heart and his soul were at stake, only he
was sure Barnes didn't see it that way.

"I've no idea what to do. I can't honorably discharge
you, but I can't give you a dishonorable discharge without setting off a press ruckus. I had hoped your explanation would save you, but you've only given me more
rope to hang you, son. Only I can't hang you, and ac-

cording to Madison, I can't send you back into active duty. Ever."

"I know." John kept his voice neutral even though the finality of the general's pronouncement stole the peace he'd been feeling up until a moment ago. He didn't know what to be if he couldn't be a soldier; he'd been raised to fill a uniform from his earliest days. He tried to remember God was in control, and his role wasn't to wrangle his future, but to stand firm and tell the truth. The old John could have invented twenty salable explanations for his actions, could have concocted a variety of stories to meet the public need. In every aspect of this situation, the truth seemed not only useless, but downright harmful. "I do appreciate your position, sir."

"'You appreciate my position.' Gallows, you pander like a confounded diplomat." The general froze. "You *are* a diplomat. You can talk out of both sides of your mouth better than half the fellows up in Washington." Barnes pointed at him. "Come to think of it, I can't fathom a worse punishment for you than to send you into a post dripping with rules and protocol. A protocol officer. If we don't have one, I'll find a reason to need one. It'd serve you right, if it doesn't kill you first. Why should I go through the trouble of Courts-Martialing you when I can send you someplace dreadful and force you to sit through endless speeches?"

John gulped. Should he protest, fortifying the general's appetite for punishing him? Or congratulate him on a creative solution? He settled for something in between. "Exactly how would I be discharged, then?" He wasn't even sure the general's current plan involved a discharge. Did it matter?

"I have no idea. It'll take me a month just to figure out how to set it all up through channels, so you can expect to be on base through November."

"That's fine, sir. I have a…commitment of sorts to keep in November."

Barnes looked up. "Commitment?"

"To the Red Cross, if you remember."

The general's laugh filled the room. "The socks? The auction of your Red Cross sock? Confound it, Gallows, you'll be the death of me yet." He waved John off. "Dismissed until I can fathom what to do with you."

John retrieved his cane and rose.

"John Gallows knits and gets religion. And here I thought I'd seen it all. Well, whatever you do," Barnes added, "don't tell me you'll pray for me. I'm not sure I'm ready to hear that talk coming out of your highly publicized mouth."

"I won't," John replied, but couldn't help adding, "*tell* you, that is."

# Chapter Thirty-Three

*Charleston, South Carolina*
*November 1918*

Mama touched Leanne's arm as the Charleston Holiday Ball was winding to a close. "You feeling all right, honey? It's been a long night."

She wasn't at full strength, but Leanne had enjoyed the evening despite so many missing people and decorations that were half as splendid as in years past. "I'm fine, Mama. Tired but fine." She sighed. "It'll be a somber sort of holiday season, don't you think?"

"Too many families have empty places around the table." Mama's sigh matched her own. "Your grandmother will be sorely missed." Nana had been in the last wave of influenza victims.

"You took good care of her," Papa said with a hand on Leanne's shoulder.

"I was glad of the chance." She had still been on medical leave, and while she wasn't strong enough to resume her hospital duties, Leanne had surprised herself by requesting two weeks' leave to come home to

Charleston and tend to Nana. Besides, Dr. Madison felt she'd have further immunity to contracting influenza—unlike her parents. It seemed, like John said of his trip to the campus, that God was clearly leading her to her Nana's side. "We had so many wonderful conversations before she passed, Mama. I thank God every day for that time."

Mama smiled through brimming eyes. "She loved you especially. She was glad to see you happy."

Leanne looked at John, regal in his full dress uniform for perhaps the final time, smiling as he accepted the gushing thanks from a group of Red Cross leaders. He'd been asked by over two dozen Red Cross Chapters to give speeches in support of the knitting campaign before Armistice Day had announced the end of the war last week. Tonight at the Charleston Holiday Ball, his famous sock had brought in a record-breaking anonymous bid to raise funds for wounded soldiers. "I am dearly happy, Mama."

"I gather you told Nana so?" Papa asked.

"Of course I did." She'd told Nana all about John and what had transpired between them. Nana and Grandpappy had been a wartime romance, too, and Leanne heard many tender stories that cast the memory of her grandmother in whole new light.

"Well, now," Mama said with a mysterious smile, "that explains everything."

"Explains what?"

Papa reached into his coat. "Why your mother owns this, of course. Only we don't think I should keep it. I believe it belongs to John." To Leanne's surprise, Papa produced a hideous olive-green sock.

"I think you ought to frame it, though—it's certainly no good for wearing." She chuckled, peering at the lopsided garment. "The top isn't even the same size as the bottom from the looks of it."

Leanne felt her jaw drop. "*You* bought John's sock?"

"Actually your grandmother did. The last time we were together, she gave me money and told me to bid in secrecy." Mama's eyes brimmed over, and a single tear stole down her cheek. "Mother always did like a good surprise, and she wanted such a marvelous heirloom to stay in the family."

Leanne pulled her mother into a quick, joyous hug. "John will be thrilled. I should go tell him."

Papa stopped her as she turned. "No need, darlin', he already knows."

"You told him Mama was bidding on his sock?" John hadn't given any hints of knowing what was afoot. He'd acted as surprised as everyone else when the emcee had announced the generous anonymous winning bid.

"It seemed only fair to let him know, seeing how he's asked for your hand and all. I told you Nana wanted the sock to stay in the family."

Leanne was having trouble breathing. "Mama, I…" She turned and looked at John, who was trying hard to pry his way out of a gaggle of Red Cross spinsters to make his way toward her. The look on his face told her he'd known everything all evening. "Papa, you…"

"Go save your beau, Leanne." Papa's voice was warm and joyous.

"Oh, he can take care of himself with those old hens." Ida's voice came from over Leanne's other shoulder. "I'm gonna get my congratulations in first." Ida's fierce hug nearly sent Leanne to coughing.

"Did *everyone* know but me?" Leanne gasped, fanning her face in stunned shock.

"Only Colonel Gallows doesn't know by now, and I expect he'll know within the hour if not sooner." Ida laughed.

Leanne wanted to shake her head and blink. God had granted her every single wish and more besides. "I'm stunned. I don't know what to do."

"I have a few ideas." John came up from her other side and took her hand. "But I hope you're not going to make me knit a second sock before you say yes."

"No! I mean yes! Rather, yes, I'll marry you but no, you won't have to knit a sock." She flew into John's arms, knocking his cane from his hand and nearly sending him reeling. "A hundred yesses!"

Ida caught the cane and tried to hand it back to John, but Leanne happily ensured the captain was otherwise occupied. "I'd rather he lean on me."

# Epilogue

*Era Magazine*
*Dateline: November 1919, Washington, DC*
*Headline: New Socks for Celebrated Knitting Couple*

The war hero and nurse who charmed the nation's heart into more Red Cross knitting have collaborated on their finest project to date. Sources close to the Red Cross told *Era* magazine that Mrs. John Gallows, now wife of diplomatic attaché and decorated former U.S. Army Captain John Gallows, will be knitting a new type of socks: baby booties. Readers will remember last year's *Era* cover featuring Nurse Leanne Sample and Captain Gallows in the Red Cross promotion to encourage boys' participation in the "Knit Your Bit" for the war campaign. That effort, and their survival of the subsequent influenza epidemic and quarantine that hit Camp Jackson, evidently joined more than just yarn to needles and the couple married this past spring.

Pink or blue? "Anything and everything but army green," Gallows remarked with a smile when cornered by reporters last week. "We've had enough of that for a while."

Congratulations, Mr. & Mrs. Gallows! *Era* couldn't be more pleased that our little project paved the way for yours.

* * * * *

Dear Reader,

Eleanor Roosevelt said, "A woman is like a tea bag. You never know how strong she is until she gets into hot water." Life's "hot waters" are indeed what makes us strong, and are often how God molds us into who He wants us to be. John and Leanne came into this story with goals very different from the experiences God gave them. But in His infinite wisdom, God not only gave them hardships, but gave them each other. Love allows life's challenges to bring out the best in ourselves and our relationships. While John's and Leanne's wounds make them who they are, their spirits reveal who they can be. It's my hope that these two brave lovers give you hope and courage for the challenges you face. As always, I love to hear from you at www.alliepleiter.com or P.O. Box 7026 Villa Park, IL 60181.

# Questions for Discussion

1. Think back to a time when your future felt wide open with possibilities like Leanne's. What caused you hope? What caused you fear?

2. Are people right or wrong to call John Gallows a hero for his airship incident?

3. Would you have said yes if you were asked to be part of the Red Cross knitting promotion photos? What would you have done in Leanne's place?

4. Did you have a time in your life where physical pain was a serious issue? What helped you cope? What made it worse?

5. What is good about Leanne's idea of waltzing? What's not so wise about it?

6. How would you help a soldier like Private Carson?

7. Do you think John recognizes the gift he's been given? Why or why not?

8. Would you have stopped John from waltzing in front of General Barnes? What would you have suggested he do instead?

9. Leanne tells John, "God's placed you in just the right place at just the right time." When have you felt this way? What came from the experience?

10. John disregards his body's need to heal. Do you agree with his approach? What are the risks and are they really worth taking?

11. Leanne says, "I am [not] free to ignore God's instructions simply because I wish differently." When have you faced this struggle? Would you change how you reacted?

12. Have you faced a large-scale crisis like the influenza epidemic? What did you gain from the experience? What was the cost of it for you or those you love?

13. If John were your son, would you have made him get on the train or let him stay with Leanne?

14. Leanne feels God close to her when she is desperately ill. Have you had such an experience? How has it changed you?

15. Is there a way you can use a craft you love to support the men and women in the armed forces? Contact your local yarn shop, fabric store, Red Cross, or search the internet to see if there's a project suited to you.

# INSPIRATIONAL

celebrating
**15**
YEARS

## HISTORICAL

### COMING NEXT MONTH
AVAILABLE JUNE 12, 2012

**A BABY BETWEEN THEM**
*Irish Brides*
**Winnie Griggs**

**THE BARON'S GOVERNESS BRIDE**
*Glass Slipper Brides*
**Deborah Hale**

**A PROPER COMPANION**
*Ladies in Waiting*
**Louise M. Gouge**

**WINNING THE WIDOW'S HEART**
**Sherri Shackelford**

LIHCNM0512

# REQUEST YOUR FREE BOOKS!

## 2 FREE INSPIRATIONAL NOVELS
## PLUS 2
## FREE
## MYSTERY GIFTS

*Love Inspired.*
## HISTORICAL
INSPIRATIONAL HISTORICAL ROMANCE

---

**YES!** Please send me 2 FREE Love Inspired® Historical novels and my 2 FREE mystery gifts (gifts are worth about $10). After receiving them, if I don't wish to receive any more books, I can return the shipping statement marked "cancel." If I don't cancel, I will receive 4 brand-new novels every month and be billed just $4.49 per book in the U.S. or $4.99 per book in Canada. That's a saving of at least 22% off the cover price. It's quite a bargain! Shipping and handling is just 50¢ per book in the U.S. and 75¢ per book in Canada.* I understand that accepting the 2 free books and gifts places me under no obligation to buy anything. I can always return a shipment and cancel at any time. Even if I never buy another book, the two free books and gifts are mine to keep forever.

102/302 IDN FEHF

| | | |
|---|---|---|
| Name | (PLEASE PRINT) | |
| Address | | Apt. # |
| City | State/Prov. | Zip/Postal Code |

Signature (if under 18, a parent or guardian must sign)

Mail to the **Reader Service:**
**IN U.S.A.:** P.O. Box 1867, Buffalo, NY 14240-1867
**IN CANADA:** P.O. Box 609, Fort Erie, Ontario L2A 5X3
Not valid for current subscribers to Love Inspired Historical books.

**Want to try two free books from another series?**
**Call 1-800-873-8635 or visit www.ReaderService.com.**

* Terms and prices subject to change without notice. Prices do not include applicable taxes. Sales tax applicable in N.Y. Canadian residents will be charged applicable taxes. Offer not valid in Quebec. This offer is limited to one order per household. All orders subject to credit approval. Credit or debit balances in a customer's account(s) may be offset by any other outstanding balance owed by or to the customer. Please allow 4 to 6 weeks for delivery. Offer available while quantities last.

**Your Privacy**—The Reader Service is committed to protecting your privacy. Our Privacy Policy is available online at www.ReaderService.com or upon request from the Reader Service.

We make a portion of our mailing list available to reputable third parties that offer products we believe may interest you. If you prefer that we not exchange your name with third parties, or if you wish to clarify or modify your communication preferences, please visit us at www.ReaderService.com/consumerchoice or write to us at Reader Service Preference Service, P.O. Box 9062, Buffalo, NY 14269. Include your complete name and address.

LIHI1B

Author

# WINNIE GRIGGS

brings you another story from

*Irish Brides*

For two months, Nora Murphy cared for an abandoned infant she found while on her voyage from Ireland to Boston. Now settled in Faith Glen, Nora tells herself she's happy with little Grace and a good job as housekeeper to Sheriff Cameron Long. A traumatic childhood closed Cam off to any dreams of family life. Yet somehow his lovely housekeeper and her child have opened his heart again. When the unthinkable occurs, it will take all their faith to reach a new future together.

## *A Baby Between Them*

*Available June 2012 wherever books are sold.*